I [illegible] steps back toward the bedroom wing and gasped. I wouldn't have to search for the house's owner after all. He lay sprawled motionless on his side behind the couch, a gag in his mouth.

My hands fumbled at the knot holding the gag, a brightly patterned scarf, while my mind registered the fact that I had seen this material before. When the gag finally came loose, it didn't help. This man wasn't going to talk to me, or to anyone else, ever again. Taking a deep breath, I grasped his shoulder and rolled him onto his back. His arm flopped without resistance and his sightless eyes stared at the ceiling. The coffee spilled in the middle of the straw-colored carpet had already left a dark brown stain. The blood oozing from his chest now added a rusty pool.

With the aid of the couch, I stood up and backed away, still clutching the gag, and held it up, trying to make sense of its presence here. My daughter had been wearing it as a belt the last time I saw her.

MURDER OF THE MONTH

ELIZABETH C. MAIN

WORLDWIDE®

TORONTO • NEW YORK • LONDON
AMSTERDAM • PARIS • SYDNEY • HAMBURG
STOCKHOLM • ATHENS • TOKYO • MILAN
MADRID • WARSAW • BUDAPEST • AUCKLAND

To
Marie Cole Colasuonno
and
Mel Pearson Lamping

MURDER OF THE MONTH

A Worldwide Mystery/July 2012

First published by Five Star Publishing

ISBN-13: 978-0-373-26807-8

Printed in U.S.A.

Acknowledgments

I thank my family more than I can say for their enthusiastic and unwavering support of my writing career.

I am also grateful to the many friends and relatives who took the time to read and offer suggestions about my manuscript.

And finally, I'd like to acknowledge Tar, my beloved one-eyed dog, who inspired the character of Wendell. Tar was my constant companion when I started writing the novel, and I'm glad he will live on in print, as well as in my memory.

PROLOGUE

VANESSA STRUGGLED hardly at all in the last moments of her life. Too startled by the unexpected attack to scream, she made no sound as she scrambled for something, anything, to break her fall. Her perfectly-manicured fingers spread like bloody talons, but they grasped nothing but air as she plummeted like a wounded bird three hundred feet to the dusty rocks below.

She made tiny, crablike movements in her futile attempt to crawl away from the ugly death that would soon claim her. Ugliness had never before been a word associated with Vanessa, but soon she'd be found dead, sprawled in an ungainly pose she'd have hated.

Vanessa's assailant studied the scene below. Yes, everything was coming together nicely. Too bad about the ugliness though. Vanessa would have made an exquisite corpse, her long black hair curved gently around delicately rouged cheeks...if, that is, she hadn't fallen so far. Now the coffin would have to remain closed.

Vanessa had started the day without even a worry line to mar her lovely, deceitful face. She had come here fully expecting her beauty to get her what she wanted, just as it always had. This time, it didn't work.

ONE

"He killed her! He killed her sure as anything!"

"Bianca? Are you all right?" Dragging myself from the fog of an afternoon nap, I struggled to comprehend my daughter's words. A whirlwind made better sense than my youngest child, even on a good day, so the task wasn't as easy as it might seem. I clutched the receiver and bolted upright, my book thudding to the floor as I did so. Its pages remained open to the fourteenth chapter of *Making Peace With Your Adult Child.* After dealing with Bianca all summer, I was even desperate enough to try the pop psychology of best-selling author Raymond Morris.

I repeated, "Are you all right? Just tell me that much."

"Of course I'm all right," came the annoyed reply. "What makes you think I'm not? Oh, you've been napping again, haven't you? I should have known. If you'd—"

"Never mind that!" I flung aside the comfortable afghan and interrupted her before she could launch into yet another lecture on my sleeping habits, which inevitably expanded into a lecture on her plan for improving my general health and character. At age forty-two, I held down a job, ate plenty of fruits and vegetables, voted responsibly, and visited the dentist regularly. Surely I was capable of deciding on the proper amount of sleep without my daughter's help. If only Bianca could see it that way, my life would be much easier. "Who's dead? What are you talking about?"

"Vanessa Fortune. It's all over the news. She fell off a cliff in the Crooked River Gorge."

"That's awful. How did she—"

"Don't say she slipped. That's what he wants everyone to think." Bianca's voice deepened dramatically. "She was murdered."

I'd had enough conversations with my fanciful child to know the importance of pinning down facts before she could dismiss them as irrelevant. "Now, Bianca, before you get carried away, tell me exactly what happened."

"I'm not the one they're carrying away. Vanessa is...and I tell you she was murdered!"

I sighed. Raymond Morris's Rule Number One: *Make each conversation a positive experience* was going to be harder than usual. "Let's start from the beginning. What makes you think Vanessa was murdered? Did someone see it happen?"

"Well, just the killer. Otherwise, she was out there alone."

"I see." Now we were getting somewhere. This was another of Bianca's unique interpretations of events. "What does Arnie say?" Arnold Kraft, the Russell County sheriff, wasn't a particularly bright light in Oregon law enforcement, but he was honest and sincere.

Bianca's unladylike snort told me that she and Arnie differed radically in their assessments of the incident. "What's he going to say? Gil's an old football buddy of his."

I was confused. Why wouldn't Vanessa's husband want to get at the truth? "Gil? Well, of course, but so what? Won't their friendship motivate Arnie?"

"Not if he killed her."

"Why on earth would Arnie murder Vanessa?"

"Not Arnie...Gil."

"Gil? That's ridiculous! You can't say that."

"I can if it's true. I know that he killed—"

"Bianca!"

"See? You won't even hear me out. Why won't you listen?"

"Because it's too improbable to consider, let alone say

such a thing." I glanced uneasily at the smiling picture of Raymond Morris on the cover of his book. In his next edition, he might want to use me as an example of how not to deal with a nineteen-year-old daughter. I was doing my best, but it was tough to sound conciliatory. "Okay, Bianca, I'm listening. What does Arnie think?"

"That it was an accident."

"And why does he think that?"

"Because she was hiking alone and Gil was supposedly somewhere else—"

"But that's not enough for you."

"Arnie doesn't know what I know."

"Which is…?"

"…that Gil killed Vanessa."

"This isn't some murder of the month novel." My words tumbled out before I remembered Rule Number Three: *In tense situations, say something totally neutral.* I need to read Rule Number Three more often. "Why do you know that Gil killed Vanessa? That's the stupidest thing I've ever heard!"

"So now you're calling me stupid. That's great, Mom. Very nurturing."

"I'm sorry, honey. I shouldn't have said that, no matter—"

"No matter if it's true?" Bianca's voice trembled. "That's what you meant, isn't it?"

She was jumping to conclusions, but she didn't deserve to be talked to that way. I was supposed to be the adult here. "I was going to say, no matter if we disagree. I'm truly sorry, Bianca, for what I said. Please, tell me what you think."

"Yeah, right. You're just humoring me now, but maybe someone at book club will listen. Vanessa's death is totally like the book I want us to read next."

"How?" I asked faintly. Bianca's favorite mystery fiction was a popular series that featured two dogs as detectives. Fortunately, she hadn't yet convinced the rest of our book club to waste time on them.

"I'll explain at book club."

Alarm bells clanged in my head. Did I really want Bianca to be talking to others about this nonsense? "Why don't you come over here now and we'll talk this out?"

"No thanks. You had your chance to be the first to hear."

I recognized that determined tone, but tried one more time. "I'll make a…tofu stir fry, with fresh broccoli. We'll have a nice, quiet evening here, skip the meeting—"

"Why would I want to spend the evening with someone who thinks I'm stupid?"

"Please, I said I was sorry about that."

"You're always sorry afterward, but you always forget."

True enough. Raymond Morris could write an entire book about my failures as a mother. "Well, I'm sorry that I'm always sorry. I don't know what else to say."

"It's okay, Mom. I know you mean well." It was a good thing that Bianca had a forgiving nature. I was a trial to her, but she kept hoping to whip me into shape. "I'll see you later. This is bigger than you know."

That's what I was afraid of. "At least promise that you won't say anything to anyone else until I arrive."

"Okay, I can do that. By the way, that's a good idea."

"Not saying anything? I agree!"

"No, the other one. The name for our book club. I can't believe we didn't think of it before: Murder of the Month. It's perfect."

Rule Number Seven: *Agree whenever you can.* Finally, something I could manage. "Right. It's perfect."

"Of course," Bianca continued thoughtfully, "we usually just read about fictional murders, but Vanessa is a real person and she's really dead. I'm not making that up."

"Well, no, but that doesn't mean—"

"And he killed her."

Rule Number Ten: *Stay quiet when nothing you say will improve the situation.* It's a useful rule, particularly when dealing with Bianca.

Exhausted as always after talking to her, I sank back onto the couch as soon as we hung up. If I could transfuse about ten percent of her energy into my veins, I could run marathons with energy to spare, but mostly I wanted to strangle her, though, of course, a mother can't ever admit that out loud. If her call hadn't startled me, I'd have found some way to avoid letting her know I'd been taking a nap. I'd learned all too well that it was best to hide from my three kids the number of hours I disposed of through sleep. They might be separated by geography, age, and interests, but they were in accord about the perceived need to "do something about Mom" after their father's death one year, two months, and ten days ago. Not that I'd ever be foolish enough to tell them I still kept track of the exact number of days since Tony's plane crash. If I did tell them, they would only take it as yet another sign that I wasn't adjusting well.

Mourning Tony's loss after twenty-three years of a good marriage was a slow, untidy process. It wasn't as simple as stowing sweaters in a bottom drawer at the approach of summer. I wasn't really fooling the kids even when I didn't say anything about being sad, of course. They knew I wasn't back to normal yet, and it made them nervous. Recently they had started making oh-so-casual suggestions about terrific activities I should try, like bowling or painting in watercolors. I loved them for their thoughtfulness, but sometimes it seemed more like nagging. When my sadness surfaced now and then over something as simple as a fondness for afternoon naps, it stirred them up again and the telephone wires hummed. I was sure that Bianca would call both of her sisters—Susannah in Minnesota and Emily in Peru—before the day was over.

What they couldn't accept was that I had to go through this adjustment process in my own way, and it would take more time than was comfortable for them. Right after Tony died, it helped that I was still a mother because mothers know the art of putting their children's needs first. We worked through those early months together, going through the shock and anger at the unfairness of our bitter loss.

After a few months, my three strong daughters started looking ahead to their own lives and activities, which was the way it should be. At that point, my motherly duties diminished, but that meant I could no longer avoid confronting my own altered future. Suddenly a great weariness overtook me, and I spent several more months hunkered down in the black Early American rocking chair, listening to the ticking of the clock as it agonized its way through the endless hours.

Resentment eventually overtook lethargy as I wondered why I was required to go on without Tony, why I would even want to go on without him. We had been happy together, but all of a sudden he was gone and everything had changed. I didn't want to start all over again, learning new ways to fill my days and my life. Recently Bianca had suggested that I consider dating, especially after she realized that several local men had already asked me out. The idea that I might be attractive to men surprised all my daughters at first, but they soon adjusted to the notion, though Bianca's description of me as "really healthy looking" left something to be desired. Tony had found me a little more exciting than that, but then he had been a sucker for my green eyes, chestnut hair, and wide smile from the moment we met. Up to now, going out with someone else still seemed quite impossible and uninteresting, but little by little I had found a few minutes each day when I wasn't thinking about Tony. I felt guilty about those times at first because it seemed that I was abandoning him, but at least those minutes didn't hurt so much.

Being a mother still helped fill a lot of empty hours. When Bianca's call had shrilled its way into my dream a few minutes earlier, it was only my motherly instinct, thoroughly ingrained, that had caused me to answer it. It wasn't that I was expecting anything interesting to come from a telephone call, but what if one of the kids needed me? The call was more likely to be an unsolicited offer to fix a cracked windshield, but old habits die hard and I had dutifully scrambled to answer it, just in case.

Motherhood was a mixed blessing though, especially with Bianca. Tony and I had felt rather smug about our parental abilities as we saw our older two daughters, Susannah and Emily, progress smoothly through their youth and adolescence. But Bianca proved that the peacefulness we had experienced with the first two was less the result of good parenting than pure luck of the personality draw.

Susannah was currently enjoying her role as wife and mother in Ely, Minnesota, thrilled with her husband and two-year-old son, and excited about the prospect of giving little Kevin a brother or sister any day now. Emily, our middle child, was having the time of her studious young life this summer as a member of a crew from the University of Oregon grubbing around a newly-discovered Inca ruin in Peru.

Then there was Bianca, the baby of the family. She wasn't so much marching to a different drummer as dancing to about nine different bongo rhythms which no one else had heard before or would ever hear again. For starters, at age fourteen she had dismissed the name we gave her at birth, Louise, declaring it too boring for words and refusing to answer to anything other than Bianca. Just like that, our dear little Louise was gone. Life with Bianca after that was anything but boring.

Unfortunately, she also decided about then that Tony and I were also unspeakably boring, and though she couldn't manage to give us complete personality transplants, she had felt no compunction about expressing her disdain for almost everything we said or did. This continued right up until Tony's death. After that, he had magically become the ideal father in her mind, leaving me to bear the brunt of her unremitting scorn for everything from my taste in refrigerator cartoons to my unfashionable political opinions.

Her determination shortly after Tony's death to travel alone around the United States had triggered my strong objections, but off she went. At least her absence had lessened the daily tension between us. I was terrified about the dangers inherent in her solitary journey, but she called in now and then and I tried to concentrate on anticipating her safe return home. However, her arrival here in Juniper late this spring had soon caused my stomach to knot even more. My lovely, will-o'-the-wisp daughter had come home, and here she had stayed with her latest mission: to "do something about Mom."

Was I supposed to be happy today that her attention had been temporarily deflected from my shortcomings in favor of a new crusade? Maybe so. If she had stuck to some of her earlier causes—boycotting Safeway because they sold beef treated with growth hormones or writing letters to the *Juniper Journal* about the lack of affordable housing for low-income workers in the tourist industry—I could live with the slight embarrassment. Those activities were harmless, but her baseless accusation against Gil was not. I feared she was about to go too far.

I looked once again at *Making Peace With Your Adult Child.* There it lay in all its best-selling glory, glossy and authoritative. I picked it up and examined the smiling, confident face of Raymond Morris on the cover. No worry lines. I was willing to bet that all his children were boys. What did he know about stress? Disgusted, I dropped the book onto the couch once more. No point in checking the index for a heading about how to respond when your daughter accuses someone of murder.

TWO

THE DUELING AROMAS OF cigarette smoke and incense greeted me as I trudged toward the heavily carpeted front staircase of the somewhat faded, but still imposing Victorian structure that housed Thornton's Books, the small independent bookstore where I worked. When I was working, I didn't mind running up and down both the front and back stairs, counting it an easy way to get exercise, but tonight, knowing that I was on my way to our book club meeting, I dragged up the stairs like a prisoner en route to the gallows.

Even without tonight's threat of Bianca's bizarre accusation about Gil, these meetings were excruciating. Each gathering of the recently formed mystery book club had grown more acrimonious than the one before, leading me to wonder why everyone kept coming. Either they enjoyed torturing themselves or they relished the prospect of torturing each other. With this bunch, either explanation was plausible. I might as well have put a sign on the door saying "Welcome, Weirdos!" A meeting between the National Rifle Association and the People for the Ethical Treatment of Animals would surely have produced a more compatible group.

The jangle of voices from above convinced me that Bianca and Alix had wasted no time in commencing their inevitable argument tonight. Alix, another charter member of the book club, was the cynical and, thus, somewhat improbable owner of a local bridal shop called "The Wedding Belle." She and Bianca mixed just slightly less well than oil and water. So far, they'd been in total disagreement on every topic, starting with the choice of books to discuss and moving on to the question of profanity in modern literature, the admissibility of Alix's cigarettes in the meeting room, and the value of seaweed as an aid to concentration. Their latest battle had been expanded to include the opinions of another member, Minnie Salter, and concerned the possible correlation between the number of grisly murders described and the effectiveness of a mystery. A couple of months into meetings with this experimental book club, my only remaining question was how long it would take before we arrived at the actual slaughter of one club member by another.

I'd been naively elated when Bianca had wanted to join the new club, thinking that this was an easy way for her to meet people when she moved back to Juniper in June. Visions of mother-daughter bonding on a new level now that we were both adults had floated through my head, but they hadn't stayed long. If Bianca and I, her own loving mother, skirmished regularly over her opinions, I should have realized that Bianca and the no-nonsense Alix, a total stranger, would likely move quickly to all-out warfare. In our initial meeting, Bianca had expressed her fervent hope that we'd all be able to get in touch with a higher spiritual awareness through studying the crime-solving aptitudes of animals.

While most of us absorbed this statement in stunned silence, the ever-cynical Alix had offered a muttered response: "If the essence of our spiritual awareness involves disconnecting our brains, that just might work." The relationship between Bianca and Alix had gone downhill from there.

The original reason for the formation of this club had been to help Tyler, my employer's fifteen-year-old grandson, adapt to his forced presence in "this hick town," as he put it, for the summer. Tyler had yet to say much, but his sideways looks regularly demonstrated his disdain for the group. He was staying with his grandfather while his mother tried yet another drug rehab facility. I hadn't decided yet whether he was naturally unpleasant or simply reacting to a situation he found totally unsatisfactory.

Only Minnie Salter, at sixty the oldest member of the book club, seemed to enjoy herself at our meetings, but then Minnie apparently loved everything she did. On Sundays she taught Sunday school classes. On Mondays she hosted an evening knitting group at the church. On Tuesdays, she arranged flowers at the local cemetery and tended gravesites that would otherwise be neglected. On Thursdays, she delivered casseroles to people just out of the hospital or otherwise incapacitated. And on Wednesday nights this summer, she had given up her usual bunco game so she could attend our meetings at Thornton's Books, where she hoped to discuss in gory detail the latest in the string of true-crime novels she churned through at an amazing rate.

These meetings were bad enough at the best of times, but with Bianca's new crusade against Gil, we were probably about to hit a new low. From the decibel level emanating from above, I judged that we were going to witness my long-predicted real-life murder in the next ten minutes. That sounded fine to me, as then I'd have a good excuse to disband this ill-assorted group once and for all. On the other hand, it would be hard work cleaning the gore off the Oriental carpets.

"Have a good meeting, Jane." My elderly employer, Laurence Thornton, spoke from his lonely post at the counter below. No customers were currently in the store, though he had stayed open on this warm summer night, just in case. Unfortunately, business had fallen off at Thornton's Books after the recent grand opening of the glossy Megabooks Plus! bookstore on Highway 97 north of town. Once the private residence of Marcus T. Konig, an early Juniper saloonkeeper, this house's Victorian charm and central location on an oversized city lot had proved an ideal setting for the quiet business of selling books for the past ten years. With Juniper's growth and booming economy, people were buying more books than ever, but our friendliness and personalized service couldn't compete with the deep discounts offered by Megabooks Plus!—nor their animal-costumed sales staff flown in from Arizona one Saturday a month.

If Laurence, a retired classics professor, had possessed even one shred of salesmanship, if he had ever looked up from his reading of *The History of Herodotus* long enough to notice the falling sales, maybe I wouldn't have been foolish enough to propose that we host a mystery book club right at Thornton's. But Laurence had been looking forlorn about his grandson's sullen inability to find something to occupy him this summer, and Tyler had shown a slight interest in mysteries, so I had offered the brilliant suggestion that perhaps starting the club would serve the double purpose of giving Tyler something to do and spurring book sales.

But anyone who would name his store simply "Thornton's Books" and stock his shelves with Sophocles and Shakespeare instead of the latest celebrity tell-all fluff was definitely not a marketing whiz. While my own degree in English literature made me sympathetic to Laurence's taste in reading, I assumed that Thornton's could improve sales by stocking reading matter that was at least a few centuries more contemporary.

And now he had the nerve to tell me to have a good meeting. I leaned against the ornate banister and shot him a baleful look. The false smile he wore made me sorry I wasn't carrying something, preferably something hot and sticky, that I could drop on his head. The old rogue was trying to soothe me as though I were a nervous freshman faced with studying Thomas Aquinas for the first time.

"I can hardly wait. We always have such a jolly time."

He ignored my sarcasm. Approaching eighty years of age,

his once tall frame was stooped and his hair had thinned, but Laurence Thornton still retained his professorial air of calm competence. "Tonight's meeting will be fine. You'll see."

"Oh, yeah. I'll see something all right, but…just listen to what's going on upstairs!"

"Well, literary discussions do tend to get heated."

"Literary? We're not anywhere close to literary. Do you want to know why?" I descended a few steps. "Well, I'll tell you." I was more than happy to delay the trip upstairs. Besides, I'd been itching to tell Laurence a thing or two about what I'd been going though with this book club. "Let me give you a few pointers about how to set up a book club that might actually have a chance to achieve a literary discussion. Point one: Don't let lunatics into your club. Point two: If they do slip in, don't agree to a minimum three-month trial period because for some reason those lunatics will enjoy coming and won't want to disband—"

"Even when—"

"Exactly! Even when it becomes clear that this group is absolutely impossible. I have no idea why. Ask the lunatics. Point three: Don't let anyone in without making him swear in blood to read mysteries from a variety of categories—"

"But aren't mysteries just…mysteries? With bodies and clues and such?"

I ticked the categories off on my fingers. "Police procedural, hard-boiled detective, suspense, cozy—"

"Cozy?"

"A big category," I said. "A peaceful little murder at the vicarage or some such nonsense that gives you a warm, fuzzy feeling when you read it. Anyway, wouldn't you think that rational people could come up with at least one mutually agreeable choice in a couple of months? Well, forget it. There are no rational people in this book club—present company excepted, of course."

"Of course."

"Everybody else is passionate about one category and detests all the others. Aren't you going to ask about 'hard-boiled,' too?"

"I'm still assimilating 'cozy.' Well, Jane, I appreciate your problem, but surely, eventually—"

"Alix and Bianca are still scuffling over Alix's cigarettes." I sniffed and grimaced. "And as you can plainly tell, even from here, Bianca has now mounted a rather intense and… pungent counter-offensive."

"You might even say Bianca was 'incensed,'" Laurence offered with a smile.

"I get it…'incensed.' Very funny." I came back down the stairs and ostentatiously lifted the portable fan off the counter. "Well, Laurence, since you find this situation so humorous, maybe you'd care to join us." I mimicked his tone of voice, "Tonight's meeting will be fine. You'll see."

At his horrified look, I relented. Besides, I didn't want any extra witnesses to whatever Bianca was going to say. "Oh, all right. Maybe not tonight, but one of these evenings. You owe me."

"I know, Jane." His faded blue eyes grew sad. "And don't think I'm not appreciative of all your efforts to help me out with…everything."

Oops. "Everything" was code for Tyler, and Tyler's troubled mother, who was Laurence's only child. I didn't want Laurence to retreat once more into the misery that had so dominated his thoughts when Tyler first arrived, and I could have kicked myself for letting the conversation stray to that painful situation. I switched into theatrical mode, left over from my career in college melodramas. Coupling an evil expression with a maniacal cackle, I said, "I know, I know… and I'm contemplating many devious ways to get even. Will it be the rack? The iron maiden? Hah! Only time will tell." I leaned across the counter to pat his wrinkled cheek and was relieved to see the beginnings of a smile. "I'll let you worry while I take care of…that." I pointed dramatically up the stairs. "Should I take a whip and chair?"

"Not necessary. You need go armed with only your charming personality, my dear. That should conquer even the most beastly members of your…er, delightful group, though the fan might prove to be of some immediate assistance as well."

The front door swung open to admit what at first appeared to be a freestanding scarf collection topped by a floppy black hat. The colorful scarves swirled into the bookstore and from their midst came a cheery voice. "Hello, hello, Jane. Why, Laurence, there you are. I didn't see you."

I avoided meeting Laurence's eye. How Minnie could see anything from under her omnipresent hat was something of a mystery, and what the hat didn't cover, one of the scarves would surely obscure.

"Am I late? I hope I'm not late, but I was filling the church box that's going to…let's see, I think it's Sri Lanka. So many places need help…I already collected the books you were donating, didn't I? Yes, I thought so. Anyway, I looked up and it was already after seven, so I just scooted right over. Don't know what Fred's going to do for dinner tonight, but I'm sure he can manage. There's plenty in the fridge. Of course, everyone at church was just in shock about poor Vanessa. Well, 'in the midst of life we are in death,' as they say. You just never know, do you? How long you have, I mean. Dreadful, dreadful." She contemplated the idea for a moment, head bowed, before switching gears. "Now, what have I missed? Has the meeting already started?"

"Not yet, Minnie. Go on up. I'll be there in a minute."

"Wonderful. I'll just…" Minnie swept by us both, then turned in a flurry of bright material. "Laurence, I can't thank you enough for setting up this club."

"Jane deserves all the credit," Laurence said.

"Well, you both deserve some, don't you? After all, Laurence, you let us use the store for meetings, and it's just the most darling place. All these dark little alcoves and spooky corridors—what better place to discuss murder? It really puts me in the mood! For our next book, Jane, what do you say to *Paint Her Dead*? The mutilation of that artist in Rhode Island? You know the one I mean...where the killer painted the stripes? Now that's a book any group would find interesting." She clapped her hands, causing multiple bracelets on each wrist to dance and clatter. "I don't know when I've had such fun! You really should join us sometime, Laurence. Well, better get along. Oh, dear," she said, halting at the bottom step with her nose twitching. "Alix is still determined to smoke? And what is—"

"Incense," Lawrence and I intoned glumly in unison.

"Goodness. That would appeal to Bianca, I suppose. If you ask me, the incense smells worse than the cigarettes, but that's just my opinion. Well, 'judge not, that ye be not judged.' That's what I always say. Good thing you have a fan." She shrugged and flowed up the stairs, her scarves trailing majestically.

"She doesn't know when she's had such fun, eh?" I asked with wonder, once Minnie was out of earshot. "Has she been at the same meetings I have?"

"Just as I suspected. You're all having a lot more fun than you've been willing to admit, creeping around in these dim hallways thinking about murder."

"You don't want to encourage me along those lines, Laurence—"

"And you wanted to install brighter lights upstairs. Shame on you, Jane."

"How could I have thought people might actually want to see where they were walking? Much more important for customers to be in the proper mood as they delve into all those—what'd Minnie call them?—'dark little alcoves.' What's a broken leg or two in our jolly quest for fun?" I shook my head. "Alix's cigarette smoke must have pickled my brain. And speaking of cigarettes—"

"Don't start," Laurence warned. "I've cut down so far already that it hardly counts—"

"To what? A pack a day? When are you going to quit?"

"I don't suppose 'when hell freezes over' would satisfy you?" Laurence asked grandly. "Your nagging has already brought me to the edge of a nervous breakdown. Isn't that enough?"

"It's not your nerves so much as your circulatory system that worries me," I said, attempting to keep my tone stern. As always, my fondness for the cantankerous old man warred with exasperation at his inability to break free of cigarettes. In the few months I had worked here, I had often listened to his tortured cough and watched him struggle for breath. My initial reluctance to intrude into his personal affairs had given way to alarm as his condition had deteriorated.

"Jane, if you don't get upstairs right away, Minnie will have *Paint Her Dead* scheduled for your next meeting."

"Over my dead body."

"Watch your word choice. Goodhearted Minnie sounds a bit bloodthirsty to me, though I do wonder...with her love of scarves, whether she might favor mysteries about belly dancing. Yes, that's it—and Bianca's incense would fit right in."

"Belly dancing! A pillar of the church like Minnie? No way. Besides, if there's a belly dancing mystery series—and there very well might be because there certainly is every other kind—somehow I've missed it. Minnie's all-time favorite book is *In Cold Blood*."

"What's a mystery without a little evil, and a bloody limb or two on the staircase?"

"No bloody limbs for me, thank you, on the staircase or anywhere else. Light on reality and heavy on whimsy, that's the mystery for me, with just a touch of blood added for color."

"You must have had a tough time with *Macbeth*."

"That's different. Shakespeare can strew bodies all over the stage because he gives his characters something poetic to say while they hack each other to bits. But, alas, today's murderers aren't as poetic as they used to be. I want my victims dispatched offstage, or between chapters five and six. No cataloguing the stab wounds centimeter by centimeter. Do you suppose Minnie has nightmares? She must."

A sudden crash from above made us both jump. "Laurence, did you let Bianca bring that dog in here again? Don't play the innocent with me. Of course you did!" My attempt to stomp up the stairs was somewhat muffled by the density of the carpet. "Oh, what's the difference? Having a one-eyed dog at the meetings makes as much sense as anything else about this club."

THREE

THE SCENE THAT GREETED me when I groped my way down the dim hallway to the converted back bedroom upstairs did nothing to restore my good humor. Even with the inadequate lighting, I could see the disarray in the book-lined lounge. Normally the deep leather armchairs and couch surrounded a scarred wooden table, but several of the chairs had been shoved away from the table and the contents of a broken pottery bowl littered the Oriental carpet beneath. Wendell, a large black dog of indeterminate breed, was industriously cleaning up the remains of whatever had been in the bowl, while the occupants of the room watched him with varying degrees of interest.

Alix Boudreau lounged against the wall by the open window, looking like a graceful beige column in her sheath as she watched the mini-drama before her. Her languid bearing and faint smile suggested that she had little to do with whatever was going on, and indeed, that her only current interest lay in extracting the most nicotine possible from every puff of her extra-long cigarette.

Tyler slumped as always in the deepest corner of the couch, doing his teenage best to let us know that he was there under duress, and he would sooner eat nails than associate with the rest of us. He pretended to study the cover of a paperback book he was holding, but his feigned lack of interest in the situation was belied by the furtive glimpses he kept shooting from under the unkempt thatch of blond hair that covered his forehead.

Minnie and her scarves fluttered around the table as she attempted to clean up the mess. "I'm so sorry, but I didn't realize…my goodness, he really is fast."

Bianca, casually beautiful in a formfitting purple tank top and the briefest of cutoff jeans, patted the dog's stiff fur. "It's all right…good dog…you didn't know," as though he were cowering in a corner, filled with remorse after having committed some unpardonable sin. Instead, he was licking the last crumbs from the rug, giving every evidence of being a dog with a clear conscience.

"Bianca, what on earth…?" I began.

"Don't blame Wendell," Bianca said. "It wasn't his fault. I brought these frosted bran bars for the meeting and when Minnie reached for one, Wendell thought she was offering it to him. With only one eye, he probably can't tell distances too well. Poor puppy."

He doesn't seem to be having all that much trouble, I thought, watching as the one-eyed dog snuffled under the chairs in search of more treats. Frosted bran bars? No one looked too upset at being denied the contents of the bowl, but then Bianca's unceasing attempts to convince us of the virtues of vegetarianism had met with a steady stream of rebuffs all summer.

A curtain of white-blond hair that any Hollywood starlet would envy framed her young face. Even had I not been her mother, I knew that the sweetness of her smile as she expressed regrets for Wendell's behavior would warm any but the coldest heart. I glanced at Alix. Sure enough, her expression hadn't changed.

"Okay, okay." I called a halt to Bianca's stream of apologies. "No harm done—unless someone besides Wendell was really hungry, that is."

Alix laughed, choking on her cigarette smoke until she finally regained enough control to gasp, "Not likely."

"How could you tell, Alix? You know that those disgusting cigarettes have killed any taste buds you ever had," Bianca retorted from the other side of the table.

Alix wiped her eyes. "Thank God my taste buds departed before your recipes went to work on them. But don't give up. Your incense will kill off my sense of smell, too. In fact, that's probably what set your dog to overturning the furniture just now. He's being driven nuts by that stuff...but then, who isn't?"

"But I read this neat article—" Bianca began.

"Ah, a neat article," Alix retorted. "Well, then—"

"Oh, no," Minnie broke in passionately. "Please don't argue. Remember, 'grievous words stir up anger.' I can't stand unpleasantness, not tonight. After Vanessa's death...so distressing...I'm sure we were all looking forward to a quiet literary discussion of...something...just as soon as we decide what to read." She spread her arms apologetically. "Of course, I've already recommended *Paint Her Dead,* so I didn't actually get around to thinking much about anything else we might consider. Besides, you have no idea...absolutely none... how much coordination is involved in getting food together after a funeral service—which will be Sunday afternoon, by the way—especially in the summer when people are melting and can only think of salads. Mark my words, if you're not careful, you can end up with thirty molded salads, and then where are you?"

Tyler looked even more blank than usual, presumably as he tried to picture the disaster that would come with the arrival of thirty molded salads. I knew that Minnie was always the first to offer help to anyone in need, but she must have set some kind of a record today, since Vanessa had fallen to her death less than twelve hours ago.

Minnie continued. "Not that there's anything wrong with molded salads, but really, even on a hot day, people need something substantial to keep up their strength. Chicken pot pie always goes well, and macaroni casseroles." Judging from Minnie's generous size, I deduced that she had often followed her own rule for keeping up her strength. As she leaned over the arm of the couch to dispense this vital information, Tyler's mouth dropped open, which Minnie seemed to take as a sign that he was about to declare his view on the relative merits of casseroles and salads. "Of course, I didn't mean you, Tyler. No one would expect you to make a casserole, dear. Boys your age don't cook, do they? It's all nachos and french fries with you, I imagine, and who ever heard of eating french fries after a funeral? Anyway, all those telephone calls took more time than I expected. Besides, I was too upset to think about reading after I talked to Gil. The man is devastated, just devastated."

"Well, Tyler," I said, "can you talk about *The Deep Blue Good-By?*"

Tyler flushed, but collected himself enough to mutter from the depths of the couch, "I'm not ready."

Big surprise. I'd made a private bet with myself that he would never actually put aside his contempt for the group long enough to speak up at a meeting, though I had chosen to consider his shrug at the last meeting as acquiescence to my suggestion that he tell us about the books of John D. MacDonald soon. During Tyler's first week in Juniper, he had found an entire suitcase stuffed with tattered paperbacks by that author in the bookstore's attic. Once started, he had been devouring them at a terrific rate and was now a walking—or perhaps a better word was "slouching"—encyclopedia about the life and times of Travis McGee.

"Are you sure?" I pressed. Anything to move the conversational topic away from Gil.

"Yeah, I'm sure." Tyler returned to studying the book in his hands.

My efforts were in vain. Alix had abandoned the window and ambled over to the group. "You really think Gil is devastated that Vanessa's gone, Minnie?" she asked. "Rumor has it that there are a few women around who would dispute that."

Minnie flicked a glance at Tyler. "That's just a rumor, Alix, and people do change."

"Not that much they don't. Doesn't the Bible say something about a leopard not changing his spots? Remember, I went to high school with Gil and—"

"Well, then," I said briskly, "if nobody is ready to talk books, maybe we should just call it a night…all things considered."

Minnie spoke as though she hadn't even heard my suggestion. "You're saying terrible things, Alix."

"Doesn't mean they're not true," Alix countered. "Maybe Vanessa is better off dead than married to Gil."

Minnie gasped. "You think that she…she jumped off that cliff?"

"No, of course not. I just wouldn't want to be married to him. Don't get all melodramatic here." Alix picked up her wallet in preparation for departure. "Could be she even loved him, for all I know."

Minnie sputtered in outrage. "And why wouldn't she? He's going to be the next Attorney General of Oregon. He's handsome, talented, intelligent—"

"All those things, and a few others besides."

"But everybody knows they'd put their problems behind them."

"I thought you said those were just rumors."

"Well, I'm sure they were. Besides, Arlene transferred to San Francisco over a year ago."

"I didn't even know about Arlene. Gil always did like blondes though. Maybe if we pool our rumors, we can each come up with a different blonde." Alix continued, "I was thinking of—"

"Don't say it. Don't say it." Minnie put her hands up as if to cover her ears, but mainly succeeded in covering her face with the scarves. Peering out from behind them, she recited, "'Let him that is without sin cast the first stone.'"

Alix gave Minnie a long, incredulous look and then shrugged. "Well, Minnie, it's certainly very Christian of you to take that attitude…in the face of all available evidence. I guess that's where faith comes in—but you'd better toss in some hope and charity to go with it. All I'm saying is that I'd be surprised if Vanessa hadn't figured out that being married to Gil wasn't all it was cracked up to be."

"Wait a minute, both of you!" Bianca's abrupt words startled Wendell into a frantic scramble to get out from under the table, where he had continued his hunt for food.

I tried to head her off. "Yes, in fact, let's wait more than a minute. We've all had plenty for one night."

Bianca continued earnestly. "No, that's not what I meant. Sorry, Wendell. Didn't mean to scare you." She stroked him before continuing. "Mom, I know what you're trying to do, but I just can't let this go." She turned to the rest of the group and said, "I told Mom something earlier, and she doesn't want me to tell you about it, but it's important. I read a book—"

"Oh, no. Not the dog detectives again," Alix said.

"You haven't been willing to read even one book in that series—"

"And I don't intend to—"

"See? That's the problem, Alix. You're just like Mom, so closed to anything new that you miss opportunities to see things from a different perspective, things that might be right in front of your face."

"And you want me to find opportunities to expand my

consciousness by studying dog droppings or whatever?" Alix asked.

"I'm not talking about dog droppings—"

"Well, that's a relief—"

"—and trying to expand your consciousness is pretty much a lost cause! But if you pay attention to what animals have to tell us, you might learn something. I'm not kidding. Dogs in particular can be very perceptive."

"Oh, my god, we're back to learning about life's truths as revealed by those famous philosophers, Bipsy and Mr. Potts."

"Now, Alix," Minnie cautioned in her Sunday school teacher's voice, trying as always to be fair and to make sure that everyone was playing well together. "Bianca is right that we haven't even tried to read one of the books she likes."

"And with good reason," Alix said. "Or maybe if Vanessa had read the doggy detective books, instead of listening to the twaddle dished out at your silly Women's Empowerment Group, she'd have learned that your canine detectives could sniff out an unfaithful husband at fifty yards."

"It's not a silly group. You have no right to call it that." Bianca paused dramatically before delivering her trump card. "In fact, it was after the last WEG meeting that Wendell growled at Gil!" She folded her arms and waited for their reaction.

"I'm afraid I don't understand," Minnie said.

"Wendell growled," Alix said slowly, nodding her head. "Well, I understand perfectly. Wendell growled. That proves what…? That Wendell disapproves of infidelity? That's some unusual dog!"

Minnie gave a small groan and turned a beet-red face to Tyler, who seemed to be hunching himself even further into the corner of the couch. "Tyler, I'm sorry you have to listen to this. It is all so very unseemly. Some day, when you're older, you'll understand that married people have their little problems, but, with love, they can work them out."

"I don't know about that," Alix said, "but when you grow up, Tyler, please at least have the good sense to choose reading matter that doesn't depend on some fictional dogs' insight into human nature."

Now it was my turn to groan. I knew enough about teens to guarantee that telling a boy that he'd understand something when he grew up was a sure-fire way to slam his mind shut to whatever you were saying. Tyler's expression didn't change, but I surmised that he had leapt—without moving a muscle—from neutral observer to Bianca's side of the argument.

"If you can stop making fun of me long enough to listen," Bianca said, "I started to tell you about a book—"

"Here we go," said Alix. "The dogs, wearing little Sherlock Holmes hats, got confused and chased the distraught wife of a philanderer over the cliff, right?"

Resolutely ignoring Alix, Bianca continued. "The book I read had a situation that was a lot like this one—"

"I'm sure that Gil and Vanessa were very happy in their marriage," insisted Minnie mechanically, still responding to Alix's comments.

"You don't understand, Minnie. Some dog in a neat book that Bianca read growled at a character in that book," Alix said. "That's very significant. I can hardly wait to find out why."

"I really don't think we need to go into this topic more tonight," I said desperately. "Let's go home. Maybe next time we can talk about Tyler's book and—"

Bianca raised her voice once more. "In the book I'm talking about, the whole thing is laid out step by step. If you'd read it for yourselves, you could see that everything is right there in front of you."

"What?" Tyler asked, sitting up straight at last. "What's right in front of us?"

I'd been right. He was rooting for Bianca now.

"Thank you." Bianca spaced her words to lend each one weight. "The dog growled. The dog knew. There was no other evidence, but the growling dog was enough to point Bipsy and Mr. Potts toward the truth. It's the same situation here."

"And the truth was...?" Minnie asked faintly.

"...that Gil pushed Vanessa off that cliff. He murdered her!"

The ensuing silence was broken by only one sound. Under the table, Wendell demolished a piece of bran bar that he had somehow missed before.

FOUR

"GIL, A MURDERER?" Alix doubled over, whooping with laughter. "That's rich. I wouldn't trust him as far as I could throw this couch, but come on! Just how much incense have you been inhaling, Bianca? And you talk about my brain being pickled by cigarette smoke."

"That's not fair," Bianca retorted. "Incense clears the mind, expands your ability to—"

"Don't start that again," Alix said, wiping her eyes, "not when I'm enjoying the best laugh I've had in months."

"This isn't funny." Minnie's distress was palpable. "That poor man…oh, Alix, how could you?"

"How could I? I'm not the one with some cuckoo notion, accusing our esteemed district attorney of…" Once again, laughter overcame her.

"Well," Minnie began uncertainly, "Bianca, you really shouldn't…I mean, I don't want to sound harsh, dear…" She trailed off. Though Minnie always put the best face on a situation, this one was stretching even her considerable abilities. The vigor with which her scarves fluttered attested to the degree of her agitation, but as always, her voice was kind as she attempted to explain to Bianca just why it was that nice people didn't go around accusing other nice people of murder. She finished with a hopeful question. "Perhaps you were only making a little joke?"

"This is no joke!" Alix said. "Let's not forget that the dog growled." Like an over-zealous attorney in a courtroom drama, she pointed a manicured finger at Wendell, whereupon the dog crawled out from under the table, wagging his tail and hoping for more food. “As you can see, Wendell is not a dog that normally growls, so, just like Mr. Pibbs—”

“Mr. Potts,” Bianca interjected. “Well, actually it was Bipsy who first heard the growling dog—”

“Doesn’t matter,” Alix said. “The dog growled and that solved the entire case.”

“No, it didn’t. It just pointed the way to the solution,” Bianca said. “I wish you’d stop making fun of them. They’re more interesting than the so-called detectives in those boring religious mysteries. Rabbi Small just sits around and thinks until he finds the killer. Or how about that Jesuit priest?”

“Father Mark Townsend,” Alix said. “What’s wrong with him?”

“Nothing, probably, but how much excitement can a priest bring to a mystery?”

“How about Travis McGee?” Tyler asked.

“Right,” Bianca agreed. “The John D. MacDonald character. From what you’ve already told us, he can’t step off his houseboat without getting mixed up with slimy Florida land developers. Probably lots more action, but who wants to read about those horrible people? Nobody is as disgusting as that!”

“You should meet my ex-husbands,” Alix offered. “I’ll bet the slimy land developers have better morals than those losers.”

“You’re missing the point,” Bianca said.

“Oh, really?” Alix asked.

As Alix and Bianca continued to argue—with Minnie continuing her fruitless attempts at mediation—my thoughts drifted to possible silver linings in this ludicrous situation. At least they were arguing about fictional murders instead of Bianca’s latest brainstorm. Besides, it was nice to see that something had broken through Tyler’s usually bland exterior. His head swiveled as he followed the volleys in the verbal tennis match before him. Also, for once Alix was participating. Never before had I seen her put down her ever-present cigarette and enter into a conversation with such relish. Even Wendell had abandoned his quest for crumbs and joined the group, wagging his tail and encouraging first one combatant and then the other as the argument raged.

I mentally constructed a score sheet, giving one point for a wisecrack, two for a remark that would cause an opponent to screech, and three for a direct hit that would cause someone to leap over the coffee table in fury. Suddenly, the room went silent. Was it over? Had someone gone for the jugular while I was setting up the rules? Nope, Alix and Bianca were both still breathing, but now they were regrouping for a combined attack on Minnie. I sank onto the couch. Not over. Just opening up another front. I added a column for Minnie onto my imaginary tally sheet.

"At least we're not wasting time reading about murder victims painted in zebra stripes," Bianca said.

"Right," agreed Alix. "We haven't sunk that low. True crime shouldn't even qualify for this club. Any fiction is better than reading that stuff."

Bianca tried a flanking maneuver. "Even Bipsy and Mr. Potts."

"I wouldn't go that far," Alix said, "but zebra stripes?"

"It's not the zebra stripes that make the story!" Minnie hotly defended her passion for true-crime stories. "It's the way they solve the crimes. These things really happened."

Bianca jumped at her chance. "Well, if you like finding out what really happened, Minnie, then give me a chance to prove my point about Van—"

"It was an accident," Minnie wailed.

"How do you know? You haven't heard me out. And you, Alix, you haven't either." She turned appealingly to Tyler, putting a hand on his shoulder. "You'll give me a chance, won't you, Ty?"

The newly christened "Ty" jumped up, a beatific look on his face, as though he'd been knighted by a queen's scepter instead of Bianca's tanned hand. I hadn't seen him move that fast all summer. What on earth? Then I saw his flushed face and knew it wasn't the force of Bianca's arguments that had galvanized him. No red-blooded adolescent could resist the direct entreaty of a young, beautiful woman, especially one who had called on him to act as her champion in the battle against their common enemy—that is, adults who talked down to them.

I knew he was a goner before he even opened his mouth. "Sure, I mean, why not? That's only fair."

"Great! You're terrific, Ty!" Bianca pressed her advantage. "Minnie?"

Still smarting from the zebra comments, Minnie nodded crisply, as though to indicate that she—unlike certain others she could name—was willing to be fair.

"Alix?"

"As Tyler says, why not? I could use another good laugh."

Bianca turned to me. "What do you say, Mom? We'll all read my book before the next meeting. Then you'll understand for yourselves. Ty, you don't mind putting off your selection one more week, do you?"

"No problem."

"See? Ty doesn't mind."

Prince Ty wouldn't mind if Bianca asked him to eat fish fertilizer. I wondered once more how I had landed in this mess. Just wait until I get my hands around your scrawny neck, Laurence, I thought, and I'll give you a murder that won't be hard to solve, even if there aren't any zebra stripes for clues.

Raymond Morris's Rule Number Seven came to mind:

Agree whenever you can. Our seeming acquiescence might keep the lid on Bianca for a while longer, and maybe her fantasy could be brought back into bounds without anyone outside the group learning about it. "Nothing public meanwhile," I insisted.

"That's fine," Bianca agreed. "As long as you give me a chance."

"Okay, apparently we're all in agreement," I said. Everyone nodded. "We'll read your book, Bianca. Give me the title and I'll order it tomorrow."

"Prove It, Puppy!" she announced happily. "How soon will it arrive?"

I swallowed hard before continuing. "If I order before noon, we should have it here by the next day."

"Great!" Bianca clapped her hands, reminding me of her excitement at age seven when she won a goldfish at the Pioneer Elementary School PTA carnival. "I'd better get started."

"On what?" I asked. "You agreed that you're not going to do anything—"

"Nothing public," she responded.

I wasn't reassured. "You know about slander and defamation of character—"

"Oh, Mom. Don't be silly. I just have a few things to do." She turned to talk to Tyler.

Usually I heard Laurence's shuffling footsteps and labored breathing long before he appeared in a room, but I'd been so preoccupied that I'd missed his entrance this time. He was leaning against the doorjamb, looking amazed to see his grandson in animated conversation with Bianca, or, as Laurence had once described her, "your colorful butterfly of a daughter."

Laurence looked even more surprised when Tyler hurried

over to him. "You won't mind if Jane orders some books for us, will you, Grandpa? We each need our own copy right away."

For a moment pure astonishment kept Laurence from answering, but I knew he wanted to encourage anything that interested Tyler. He finally stammered, "No, of course not, Tyler, but maybe we already have the books you need."

I gave Laurence a look that told him most definitely that these books would not already be on our shelves. That wouldn't matter though. Tyler had shown a spark of life and Laurence wanted to fan that spark into flame. He continued smoothly, "Or if we don't, Jane can order them right away."

Bianca fluttered over to him and said, "Oh, thank you, Laurence. Ty said you wouldn't mind. I already have my copy, but the others will each need one, so that makes four."

I always expected that courtly old Laurence would be taken aback by such a young woman calling him by his first name, but he was as mesmerized by Bianca as his grandson. "We'd be glad to...er, Bianca. What's the title?"

Bianca favored him with an incandescent smile and said, "It's by Laddy and Lady. Those are the names on the book jacket anyway, but that's sort of an 'in' joke. I mean, Laddy and Lady aren't really the authors."

Apparently still drowning in that smile, Laurence said weakly, "Of course not. You're just making a little joke... and the title is...?"

"*Prove It, Puppy!* It's a really good book. You might want to get an extra copy for yourself."

Belatedly, I realized that Laurence didn't normally make the trek upstairs without good reason. "Is something wrong, Laurence?" No answer. Whatever the original reason for his hike, it apparently had fled his mind at the mention of a book called *Prove It, Puppy!* He was opening and closing his mouth like a bass out of water.

I crossed the room to him and put my hand on his bony arm. He turned slowly, his attention clearly elsewhere. "Wrong? What makes you think anything is wrong?"

"Well, you normally don't come up here—"

"Are you implying that I can't make it up the stairs whenever I—"

"Of course not, but are you feeling all right? You look a little flushed." I led him back toward the couch. "Here, why don't you sit down?"

"No, I don't want… Stop mothering me, Jane. I won't have it. Did she say *Prove It, Puppy!* is the book she wants? I can't believe—"

"Maybe you'd like a frosted bran bar," I interjected.

"A frosted bran bar?" he repeated. Distracted, he sat down. "Why would anyone frost a bran bar? Why would anyone want a bran bar, frosted or not?"

"Oh, sorry. They're all gone, of course," I said, glancing at Wendell, who was now stretched out on the carpet, legs twitching as he dreamed. At least I hoped he was dreaming, and not going into spasms as a result of an overdose of fiber. "Just sit here a minute until…uh…until you remember what it is—"

"I'm not senile, Jane. I know why I came up here. It was just that I couldn't believe I heard right when—"

"Yes, yes, I'll explain later. Now, you were saying…?"

"It was Susannah."

"Susannah?" Several days had passed since I'd talked to my oldest daughter, and her due date for this difficult pregnancy was fast approaching. "She called?"

"Well, that's what I'm trying to tell you. Yes, she called, and she wants you to call her right back. Those were her exact words."

Bianca said, "I left a message on her machine earlier. Maybe she was calling me back."

"She specifically asked for your mother," Laurence answered.

"Was she all right?" I asked. "Has she started labor? Why didn't you tell me sooner?"

"That's what I was trying to do when you dropped me into this black hole of a couch." As he spoke, Laurence attempted to lever himself back to a standing position, finally heaving himself to his feet with a Herculean effort borne of frustration and embarrassment at his obvious frailty. "You'd better get downstairs and find out what she wanted." He waved off my help. "No, no, I'll be fine. Just go."

"I'll help you, Grandpa," said Tyler.

"So will I," Bianca chimed in.

"No, thank you…er, Bianca. Tyler's help will be sufficient."

"Want me to call Susannah, Mom?"

"I'd better do it, as long as she asked for me," I said. Limiting Bianca's conversations with anyone outside this group was a high priority for me at the moment.

"Well, in that case," Bianca said, "come on, Wendell. We have things to do."

"What kind of things?" Minnie asked. "Remember, it's not nice—"

"Don't worry," Bianca replied. "Now that you've agreed to read the book, I can take my time and do this right."

"Don't be dense, Minnie," said Alix. "She's going to get a trench coat, of course. Probably didn't think to pack one with her summer cottons."

"Not that it should matter to you, Alix, but after I straighten things up here, I'm going to the Good Food Store to get the ingredients to make Wendell's dog food." She looked around in some surprise at the disarray caused by Wendell's quest for the ill-fated frosted bran bars.

"Ah, I see," Alix said. "He's such a picky eater. Clever girl. Apparently, you did remember to pack your trench coat. I have to get a few groceries, too. Perhaps we'll meet over the wheat germ."

Minnie said, "Well, that's all right then. We'll clear up everything after we get a look at this book of yours, Bianca, though I don't think for a minute that—"

"Walk downstairs with me," I said, gripping Minnie's arm. "Coming, Alix?"

"Might as well," said Alix. "Today's show seems to be over. Call when my copy of the book arrives."

I hustled them out the door and down the hall. "I'll let you know." With any luck at all, Ingram's Roseburg warehouse wouldn't have any copies of these books, and by the time we could order them from a secondary warehouse, maybe Bianca would have forgotten this whole thing.

But right now, I needed to call Susannah.

FIVE

BECAUSE OF MY SHAKING HANDS, it took me several tries to dial Susannah's number correctly. I should have packed a bag before this so I could be ready to leave the minute she called, but Bianca's accusation had put it completely out of my mind. How could I fly to Minnesota with things here so unsettled, but how could I not? Susannah was counting on me to take care of Kevin while she was in the hospital. The answering machine picked up after the sixth ring, leaving me time to envision a breech birth, trips to the emergency room, pools of blood, hastily arranged plane tickets…

So deep was I into disaster mode that I almost missed it when the recorded messaged segued into Susannah's voice, barely audible over the screams in the background. "Mom, if that's you, don't hang up!"

"Is that Kevin? What's happened?"

"Kevin's fine, or he would be if I could get the peanut butter out of his hair. Just a minute." The continuing background commotion told me how Kevin felt about the situation. Finally, the wails died away and Susannah was back. "Okay."

"Should I call the airport? It won't take more than—"

"Relax. The baby's not coming yet, Mom."

"But Laurence—"

"Sorry if I scared you, but your situation sounded serious."

"What situation is that?" I asked, stalling for time.

"The Louise situation, of course." Always the impatient older sister, Susannah refused to use the name Bianca had chosen for herself. The two of them had never been compatible, and the considerable distance between Minnesota and Oregon suited them both. Susannah's tone of voice when speaking of her younger sister veered primarily between disapproval and disbelief. We were in disbelief territory at the moment, but I expected that to change soon. "Some wild story about a murder? She's not answering her phone at home, but I thought you'd know what she was talking about."

"Well, you see—" I started to explain, but broke off as Minnie swept back into the store.

Minnie's color was high and she wore a frown on her normally cheerful countenance. "I know that 'a soft answer turneth away wrath,' Jane, but I'm not sure how long I can continue to remain calm if Alix doesn't stop making unkind remarks about poor Gil. I've decided to go straight over to his house with some of my peanut butter cookies…well, right after I pick up some peanut butter and bake the cookies. I just wanted you to know that I don't blame your daughter though. Bianca is just young and foolish. We'll soon set her straight, but Alix should know better. Her attitude is outrageous!" Belatedly she noticed the telephone I held to my ear.

"Susannah?" she asked. At my nod she started backing out the door. "Everything all right?" Another nod. "Don't let me keep you then. Just order those books, Jane. The sooner we clear this up, the better. Poor Gil."

"Susannah? Sorry. That was Minnie Salter. Look—"

Wendell hurtled down the stairs and out the open door, with Bianca in hot pursuit. She paused long enough to ask, "Is everything okay with Susannah?"

I gave her the thumbs up signal.

"Great! Fill her in, will you? I need to catch Wendell. He kept getting under my feet, so I just called out, 'Wendell! Dinnertime!' and he took off. I was afraid he'd break Laurence's leg or something. Gosh, that man is really decrepit, isn't he? Talk to you later. Say hi to Susannah and the sprout."

She paused in the doorway to locate Wendell before sprinting across the lawn. "Wendell, drop it!"

Susannah's voice came through the receiver again, bringing me back to the conversation I'd been hoping to avoid. "What's going on?"

"It's complicated. Vanessa Fortune had an accident at the Crooked River Gorge this morning…and she died. Everyone's very upset, of course."

"Any chance she was pushed?" Susannah asked.

"Uh…not really. She was alone."

"And…? Oh, I see. Let me guess. In spite of that fact, dear Louise has concluded that Vanessa was murdered."

"Well, yes." Susannah really did know her sister well.

"Do the police agree?"

"Uh, apparently not."

"And, according to Sleuth Louise, this murder was committed by…?"

I really didn't want to tell her, so I said the name in a very quiet voice.

Unfortunately, she heard me anyway. "Gil? Louise thinks Gil murdered Vanessa?"

"I told you it was hard to explain. Apparently the plot of a book your sister was reading resembles the situation with Vanessa."

"I'll just bet it does."

I ignored the sarcasm and plodded on with my explanation. "In the book something looked like an accident, but it really was a murder. We're going to discuss the book at our next meeting."

"I can't believe it! Don't let her walk all over you, Mom. You have to do something about her. She can't just go around accusing people of murder."

"I know."

"What planet is she on? Can't you try to get her back into the real world for once?"

"I think maybe she's simmered down since she called, but you know your sister."

"I certainly do." Susannah's disapproval dial was set on high. She had never encountered a rule she wanted to break, never looked at a pond she wanted to rile, so Bianca's penchant for stirring things up was a constant source of friction between them. As someone who loved them both, I found it hard to watch them clash, though there was little I could do. It was easier for me to understand Susannah's more rational viewpoint, but that merely made me redouble my efforts to make sense of Bianca's need to break free of restrictions. Each of the girls, of course, thought I took the side of the other, so I couldn't win.

Between Bianca telling me to loosen up and Susannah urging me to tighten up, I found myself doing quite a balancing act. Thank goodness Emily was off in her own little world, one that counted Inca civilization far more fascinating than anything since the sixteenth century. Emily noticed people only if they had been covered with dirt for a few centuries and then discovered as a pile of bones.

When I tuned in once more to the current conversation, Susannah was still giving directions. "Well, she's your daughter. Talk to her..."

"Don't you think I've tried?"

"Do it some more."

The fact that I'd been talking to Louise/Bianca for nineteen years without result seemed to have escaped Susannah's notice. Susannah used to line up her dolls and order them to behave, so presumably she'd mastered a better maternal technique than I had. Thank goodness she'd married a nice, relaxed man like Mike, or Kevin and his soon-to-be-born new baby sister or brother would have stood a good chance of being pressed into little robot molds.

"How about Emily?" Susannah apparently had decided we needed reinforcements. "Have you talked to her?"

"About this? Well, it only came up today, and besides…"

"You're right. She hasn't noticed anything that's happened in the past five hundred years, so she wouldn't be much help. You need to talk to her about being a more active member of this family." Another failing of mine. Susannah had a whole list of improvements in mind for me, just as Bianca did. The only trouble was that they were two entirely different lists. Apparently I needed improvement in an astounding number of areas. I imagined that the items on Susannah's list were alphabetized and arranged in order of priority.

At times like this, I missed Tony more than ever.

SIX

"WHAT'S THAT ALL ABOUT?" Harley Cunningham, Gil Fortune's best friend, stood in the open doorway and watched Bianca chase Wendell across the grass. Harley's words were light, but his handsome face was etched with strain, his dress shirt open at the collar, and his short blond hair uncharacteristically disheveled. As the manager of the Juniper Frontier Bank, he usually looked as though he'd stepped directly out of the pages of *GQ,* but he'd obviously put in a rough day.

"Just Wendell being Wendell," I answered.

"Bianca signed him up for obedience school?" He tried for the small joke, but his heart wasn't in it.

"Well, no, but maybe she should." This poor man. My thoughts were in an uproar, but it seemed better to blame Bianca's precipitous exit on her unruly dog than to tell Harley that Bianca was probably off to gather evidence against his best friend. There was no way to ignore the subject of Vanessa's horrible accident though, so I waded in. "Harley, I'm so sorry to hear about Vanessa. How's Gil doing?"

"About the way you'd expect. He's just basically in shock." Harley rubbed a hand over his eyes. "I guess we all are."

"I can imagine," I said. "Especially since you grew up together—"

"Since the eighth grade. That's when Vanessa's family moved here. You know how most girls that age are sort of awkward? Not Vanessa. Every boy in school was in love with her, including Gil. Vanessa fell for him, too, and that was that. Like a fairy tale romance." Harley's deep voice grew husky as he struggled for control. "Who'd have guessed it would end like this? I don't know how Gil's going to make it."

I didn't know how to respond. If Bianca could see the sadness on Harley's face when he described Gil's anguish at Vanessa's death, maybe she'd drop the nonsense about murder. Vanessa's fall was part of the same cruel reality that explained—or failed to explain—Tony's accident a year ago. People mostly don't die by getting murdered. Instead, their planes crash or they fall off cliffs or they get sick and die sad little deaths that leave everyone around them scrambling to find satisfactory explanations.

Bianca hadn't yet lived long enough to gain the perspective to grasp that. Though her father's death had certainly wounded her, she was young enough to believe that death didn't really have all that much to do with her. She still had the luxury of making a drama out of death and then going on with life, instead of undertaking the long, slow healing that must be endured after your life's partner has been wrenched from you. I had faced that situation and now Gil was about to start through it. I pushed from my mind Alix's comments about Gil's alleged infidelities. After all, Alix's cynicism about most things was well known.

"If you're able to talk about it," I said, "do they know yet what happened?"

"I don't mind," Harley answered. "We'll have to get used to it sooner or later, and I can't think of anything else right now anyway. Arnie thinks it was a freak accident, that she somehow slipped off the trail while taking pictures. She was alone, so we'll never know for sure, I guess." He appeared lost in contemplation for a moment before resuming his train of thought. "She was always so graceful and light on her feet that it's hard to imagine her falling. I always thought she should have been a dancer."

"I know what you mean," I said. Even women responded

to Vanessa's porcelain beauty. Her dark cloud of hair had framed features so lovely that they were almost unreal. "She seemed to float in a world of her own. In fact, just yesterday when she was here in the store for the Women's Empowerment Group meeting upstairs, she was so alive, so vibrant—"

"I know, I know," Harley cut in, as though he couldn't bear to hear more. It struck me that maybe he hadn't ever quite gotten over his schoolboy crush on Vanessa. He had been briefly married long ago to someone else, but no one ever talked about it and he had never remarried.

"Well, I'm sorry for all of you who were close to her, Harley. It's just a terrible tragedy."

"Thank you. She was the best. No doubt about it. Look, Jane, there's a reason I came. I hate to bother you with it, but—"

"Still open?" Nick Constantine's stocky frame almost filled the doorway. "Sorry to interrupt your conversation," he added politely. Nick was an attorney from Santa Monica taking an extended vacation in Juniper this summer. His taste in reading was wide-ranging, and I always enjoyed seeing which books he'd choose next.

"That's okay," Harley said with a frown. "Go ahead, Jane."

"We're not open, technically," I answered Nick, "but as long as you're here—"

"Thanks." Nick grinned and made straight for the sports books. "I hope you have more copies of those *100 Hikes in Central Oregon* books. I bought the first one for Pete, but now Theo wants one, too. That's the trouble with twins. Sometimes they like the same things and it gets expensive."

"They're both coming to see you?"

"Yep, and they want plenty of activities lined up. They don't want to be stuck in the house listening to me the whole time they're here."

"Oh, wait. I sold the last copy earlier. More due in tomorrow though. Is that okay?"

"If you don't mind, I'll just check to see if anything else might work."

"Sure."

He disappeared behind the shelves and I turned back to Harley.

"Sorry. You were saying—"

"Really a couple of things. The reunion meeting, for one."

"Oh, of course. That's what…? Tomorrow night?" Once Bianca had discovered that Thornton's Books was in financial trouble, she had suggested that Laurence offer the upstairs as a place for other meetings in addition to those of the mystery book club, hoping the increased foot traffic would bring in new business. Laurence had agreed without a murmur. Thus, both the Women's Empowerment Group and the Class of 1984 Reunion Committee had recently started trooping through the bookstore on a regular basis. Unfortunately, the WEG members tended to buy only the kind of self-help books that Laurence detested. I always hustled him off to the back room to keep him from telling customers that they were reading tripe when they came to pick up any books they had ordered.

On the bright side, however, at least the WEG members bought books, whereas the members of the reunion committee didn't pause to buy anything in their haste to get upstairs to their meetings. They were far more interested in trying to remember whose cousin it was that Sandi Millican had gone skinny dipping with in Tumalo Reservoir after the senior prom, or chasing down the latest lead from long-retired custodians about the whereabouts of the time capsule supposedly buried within the walls of Juniper Senior High School the year they had graduated. They were having such a fine time reliving their high school years that they had no time for buying books. Gil had been senior class president, and

Vanessa the secretary, so they had been the natural choices to co-chair the reunion committee. "I assume the meeting is cancelled?"

"No, we're going ahead...without Gil, of course. Just let people know, if you wouldn't mind—"

"But what about the reunion itself? It's supposed to be held—"

"Two weeks from now, and we're not cancelling." Harley's voice was firm. "Gil was adamant. He didn't immediately think of it, but he was all in favor of going forward, once I mentioned it to him. He doesn't want our classmates to forfeit all their hard work, and he doesn't think Vanessa would have wanted it either."

"Tough for the committee."

"We'll just do the best we can. I'm sure it will all work out. I was the vice-president of our class, so I've had plenty of practice filling in for Gil before this."

"I didn't realize that. But won't you be busy helping Gil with—"

"The funeral arrangements? Yes, that, too."

"Not to mention your job."

"This is one time when being my own boss will come in extremely handy." He shrugged. "Anyway, helping Gil is my top priority. We can't always pick the times our friends need us."

"Let me know if there's anything more I can do..."

"Really? That's great. I don't suppose—"

"Ask it."

"Would you reconsider going to the reunion as my date?"

Though I had begged off when he'd asked me the same question last week, now I hesitated only briefly before replying with as much warmth as I could muster. "Well, sure, Harley. I could do that." I wasn't interested in going out with Harley, though my kids had been teasing me all summer about the attention he paid me. Besides, Harley was five years younger than I, and even though he was the nicest guy in the world, I couldn't see him ever being more than a friend. Still, it seemed important to him, and it wouldn't hurt me to go out with him just this once. "That'd be great, if the offer's still open."

"Of course it is." His face seemed to lose some of the strain now as he smiled, and I felt bad for having turned him down before.

"Let's do it then. What else?"

"My chess book, or isn't it here yet?"

"Sorry, you need to choose a less esoteric title if you want it to be in stock. This one's been hard to find."

"That's okay. I don't really have time for it right now anyway. I'll call you. Meanwhile, if you'd just tell people that the reunion—"

Harley's expression changed from friendly to guarded the moment he saw the beefy man barrel through the still-open door. This place was Grand Central Station tonight.

"Is my son here, Jane?" Kurt Wendorf's eyes were wide and his face red, as though he'd been running.

"Well, no, I haven't—"

"Tyler then?"

"Upstairs. I don't think he's seen Max this afternoon, Kurt. Is something wrong?"

Kurt's expression darkened as he finally registered Harley's presence. He pointed a thick finger in his direction. "Now don't you go running to Gil, making something out of nothing, Harley. Max is probably home, but—"

"But what, Kurt?" Harley asked. "Is there some other problem...again?"

"There wouldn't have been one in the first place, if people'd kept their heads and—"

"And ignored the fact that Max tried to burn down a school?"

"No!" Kurt thundered. "And let kids be kids!"

"A bomb isn't kid stuff," Harley countered. "What'd you expect? Gil's the district attorney. He did his best, but—"

"His best? God, you never were a kid, were you, Harley? Ah, forget it—" Kurt made a dismissive motion and turned back to me. "Jane, if you see Max…"

"I'll tell him you're looking for him."

"Thanks." He lumbered back out the door.

Harley said, "That's one classmate I don't think will make it to the reunion. Kurt never was famous for his brains, but this has really brought out the Neanderthal in him."

"The urge to protect your child doesn't always square with reason," I said, thinking about my own situation with Bianca.

"I guess," Harley said. "Well, I'd better get back and run interference for Gil, in case Kurt decides to pay him a visit. Want me to close the door?"

"Just leave it. We can use the breeze. Tell Gil…well, you know what to say."

After Harley left, I turned to the mundane business of counting the money in the register, sighing at the meager total for the day.

"Long day?" The voice came from the shadows.

I jerked upright, momentarily disoriented. "Nick! I'd forgotten all about you."

"Obviously." He tossed two books onto the counter, along with a Visa card. "Am I too late to buy these?"

"No, of course not." I started ringing them up. "I hadn't finished closing out yet and every little bit helps. Interesting combination you have here, *Reptiles of the Northwest* and *Lincoln's Greatest Speech*."

Nick shrugged. "I like to read. Not that it's any of my business, but were you sighing over business, your friends' argument, or your date for the class reunion? Sorry, but I couldn't help overhearing. This place isn't that big."

"At least you're honest about the eavesdropping. I guess the answer is yes to all of the above. It's just been a really bad day."

"I'm a good listener."

I ticked off the topics on my fingers. "Well, the problem with business can be summed up in two words: Megabooks Plus! No surprise there. It's the classic big impersonal store versus the friendly little one."

"Don't worry. There are plenty of people like me who want to talk to real people in a friendly little bookstore."

"I just hope there are enough of you."

"If there aren't, I'll buy more books. Problem solved. Next?"

"Have you been reading the local papers? Do you know what Harley and Kurt were talking about?"

"Harley's the stuffed shirt and Kurt's the hothead with the delinquent son?"

"Well, I wouldn't describe them that—"

"Close enough. This is about a smoke bomb at a school?"

"Right, at Juniper High School. And the indictment just came out, so Kurt's got a lot on his mind right now. He's usually a very nice guy."

"And the district attorney, the one who prosecuted the kid, he's the one whose wife fell off the cliff today?"

"Right. They all went to Juniper High—Gil, Vanessa, Harley, and Kurt. They were even in the same class, which seemed to make Kurt particularly mad at the indictment."

"So I gathered. He thinks the D.A. was too hard on his son?"

"Max did set off a bomb in the school."

"A smoke bomb. There's a difference."

"But people can't just go around setting off bombs. You're an officer of the court, aren't you? You must agree with that."

"I was also a boy once, and I have a couple of rambunctious sons. Maybe I'd like to hear the defense's side of things before I decide whether to hang this kid out to dry."

"The case was supposed to be pretty clear-cut."

"I didn't think anything relating to kids was clear-cut," he countered.

"Spoken like a true parent," I acknowledged. With everything that had been going on since the book club meeting, I'd been able to put Bianca out of my mind, but now she was back.

"That's two down," Nick said. "Now, what's the problem with your date for the reunion, other than that he's a stuffed shirt?"

"Would you quit saying that? Harley is a very nice man. Anyway, I think I can handle dating questions without your help."

The phone on the wall behind me rang, and Nick waved a hand in farewell as I turned to answer it. The hollow, crackling line told me immediately that Emily was weighing in from Peru.

"Mom? Mom? What's all this about Bianca?"

SEVEN

EARLY THE NEXT MORNING I drove toward the dilapidated trailer Bianca called home, rehearsing my pledge not to confront her. If I failed to remain calm, she wouldn't hear a word I said. Raymond Morris's Rule Number One would be my mantra: *Make each conversation a positive experience.* Usually by the time I heard Bianca's first three words, my resolve to be conciliatory had disappeared like apple pie at a potluck. Today though, I vowed to pry open the gates of communication and hold them wide until I could get my message across.

This time I wasn't talking about something as simple as her recent stunt of lying down in the road to hold up traffic in protest of the shortage of "duck crossing" signs at Drake Park in nearby Bend. Raymond Morris said such actions merely proved that Bianca was testing her own values as she learned to separate from her childhood home. I understood the concept, but couldn't she test with green hair or something?

I soon covered the ten miles east of Juniper on Highway 28 and bumped my way down the track to Bianca's trailer. A cloud of dust enveloped my tan Volvo as it bounced to a stop. It was an old car but, thanks to Tony's care over the years, still dependable. I grabbed a dirty envelope from the floor on the passenger side and wrote, "Tune-up?" Now that Tony was no longer here to take care of such things, I wrote many such notes to myself. How often did cars need tune-ups anyway? It had already been over a year.

I squinted through the now grimy windshield, trying to make out whether Bianca was home. Of course, there was no car parked out front, as Bianca had informed me recently that a bicycle was the most acceptable mode of private transportation if one were serious about wanting to avoid polluting the environment. Too bad she hadn't taken that attitude in high school when she and her friends spent most of their time racing off to the Juniper Park Mall in our car.

Watching our sunny, scatterbrained daughter grow up, Tony and I had at times suspected that we had brought the wrong baby home from the hospital at birth. When Bianca announced her plan to embark on a photographic tour of the United States after her high school graduation, we concluded that our suspicions had been right. We didn't want her wandering across the United States by herself, and we were still arguing with her about it when Tony died.

Under the circumstances, I'd hoped she'd forget the trip, and she actually did start a summer job at the cozy Sagebrush Café, where unforgettable home cooking and the eccentricity of the owner, Dot Jannings, went hand in hand. Dot valued Bianca's adventurous spirit, and Bianca loved working for someone who appreciated her, but Bianca didn't want to stay in Juniper and Dot knew it. A few weeks after Tony's funeral, with Dot's full support, Bianca hung up her apron and set off toward Idaho on a Greyhound bus, with only a vague notion of where she was going and when she'd return.

After Dot died this past spring I found out just how much she'd thought of my daughter. Without a word beforehand, Dot had deeded over her old trailer to Bianca. When I told Bianca about this in one of our infrequent phone calls, she was saddened by her friend's death, but thrilled that Dot had left her the trailer. Impulsively, she made immediate plans to come home and take up residence in it. Her first decision as an owner was to move the trailer from the Sunny Trails Trailer Park out of town to where she could see the stars.

As I stepped out of the car, I saw her bicycle lying beside the trailer. Looking past it, I caught a glimpse of bright color on the gentle slope beyond and realized that Bianca was probably meditating. This was the daily routine she had adopted after discovering Bhatami Rhami's book, *One With The Earth,* discarded on a park bench in Taos six months before. According to her, she'd picked it up casually, but had immediately become engrossed in its message, so much so that by the time the day—and the book—ended, Rhami had a convert. Our conversations about his teachings had been conspicuously lacking in agreement, mostly because they sounded like total claptrap to me.

"A part I just love, Mom," she had once explained, "is when I face in the direction of the approaching sunrise, close my eyes, and meditate until I feel the warmth of the sun on my face."

"A Central Oregon sunrise doesn't have all that much warmth," I'd answered. "I hope wearing a sweater figures prominently in his instructions."

"It's easy to mock, but you haven't even tried it. If you'd just allow yourself to absorb the sun's energy, you'd start the day in harmony with the rhythm of the earth instead of having to put on a sweater to keep yourself warm."

"Give pneumonia a chance, is that it?"

"Look, I'm not asking you to do anything your inner spirit doesn't command, but really, the rest of your day would flow so much more naturally if you'd give this a try. If you don't ever try anything new, how will you know whether it works?"

After I told her that my inner spirit often commanded sweaters, the conversation started to deteriorate, and it clanked to a complete halt when I suggested that it probably wasn't an accident that Rhami had developed his philosophy in the warmth of sunny Bombay, India, rather than in Fairbanks, Alaska. Before removing herself from my unredeemable presence, Bianca had informed me that Rhami had followers everywhere, and he had addressed this very issue in the foreword to the second edition of the book. Those unfortunate people who couldn't see a sunrise—due to smog or tall buildings or igloos—should meditate until they could visualize the sun's rays. It was mind over matter. However, Bianca had little need for this backup method, since Juniper had few igloos, little smog, and hardly any buildings over three stories high, except for the eight-story High Desert Community Hospital.

Remembering my vow not to antagonize her this morning, I waited until she sauntered toward me before raising my arm in a tentative wave. She waved back enthusiastically and I relaxed a notch. Never one to hold a grudge, Bianca appeared to have rebounded from last night's rebuffs at book club. She'd probably concluded, as usual, that we weren't bad people, merely unenlightened. She had encountered the same resistance to her attempted reformation of our eating habits, reading preferences, and of course, politics, but as she had once confided, "I'm willing to cut some people a little slack. After all, Minnie is sixty, and that's…eighteen years older than you are." The incredulity in her tone at my advanced age of forty-two would normally have sparked a response, but I kept quiet, waiting to hear why the elderly Minnie was allowed so much latitude. "Minnie can't be blamed for being slow to pick up new ideas. She's probably thinking about varicose veins or cholesterol, though if she'd eat more flax and raw vegetables, she wouldn't have to worry so much.

"Hi," she said now as she came near enough to talk. "I've been thinking about you."

Was that good or bad? "Me, too," I answered. "How are you this morning?"

"I'm fine," she said absently before moving on to what was apparently on her mind. "Did you notice that Ty, the youngest person in the group, was the only one willing to listen to me last night?"

Ah, so we were back to last night. "Tyler would listen to you read the ingredients on a can of soup," I said. Raising a hand to forestall her probable next comment, I added, "Though, of course, you would never eat a can of soup."

"And you wouldn't either, if you read the ingredients—"

"—particularly the sodium content," I finished. I didn't want to tread the same old path this morning. We could argue about nutrition anytime.

"Exactly. Well, I'm glad you're at least pretending to listen. Tyler was really paying attention last night though. I could tell. Sometimes it gets discouraging when no one will hear me out about really important things."

Choosing Morris's Rule Number Ten about silence from my arsenal, I said nothing. It would be unkind to tell her to lighten up, but hearing her out could usually be translated into being harangued about one "important" cause or another. Her unremitting seriousness was wearing. Meanwhile, I'd just keep quiet and let her think that Tyler's young brain was eager to absorb her insights into human nature. After all, he had probably even been willing to eat the frosted bran bars, before Wendell took care of them. Maybe next he'd join her for meditation. Let her think, in her naiveté, that he just hungered for knowledge. In the long run it was probably better for everyone if she didn't realize the electrifying effect she was likely to have on young men. All I cared about right now was deflecting her from her cause of the week, Gil Fortune.

Her next question told me that it wouldn't be easy. "Did you catch the KPHD news this morning?"

"Well, no. Did you?" The last I heard, Bianca hadn't hooked up the old black and white portable TV that had come with the trailer. "Can you get a signal way out here?"

"I strung an antenna and wire to a juniper tree on the slope out back."

"How clever of you. I wouldn't have thought…"

"Dad showed me once. Anyway, it worked well enough to get the news. Gil was on, claiming he was at an open house for a place he and Vanessa were thinking of buying, claiming he loved her, claiming blah, blah, blah. Obviously, not true."

"What's obvious is that he was somewhere else."

"He claims he was somewhere else."

"Fair enough, but no doubt someone saw him at the open house." I was determined to take this step by step and force a logical conclusion. "Why do you assume the police haven't checked that out?"

"They're all friends of his."

"Of course they know him, but they'd still follow standard police procedure." I could hear my voice rising, so I collected myself before continuing. "If they did, and someone saw him somewhere else…" I paused to let the logic sink in.

Bianca shrugged. "That doesn't explain Wendell's growl. You're just hung up on Gil being a prominent member of this community—"

"He's lived here his whole life. He's the district attorney."

"Does that disqualify him from being a killer? Maybe he went into a career in law because he had these dark impulses."

"Oh, Bianca, that pop psychology is just, just…"

"Stupid?"

"I didn't say that."

"No, you didn't, for once. Well, Mom, did you see Vanessa fall?"

"No, and neither did you…or anyone else."

"But I did see it when Wendell growled at Gil. That's secondary evidence."

"Evidence? Wendell is a dog. Dogs sometimes growl."

"Not Wendell." We both looked involuntarily at the black

dog stretched out asleep in the dust. He didn't look capable of moving, let alone menacing anyone.

"Maybe Gil stepped on his tail."

"Nope, he didn't even touch Wendell. Gil walked up to Vanessa after the WEG meeting when I was talking to her and Wendell growled, clear as anything. Wendell knew even then. And the next day Vanessa was murdered."

"Vanessa fell. The growling the day before was a coincidence. You're making something out of nothing. Gil could sue you for slander!"

"And I could be hit by lightning, but this is different. This is a matter of justice." She was in her Joan of Arc crusader mode now. "I can't believe you'd want me to walk away from this. Look, it's easy to slip in and out of sight at an open house. Who's to say for sure where Gil was at any given time?"

"Let Arnie—"

"Arnie grew up with Gil."

"Yes, but it's his job to investigate."

"You believe that he'll really do it?"

"Give him a chance."

"Give me a chance, too. You've made it clear many times that you don't believe in the intuitive powers of animals. Fine. If I hadn't seen Wendell's reaction to Gil after the WEG meeting, I might not have given the 'accident' a second thought either, but animals are—"

"Animals. Please, just let Arnie conduct his investigation."

"I'll watch the noon news and see what they're saying, but I can't promise anything past that. Do you want to stay and help me cut out quilt blocks?"

"Quilt blocks?" Her shift of focus took me by surprise.

"For the senior center. I told them I'd bring some for one of their classes."

"What a nice thing to do," I said. I was encouraged that her often misplaced energy was being directed at something so beneficial. Maybe her positive impulse would carry over through the noon news.

AFTER WE'D SPENT SEVERAL hours cutting yards of colorful fabric to the proper size, Bianca set up a couple of rickety folding chairs outside the trailer. It wasn't quite time for the noon news yet, but already the morning coolness had evolved into the usual hot August day on the high desert.

"Carrot juice?" Bianca stuck her head out of the doorway as she spoke.

"Um, sure." I'd start with being agreeable about juice and work my way up to murder accusations later.

"I have V-8, too..."

"Even better." I smiled. She was trying to meet me halfway. Bianca returned, glasses in hand, and sat beside me in the tiny patch of shade at the side of the trailer. "Thanks," I said. "Do you ever wish you'd left the trailer in town, where there were trees to cool it?"

"I like the silence out here, and the view."

We drank our juice and contemplated the dry soil and sagebrush that stretched in all directions. "It's silent all right," I offered, "and it does have a stark beauty."

"It grows on you. Really, it does. I watch the hawks during the day and listen to the coyotes at night." Bianca stroked Wendell's glossy black fur as she spoke. "And, of course, I have Wendell. Good thing this trailer started out in town though or I wouldn't ever have met him." She laughed. "When I first saw him, it took me a while to figure out just what I was looking at. His dark fur blended perfectly with the shadows under the trailer. Finally I got close enough to figure out that I wasn't looking at a monster, just a one-eyed dog. You were waiting for me, weren't you, boy?" Wendell thumped his tail.

"He must have had an owner at some point."

"Not that I could find. That trailer had been sitting empty

for a long time. I checked at the office with Richard, who was supposed to be the park manager." Her tone left no doubt that Richard, like most people Bianca met, needed some shaping up. "When I showed up to ask about Wendell, Richard was eating his lunch, which consisted entirely of a store-bought frozen peach pie. Can you imagine?" She drank some carrot juice and shook her head. "After I demanded to know the name of the criminal who had left that poor dog to fend for himself, I warned Richard about the preservatives that go into frozen pies. Have you read those labels?"

"No, and I'm guessing that Richard hadn't either." I resisted the urge to call him "Poor Richard." Bianca on a tear was something to behold.

"You're absolutely right. He didn't have much to say for himself, but he swore that he didn't know anything about Wendell. By the time I left, he did say he'd try to improve his eating habits."

"I'll bet."

"Turned out to be a pretty nice guy. I went back later and dropped off some fresh broccoli and a pamphlet on preservatives. When I moved the trailer from the park, he was real friendly."

"Broccoli works wonders." Bianca was so focused on her story that she let that one pass. Usually she picked up my sarcasm better than this.

"I wrote a letter to the *Juniper Journal* about responsible pet ownership, but, of course, they didn't print it."

Bianca had already written to the *Juniper Journal* twice since her arrival in town this spring: the first time about the officious police cadet who told her she couldn't cool her feet in the swan fountain in nearby Bend's Drake Park, and the second time about the lack of organic foods available locally. Her letter about pet ownership had been returned bearing a scrawled note informing her that only one letter to the editor per person per month was allowed.

"I know they just made up that rule because they don't like my ideas, but I'm sending letters anyway whenever I have something to say. Even if they don't publish all of them, at least the editor gets to read them."

I said nothing and concentrated on the kindness my daughter had shown to a stray dog. "It took you a few days to coax him out from under the trailer, didn't it?"

"And another week before he'd trust me enough to get close. Now he follows me everywhere."

I noted his sleek sides and glossy coat. "He's filled out a lot."

"But he doesn't know it. He still goes at every meal as though it's his last. You're looking good now though, aren't you, Wendell? Oops!" She turned to me and whispered, "That was insensitive of me. His eye, you know."

Wendell certainly hadn't reacted, and I couldn't believe Bianca actually thought her choice of words might hurt her one-eyed dog's feelings, but maybe she did. She had told me before that she had originally thought of naming him "Winker," for obvious reasons, but feared he might take it wrong. Then she'd thought of "Patsy," since for some unknown reason that seemed to her the perfect name for a dog, but his gender ended that plan. Finally she settled on "Wendell" because she thought the name gave him a certain dignity.

Now she gently stroked the underside of his smooth muzzle, studying the concave socket where his right eye used to be. "So, how did you end up under a trailer in Juniper, Wendell?" she asked. He looked at her steadily with his one good eye, but said nothing. It had taken most of Bianca's small cache of money to have Wendell checked out at the Sagebrush Veterinary Clinic, but she had done it without asking me for help. She was radiant at Dr. O'Hara's pronouncement that Wendell would be fine once he got a few good meals in him.

Bianca had a good heart, and Raymond Morris urged me to remember that with his Rule Number Five: *Focus on every admirable trait your child possesses.* Bianca had many admirable traits, and as we moved inside to watch the local noon news, I hoped that she'd add tolerance for Gil Fortune to the list.

EIGHT

TINA MARQUETTE'S BLOND good looks were somewhat diminished by the make-up she wore, causing me to miss part of her words as I tried to figure out whether our local channel had actually intended their reporter to look like a raccoon with a fever, or if that had merely been an unfortunate side effect of the lighting. Tina read the lead-in to the news too fast, stumbling over words in her excitement at being allowed to report something more exotic than the dates for the upcoming Oregon State Fair. I could hardly blame her. She looked fresh out of school, like most of the KPHD reporters who came and went so rapidly. Some showed up eventually on Portland channels and some quickly dropped off our screens forever. She rocketed through the predictable "the investigation continues" phrases from Sheriff Arnold Kraft about Vanessa's fall as though she had a hot date waiting off camera. If she did, I hoped she planned to remove a pound or two of make-up before she met the young man, so she wouldn't scare him.

When she muffed the words "rising Republican star" while describing Gil, I mentally moved her into the category of those reporters we wouldn't be seeing for long. Mercifully, she finally finished her segment and introduced Jamie McBride, an experienced reporter who had been sent to interview Gil at his home. Jamie was more coherent than his young colleague, though his awe at covering this story still showed through.

"I'm speaking to Gilbert Fortune, Russell County District Attorney, at his home just outside Juniper, in the heart of Central Oregon." After a badly-choreographed gesture in the direction of the snow-capped Three Sisters mountains visible in the background, he continued. "However, this beautiful country contains hazards as well as the breathtaking vistas you see behind me. It was here that Vanessa Fortune, Gilbert Fortune's wife, fell to her death only yesterday from a trail along the three-hundred-foot deep Crooked River Gorge." He turned to Gil and spoke with hushed earnestness. "Mr. Fortune, please accept our condolences on your loss, and our thanks for agreeing to talk to us at such a painful time."

Gil nodded his head in acknowledgment and faced the camera. The grainy picture on Bianca's black and white TV screen made his eye sockets appear deep-set and hollowed, giving him a villainous look. No wonder Wendell had growled. I'd growl at this scary stranger myself. Too bad that Bianca was looking at this image of Gil instead of the handsome, smiling man I used to see at Thornton's, before he defected to Megabooks Plus! to buy his books.

"See?" Bianca said. "He even looks guilty."

"It's just your TV," I replied. "Besides, he probably didn't get any sleep last night."

She nodded. "Guilty conscience."

We lapsed into silence as Gil spoke. "That's okay, Jamie. As you know, Sheriff Kraft continues his investigation. I don't know much about what happened, but I'm always available to the press." He took a step closer to the camera. "To begin with, I want to thank Vanessa's many friends for your concern. It helps more than you know."

"What a phony." Bianca wasn't buying it. I kept quiet.

"Sir, I know this is painful, but could you please tell us what you've learned so far about what happened yesterday?"

"As I said, I don't know much yet, but Vanessa has—had—recently developed an interest in videography. Arnie—Sheriff Kraft, that is—thinks she lost her balance while using her new camcorder, which I gave to her on our last anniversary."

He gave a small, sad smile. "She was just learning how to use it, so perhaps she lost a sense of where she was standing in relation to the edge. Or possibly her shoe rolled on some loose rock. The camcorder was at the bottom of the gorge, near where..." he paused and swallowed a couple of times before finishing quietly, "...It was broken, of course."

"Did you know she planned to go to the Crooked River Gorge yesterday?"

Slowly, as if fumbling for words, Gil continued. "No, but that wouldn't be unusual. With the time demands of my job, she was on her own a lot. I've been working on a major case—"

He paused long enough for Jamie to fill in the gaps. Jamie had been to journalism school and understood the need for background information, so he jumped right in. "You're referring to the recent Wendorf case, in which a local high school student, Max Wendorf, set off a smoke bomb at Juniper High School, a case which you personally have pursued vigorously—"

"Yes. It's taken a great deal of my time, but I'm proud that I've been able to take a strong stand for safety in our schools."

"I understand that you and your wife were once students at Juniper High School, where Max Wendorf's father, Kurt, was a classmate of yours. That old friendship must have made the case a difficult one for you to prosecute."

"Nothing is too difficult when the safety of our students is at stake. Vanessa understood the importance of this case, and she supported my work fully. One way she helped me was by pursuing her own wide range of community and personal interests so that I would be free to discharge my obligations to the people of Russell County as necessary." Gil spread his arms expressively. "She was truly my partner in every way."

"Can you believe that hypocrite?" Bianca jumped from her chair and started toward the TV, as though she couldn't bear to watch another minute. Seeing the look on my face, she stopped short of snapping it off. "Okay, okay, I'll watch the rest." She folded her arms and stood there, seething, while the interview wound to its conclusion.

"Do you blame the State of Oregon for not placing a guard rail at that spot on the trail?"

"I'll leave the assessment of blame to others," Gil said kindly, "but, yes, I'd like to see a barrier there. I plan to offer to put one there myself, if the law will allow it, in the hope that no one else will ever have to suffer the loss of a loved one on that treacherous path."

"And finally, Mr. Fortune, in the face of your personal tragedy, will you continue to pursue your candidacy to fill the vacancy created by Ted Bergan's recent, unexpected resignation as Oregon's Attorney General?"

"I can't think about that now, but it's certainly what Vanessa would have wanted. She loved this country so much," he said, "and so do I. How can I not do my best for them both?" The cameras swung wide to get a shot of the mountains in the background just as Bianca punched the off switch and the TV screen went black.

"Okay, I've watched. I said I would and I did."

"And you'll wait…?"

"…until Arnie gets done playing sheriff. Then it will be my turn to run a real investigation."

NINE

I ARRIVED EARLY FOR Vanessa's funeral Sunday afternoon so I'd have time to visit Tony's grave. I had come here often this past year to talk to him, knowing with greater certainty each time that he would never answer me again. Even so, the Juniper Memorial Cemetery was a peaceful place.

It lay nestled at the foot of Wild Horse Butte on the east side of town, a prominent cinder cone left over from some long-ago geologic eruption. This cemetery had served as the final resting place for Russell County citizens since the days when early settlers had succumbed to typhoid and childbed fever. Over the years, large elm trees had spread their foliage into a comforting canopy over the uneven rows of headstones in the oldest part of the cemetery, that area lying nearest to Wild Horse Butte. It was laid out in no particular pattern, for early families hadn't realized that Juniper would one day grow large enough to make cemetery space a problem. Already, however, the topmost part of the cemetery was full and the headstones cascaded down the gentle slope in ragged disorder. For years Ned Jenkins, noted neither for keen mind nor industrious nature, had been paid to mow the grass once in a while, but the haphazard placement of the stones thwarted his modest efforts, and some stones had disappeared altogether into the spreading knapweed mixed in with wildflowers.

The newer part of the cemetery further down the hill had been taken over by the City of Juniper, which had immediately imposed a strict order on the placement of graves and a regular schedule for mowing the grass. On the whole, I would have preferred to rest among the wildflowers when my time came. Having my eternal resting place regimented, trimmed and mowed all the time didn't sound very restful. It wouldn't have been Tony's choice either, but there was no space further up the slope.

I glanced down the hill to make sure I still had time before the arrival of others for Vanessa's funeral to climb to the older section and wander among the stones. The flowery messages so popular a century before were everywhere. I paused to consider the grave of Hettie Margonis, "beloved wife and mother," beside the cherub-topped stone of Sarah Margonis with the words "called to God too soon" guarding the tiny plot. Both the birth and death dates for Sarah were October third, 1891. Where was Mr. Margonis? No nearby marker completed the story about this little family, and I didn't know anyone with that surname among the current residents of Juniper. Maybe the deaths of his wife and infant daughter had caused him to push on to the Oregon coast, or maybe, like so many others, he had become discouraged with his pioneer adventure and returned east.

At the very top of the hill I found the grand tomb of Marcus T. Konig, saloon proprietor and original owner of the stately house that had become Thornton's Books. His monument would have been hard to miss, though the winged angels overseeing his sepulcher seemed somewhat at variance with his reputation, which hovered between legendary and scandalous. Since starting work at Thornton's, I had been treated by old-timers to colorful descriptions of Mr. Konig's activities in the room upstairs, which currently held military books. It used to have an outside staircase, which explained a lot about the origin of the more colorful tales. Apparently Mr. Konig had been no stranger to military-style campaigning himself. No wonder he had gone through three wives, none of whom seemed to be buried by his side. I doubted that Mr. Konig deserved an angelic escort through eternity, but he had certainly surrounded himself with enough angel statuary to create the illusion of piety.

Putting aside thoughts of Juniper's past, I finally made my way back down the hill to join the people who were now gathering for the latest chapter in the town's continuing story. Vanessa Fortune's fatal fall would enter Juniper's folklore soon enough, but right now it was an open wound.

A mahogany pedestal had been imported from Morrell's Funeral Home to provide a podium for the minister. The base concealed a gleaming CD player, from which the stately chords of "The Old Rugged Cross" rose and drifted across the still afternoon air. A nearby card table covered in purple velvet held the book in which those in attendance could record their presence.

After signing in, I took a seat on a folding chair toward the back. Listening to the familiar hymn, I felt a calmness steal over me for the first time since Wednesday. Bianca's ravings had thrown me temporarily off stride, but this peaceful old cemetery was helping me to regain perspective. Surely by next week's book club meeting Bianca would have simmered down. I knew I had the bad habit of letting other people dictate my response to things, and I felt a pinprick of annoyance at the way I had allowed Bianca's accusations to upset me. I hadn't known Vanessa well, and I might very well have skipped the services today if I hadn't been prompted by some vague notion of showing support for Gil. Judging from the size of the crowd, he was receiving plenty of support from others. Still, how awful for him if he happened to hear anything about Bianca's ridiculous theory.

Uniformed members of the Juniper City Police and the Russell County Sheriff's Department were sprinkled through the crowd today, some sitting in the audience and others controlling traffic. The perimeter of the cemetery was lined with media trucks, some of which had traveled over the mountains from Portland and Eugene stations, judging by the call letters emblazoned on their sides. Only people on foot were allowed past the barricades. Though Morrell's had probably brought every chair they owned, they hadn't brought enough for this crowd.

The front row contained Vanessa's somber parents. Gil took his place beside them, though I noticed that Vanessa's mother moved further away than necessary to give him room. Apparently no love lost there. Perhaps she too had heard the rumors Alix had mentioned...or perhaps I was getting as fanciful as my daughter, building something out of nothing. I wondered idly whether Gil had any relatives in attendance. I didn't see anyone I didn't recognize in the front row, but Gil was an only child, and his parents were long dead, so maybe he didn't have any. Harley sat solidly beside him on the other side. Right behind Gil sat Jonathan Roose, the local Republican representative to the U.S. House of Representatives, and Adele Nassley, the Republican State Senator from our district. No wonder the reporters had stayed. Further down the row I recognized some of Gil's colleagues from the local district attorney's office. At the far end sat the competent new assistant D.A., Linda Sanchez, whom I'd met often when she bought books at Thornton's. If, as everyone expected, Gil wound up as Oregon's next Attorney General, it was common knowledge that Linda hoped to get Gil's current job. She was young, only thirty, but if she practiced law as intelligently as she assimilated the contents of the books she bought, she had a bright future.

A swirl of color caught my eye and I knew from the paisley scarf blowing in the suddenly freshening breeze that Minnie had arrived. With great dexterity, she made her way through the crowd of mourners, holding her hat with one hand while she patted and hugged people of all ages and descriptions with the other. Minnie was a well-known patter and hugger, taking care to acknowledge everyone, particularly anyone standing alone. She washed church supper dishes until the last plate was back in the cupboard, and she was always the first to offer help when trouble surfaced. In fact, if someone hoped to deal privately with a difficulty and Minnie got wind of it, the only way to fend off her concern was to leave town until someone else in trouble diverted her interest. More than one Juniper resident had been alerted to the fact that a personal trauma had become a public concern when he had opened the door to find Minnie on his doorstep, a savory pot pie in her outstretched arms.

Minnie started to sit in the row ahead, but when she spotted me, she gave a significant nod and proceeded to pat and hug her way back out to the aisle and into my row. After settling her considerable bulk in the seat beside me and taming the wayward scarf as best she could, she raised her carefully plucked eyebrows and leaned over to ask in what was, for her, a low voice, "How's it going?"

"Going?"

Minnie nodded enthusiastically and her voice rose in volume. "Chicken casserole, right? Just bring it by the church when we're done here." I was momentarily confused until I realized that this comment was directed to the woman sitting on the other side of me.

Minnie explained, "Food for after the service. I just hope we have enough. I'm about done in. 'Many hands make light work,' they say, but probably that's some man's idea. Men just stand around and look sad when something like this happens. They don't have to round up casseroles and salads and silverware. Would you believe it? I don't know what happens to the church silverware, but it's never there when we need it. I've been chasing knives and forks all over town. Everyone borrows it when visitors come—which is just fine, of course—

but do they think to return it? Good thing I spotted some when I was doing dishes at Grabels' house last week—after Marge's surgery, you know—or I wouldn't have thought to call them. You're coming to the dinner, aren't you?"

Giving me no chance to answer, she swept on. "Such a day, such a sad day. I'm not complaining about the work, mind you. It's wonderful to see such an outpouring of emotion… the whole community coming together to pray for Vanessa—and to support poor Gil. I guess I should have realized, after all those news people arrived, that Gil has lots of friends, not just here, but all over the state. Did you see him on TV the other day?"

"Well, I—"

But Minnie was off again at full throttle. "Once I saw all those news trucks rolling into town, I just said to myself, 'Minnie, you'd better double every recipe you own, so I did. And I called all the members of the Serve and Share Committee to ask them to do the same. Every one of them said they were willing. Can you believe that? Every last one, bless their hearts. It's a good thing, too, with so many people here.

"If you had seen Gil at church last night, trying to help with the arrangements…well, he wasn't able to focus on the simplest detail. He's just so broken up. 'Minnie,' he said, 'you're an angel. Do whatever you think best to make things nice for Vanessa.' Can you beat that? Bless his heart. It was all I could do to keep from telling him right then and there about this outlandish idea of Bianca's. I'm mortally ashamed for being even half associated with it."

"You aren't really—" I began.

"I know, I know," she said, "but it sort of feels like I am because I was listening to Bianca. Where was I? Oh, yes, we worked until after midnight last night trying to make order out of the flowers pouring in. See all those vases up front? Those are just a few of them. Every nursing home in the county is taking in the overflow, on Gil's orders. Doesn't that beat all? In the midst of everything he's gone through, he thought of the old folks—some of them all alone—in nursing homes." She lowered her voice again. "So, how's it going? Have you…?"

"Talked to Bianca? Yes, some. Have you?"

"Heavens, no. I've been in the kitchen for days—at home and at church—arranging things for the meal after this service."

"She hasn't changed her mind, as far as I know."

"Well, 'none are so blind as they that will not see,' but don't give up. You're our best hope, Jane. Frankly, I think she sees me as an old fuddy duddy."

"She sees me the same way."

"Really? You don't look old enough to have one grown daughter, let alone three. You're just a pup."

"Not to Bianca. Look, I know Bianca's young and headstrong, but she thinks it's important for us to read that book. I'm hoping that if we humor her, she'll feel that we're taking her seriously, and maybe that will be enough to calm her down."

"How can we take anyone seriously who starts with a crazy accusation of…well, you know…against…rice pudding?" Again Minnie raised her voice to address someone passing by. "Yes, that's wonderful, Ardell, even if you were out of raisins. A double batch? Wonderful." She turned back to me, triumphant. "What did I tell you? This just gladdens my heart."

Minnie did another of her quick subject changes, but by now, I was catching on to her signals. When Minnie's voice went down, she was talking about Bianca; up meant she was back to food. Her voice was currently low. "How anyone can think… It's just plain crazy. Reading a book isn't going to change that fact."

"Well, you know that and I know that, but I gave my word."

I threw in the clincher. "Just think of her as a lost lamb that needs to be brought back into the fold. She needs our help… your help, Minnie. If we can keep her focused for a few days on the book instead of running around town—"

Minnie smiled. "I get it. Then after we listen to her, we tell her she's nuts—but gently."

"Er…exactly. And no harm done."

"Well, okay, but I hope she drops the whole idea before we get that far."

"I wouldn't count on it. Ever since Arnie declared the investigation complete yesterday, she seems more determined than ever to track down some evidence."

"How can she find evidence about a crime that didn't happen?"

"Well—"

"Oh, no," Minnie's voice rose and she looked stricken.

"What's wrong?" I asked. I was getting good at reading Minnie's signals and deduced that we were back to food again. "Did you forget to tell someone to heat up the oven?"

Minnie half rose from her seat, her mouth hanging open. "Jane," she croaked.

After casting a quick glance in the direction that Minnie was pointing, I clamped a hand on her arm, forcing her back into the chair. She had switched signals on me. "Don't look. You'll make it worse."

"How could it be worse? Look at her."

"I just did, but we don't want everyone else doing the same thing."

"Oh, right, right. The fewer, the better."

The music swelled with one last magnificent chord and stopped. Thank goodness all eyes turned dutifully toward the Reverend Roger Marshall, who stood at the podium shuffling papers. Finally, he looked up. "As we have been taught, 'ashes to ashes and dust to dust....'" His powerful voice carried the ancient words easily to the large crowd.

I wanted to concentrate on the calming message of hope and redemption, but found myself more inclined to violent thoughts about wringing Bianca's beautiful neck. Ignoring my own excellent advice to Minnie, I sneaked a glance toward the grove of elm trees along the far side of the cemetery away from the road. A long lens protruded first from one leafy branch and then another, high one time and low the next, making it look for all the world as though a sniper were hiding in the trees. Wendell lay in the grass in front of the grove, panting in the heat. What was Bianca doing over there with that camera? I stifled a totally inappropriate impulse to laugh as I pictured the next logical step—Bianca in a leafy combat helmet rising to advance grimly on her subject to shoot a few close-ups.

I pressed a handkerchief to my mouth and struggled to regain my composure. Apparently assuming that I was overcome by the power of the Reverend Marshall's oratory, the kindly chicken casserole woman sitting next to me patted my arm. "There, dear, I know."

Though she was half hidden by the branches of the trees, I could see Bianca alternately swatting at flies and snapping pictures. She was swathed from head to toe in black. I didn't hear a word of the service from that point on. Bianca's beloved Rhami taught that it was necessary to rise above trivial aggravation, but I didn't seem able to do that at the moment. Minnie wasn't all that relaxed either. I could practically feel her vibrating with anger.

The minute the service concluded, Minnie shot out of her chair and raced toward the grove of trees sheltering Bianca. With her paisley scarf streaming behind her like a battle flag atop a destroyer, she bore down on her unsuspecting target vessel with surprising speed. Somewhat numb, I bobbed along in her wake. “I don’t believe it. I absolutely do not believe it,” Minnie said, pausing between words to catch her breath from the unaccustomed exercise.

“How did you know I was here?” Bianca asked.

“The next time you’re trying to hide,” Minnie advised, “don’t be the only person at a funeral wearing a floor-length black dress and a veil on a hot August day. You look like a movie star hiding from the paparazzi.”

“How did you know it was me under all this?” Bianca asked, throwing back the veil to reveal dark glasses underneath. “It was really hard to take pictures with both the veil and the dark glasses, but I wore them the whole time, except when I was talking to the police.”

“Do you see anybody else here with a black, one-eyed dog?” I asked.

Bianca looked behind her for Wendell, but then located him out in front of the trees, watching people as they left the cemetery. “Oh,” she said. “I didn’t think of that.”

“What did you say to the police?” I asked.

“Don’t worry. I didn’t give anything away. I just talked about freedom of the press and stuff…told them I was doing a feature I hoped to sell to the *Juniper Journal.* They already know I’m a photographer because of that incident with the swan fountain. Remember, Mom?” She paused until I acknowledged with a curt nod that I did, indeed, remember that most embarrassing event, before she continued. “I don’t think they believed me about the feature, but it doesn’t matter. After seeing I didn’t have a gun or anything, they sort of rolled their eyes and left.”

“What were you thinking?” asked Minnie. “Or were you thinking, Bianca?”

I stepped between them. Minnie’s resolve to help the lost lamb seemed to have evaporated. I tried for a less confrontational tone. “What were you hoping to accomplish?”

Bianca lifted her chin. "I was gathering evidence, of course, which I will show you in due course." She turned away, tripping on the hem of her long dress in the process. "Come on, Wendell. Let's go."

"Now I've heard everything," Minnie said.

"I doubt it," I said wearily.

TEN

MOST OF THE WOMEN arriving at Thornton's for the regular meeting of the Women's Empowerment Group two days after Vanessa's funeral marched straight up the stairs, stopping neither to browse for books nor to give more than a cursory greeting. That was fine with me. I'd been fearful that Bianca's recent performance would elicit questions from people who knew she was my daughter. Of course, maybe they were galloping up the stairs to ask her about it directly. I'd been busy with a customer when she'd arrived today so she and I hadn't spoken.

The WEG members came in all shapes and sizes, but the cumulative effect was one of determination and energy. No wonder Bianca enjoyed their company. Mostly, they made me tired when they started preaching about empowerment and rights. I agreed with some of their complaints about the world, but a few of these women were so generically angry at men that I felt like a traitor to my gender when I admitted that I had actually liked my husband.

Theoretically, men could join the group, but so far none had dared. Probably afraid of being devoured, I thought. However, Bianca actively sought out men as potential recruits. She felt sure they would benefit from hearing the ideas presented at the meetings. Early last week—though it seemed years ago after all that had happened since—she had eagerly approached Laurence about attending today's session.

"Why don't you come?" she'd asked. "We'd love to see some men at the meetings. You don't have to put men down to raise women up, so there's no reason men can't join. In fact, we're having Gil Fortune next week as our guest speaker to talk about opportunities in the legal profession for women."

Laurence had muttered something vague and scuttled away to the back room as fast as his spindly legs could take him, wearing the same bemused expression he always got when talking to Bianca.

"Hi, Jane." Linda Sanchez's arrival today, announced by the click of her high heels, brought me back to the present. She was wearing a navy blue St. John's ensemble that whispered elegance, femininity, and competence. No mean feat.

"Hello, Linda. Nice to see you again. Is Gil really going to be here today? I thought—"

Linda shrugged. "Haven't talked to him since Sunday. He hasn't been back to work yet."

"If he doesn't show up here today, no one would blame him. Maybe you could pinch hit. I can't think of a better example of a successful woman in your profession. Talk about a role model."

"Well, thanks, but I don't think Gil would appreciate that. He'll probably be here." Her voice lacked its usual animation, leading me to wonder whether the rumor of tension between them was true.

We both turned at the sound of the door opening again, but it wasn't Gil who entered. Nick ambled up to the counter, looking about as rumpled as I felt next to Linda.

"Been out fishing?" I asked. Nick always looked as though he spent more time admiring the Central Oregon scenery than studying himself in a mirror

"How'd you know?" he answered.

"Lucky guess. I don't suppose you two have met. Linda Sanchez, assistant Russell County D.A., meet Nick Constantine, who's an attorney in Santa Monica when he's not vacationing here."

Linda said, "An old friend of mine works in the Santa Monica D.A.'s office. Do you happen to know Amy D'Agostino?"

"Sure, I know Amy. Small world."

As they chatted, Nick showed a certain attentiveness to Linda that I hadn't noticed when he talked to me. Not that it mattered, of course, but I ran a mental check of my own appearance and vowed for the hundredth time to do something about my wardrobe. I might not be interested in dating, but I didn't like being invisible to men either.

"My book here?" Nick asked at last.

"Not yet. I'd have called you."

"Just thought I'd check."

"Then you aren't here for the WEG meeting?" Linda asked. "Women's Empowerment Group," she elaborated with a mischievous smile. "Today's topic is women in the legal profession, and men are welcome to attend. I'll bet you'd have something to add to the discussion."

"I don't know about that, but since I'm here, I couldn't possibly pass up such a fascinating subject. Lead the way," he said. "Coming, Jane?"

"I'm working, but you go ahead."

As they disappeared up the stairs, still in animated conversation, Harley swept into the bookstore, checking his watch as he came. Even on this warm summer afternoon, his blue pin-striped suit and grey tie looked just right. Nick could take clothing tips from him. "Jane, I'm glad you're alone. I need your help. It's about your daughter."

"Bianca?" My voice sounded faint, even to me. I swallowed and tried again. "I was…I was hoping no one had noticed. Did Gil see her?"

Harley looked at me pityingly. "Everybody saw her."

"Oh, I'm so sorry. I've already talked to her—"

"Gil knows about Bianca's interest in photography from that project she and Vanessa were putting together for the

Women's Empowerment Group, so he…well, let's just say he already knows that she's intense and…unusual."

"That's very generous of him. I can't tell you how upset I was about that stunt. Bianca is just—"

"—impulsive. I know." He placed a hand on my arm and leaned closer. His touch was oddly cool on this warm day. "Everyone understands that you've been through a lot this year, Jane. Would you like me to talk to her? I wish you'd let me help you more."

"Oh, no, thanks," I said. "That's kind of you, but I can manage."

"All right, but let me know if you change your mind. I'm a very patient man, as you know." He smiled and looked meaningfully at me.

I immediately broke eye contact and straightened some pamphlets on the counter. That long look told me that he'd probably taken my acceptance of his reunion invitation for more than it was. Oh, no. Now what?

Harley looked at his watch again. "Look, I have to deliver the speech Gil was going to give, but—"

"No one really expected Gil to be here today," I said quickly.

"To be honest, I wrote most of it. He's still not quite himself, as you might expect. I need to talk to you about one other thing though, and that's this 'Murder of the Month' business." Seeing my blank look, he amplified, "Your book club."

"Murder of the Month," I repeated, stalling for time as I tried unsuccessfully to think like Bianca. I didn't have any idea what she had done, but Harley didn't keep me in suspense long.

"Didn't you know? She invited Gil to speak to your club next week." Harley pulled a crisp white envelope from the inside pocket of his suit coat and extracted a typed note. "Read the invitation for yourself."

I reached for the paper as though expecting an electric shock. After reading the words, I decided I'd have preferred the shock. Bianca certainly hadn't wasted any time starting her own investigation after Vanessa's death had been officially ruled an accident. I read the note several times, trying to think what to say to explain it.

Dear Mr. Fortune:
We would like to invite you to be our guest speaker at the next meeting of Murder of the Month (a mystery book club) at Thornton's Books, seven o'clock p.m. on Wednesday, August twenty second. With your particular background, we think it would be VERY interesting to hear you discuss fictional vs. real-life crimes.
Bianca Serrano
Secretary
Murder of the Month Book Club
P.S. Healthful refreshments will be served.

"Surely you can see that this invitation is in the worst possible taste," Harley said. "If she thinks that Gil wants to be kept busy right now—"

"That's it!" My relief at his erroneous explanation for Bianca's invitation spurred me to respond enthusiastically. "She's too young to comprehend the magnitude of the loss Gil has sustained. I'll talk to her again."

"Thanks, Jane. Gil would appreciate it. I seem to be doing nothing but asking you for help these days. First, the reunion, and now, this."

"The reunion, yes! How's it coming along?" Never had I felt more interest in a change of subject.

"Fine, fine. I'll get back to you on that, but right now I need to deliver Gil's regrets...along with his thoughts about women entering the legal profession."

"There's a good crowd today, and if you need any legal expertise, Linda Sanchez is there."

"Good idea. A career in banking hasn't prepared me particularly well for this occasion, but I don't want to let Gil down, not now." Harley started up the stairs.

As soon as he was out of sight, I let out my breath with a rush and sagged against the counter. They hadn't recognized the taunting invitation for the challenge it was. We still had time to make Bianca see reason.

Yesterday's book shipment had contained the requested copies of her beloved *Prove It, Puppy!* and I had started on it immediately, discovering that it was every bit as bad as I had expected. Still, I had promised. Now, with a sigh, I pulled the dreadful book once again from under the counter and attempted to force my way through a few more pages while the store was quiet. Normally I don't read for pleasure while I'm working, but since it was Thornton's on-site book club that had forced me to read it in the first place, I could justify a few minutes with it now. Besides, by no stretch of the imagination could this be considered reading for pleasure. Raymond Morris's Rule Number Four was a seemingly simple one: *Show an interest in the interests of your child.* Hah! Easy for him to say. He wasn't being forced to read about two corgi detectives. Bipsy and Mr. Potts were well on their way to sinking their sharp little teeth into the murderer's plans when Nick's voice startled me back into the present.

"Want me to take over so you can go listen?" Nick looked around at the empty store as he descended the stairs. "I think I can handle the mob."

"No, thanks. That group doesn't particularly interest me."

"Me either," he said. "A couple of those women are ready to man the barricades."

"Is one of them a young blonde?"

"Tall? A real stunner? Yeah, she has a lot to say."

I nodded. "My daughter, Bianca. She's a good kid, but..."

"...she has more opinions than experience? Don't worry. She'll grow out of it. It's actually refreshing to hear such enthusiasm."

"Bianca does not lack enthusiasm," I answered.

"Well, that's good. Take my kids, for example. Theo and Pete are twenty-three. They're busy ripping up and down the California beaches right now, but I expect they'll settle down and be decent citizens eventually. Most kids do. But, from what I read, boys are easier on the nerves...if you don't mind a few trips to the emergency room, that is, and frogs in the toilet bowl."

"Your wife must have loved that."

"She mostly left the boys to me," he said, his smile fading. "She had other priorities. And then she left us entirely about ten years ago. Worked out pretty well in the long run though. We did okay and they're great kids." After an awkward silence, he slapped one hand on the counter decisively. "Well, if you don't need me here, I'll get going. Harley's speech about opportunities for women in the law isn't exactly riveting."

"Gil was supposed to be the speaker today. Harley's just doing him a favor."

"So he said. Still doesn't make his speech more interesting than a trip to Elk Lake. Too heavy on 'poor Gil' and not enough facts."

"You're like Joe Friday. 'Just the facts, ma'am.'"

"That's me."

After Nick left, the store fell quiet again until a burst of chatter preceded the departing WEG group down the stairs. The animation evident in the snatches of conversation I heard suggested that Harley's presentation had gone over better with the others than it had with Nick. I was glad since Harley had made a special effort to be here.

I gave him the thumbs up sign as he went out the door in

the center of a group of women asking him questions. Behind them came Linda Sanchez and Bianca in deep conversation. I didn't even want to think about Bianca talking to someone in Gil's office, but, short of tripping and gagging Bianca, I couldn't think of a way to stop her.

The store cleared at last and I was left with the nauseatingly clever corgis again. Not another soul entered Thornton's, even to browse. Tuesdays were normally better than this, but Megabooks Plus! was hosting a book signing today for Mimi Lexington, a Seattle romance author famous for her scorching love scenes. The reviews of her latest book, *Caress My Heart,* left no doubt that the heroine's heart wasn't the only part of her anatomy being caressed.

I struggled through a few more pages of *Prove It, Puppy!* but when I reached the part where Miss Pittimore invited all the doggy friends of Bipsy and Mr. Potts to a gala party in the corgis' honor, I gave it up for the day.

Casting around for something better to do, I dialed Laurence's number to see how he was getting along today. Yesterday morning he'd been under the weather, which I'd discovered only by accident when Tyler had slouched into Thornton's while I'd been unpacking books.

"Hi, Tyler. Where's your grandfather?" I'd asked. "I expected him a while ago."

"He seems sort of out of it this morning. Not exactly sick, just...I don't know." Tyler shrugged and looked at his feet.

"Maybe I'd better go take a look. Can you watch the store?"

"Sure, if you want." His voice was offhand, but his look of relief told me that I was doing exactly what he had wanted all along. Why hadn't he just said it straight out in the first place? I'd tossed him a copy of the recently unpacked *Prove It, Puppy!* on my way out.

When I'd arrived at the grounds of the imposing Paulson residence, I circled the block to the far corner of the property in search of what had originally been the carriage house. There, I found Laurence sitting in the sunshine that streamed through the open windows of his apartment. Mr. and Mrs. Paulson had donated the main house to the Oregon Historical Society some years ago, and that organization had converted the carriage house to a rental. The place was small, but it suited Laurence's simple needs.

"Hi, Laurence. Coming to the store today?" I deliberately kept my tone calm, though I didn't like the unnatural pallor of his skin.

He slowly turned his head and spoke without smiling. "Probably won't be anyone buying books, and it's too damned hot to go anywhere anyway."

"But you said—"

"I know what I said, but I've changed my mind. Can't a man change his mind?"

"Of course. It's your store, but…maybe you should see Dr. Pomeroy."

"Just because I've decided not to work today? Maybe you should mind your own business."

Ignoring his rudeness, I spoke in my most soothing tone. "You seem not quite yourself this morning."

"That ought to please you, the way you're always badgering me to change. Say, what are you doing here anyway? The store can't run itself."

"Tyler's there."

"Tyler? What does he know about selling books?"

My exasperation finally broke through. "I don't know, Laurence. Probably nothing, but he was worried about you, okay?"

"Did he say he was worried?" He half smiled for the first time.

"Not in so many words, but, yes, he was worried."

He digested this new concept before speaking again. "I

didn't think he worried about anything except getting away from here as soon as possible, though I don't know where he'd escape to, since it'll be a while before Carrie's well enough to have him at home again." At the look on my face he said irritably, "I know, the chances aren't good, but Tyler shouldn't be stuck living with some old goat he hardly knows."

"Don't talk like that! You care what happens to him, and that's important. He needs stability and I'm sure he likes being here more than he lets on. Why, he practically jumped at the chance when I asked him to help out at the store today." Remembering Tyler's laconic "Sure, if you want," I knew I was shading the truth on this statement, but the pleasure it brought to Laurence's face was enough to clear my conscience.

"He did? I never thought of asking him."

"Probably because you're such an old goat. All I know is that he's down there working right now—by his own choice. Maybe he could work there part-time on a regular basis. Give him something to do and let him know he's useful."

"He'd probably foul everything up," he said gruffly, "but it might work. Maybe you could sort of teach him the ropes?"

"Sure, and you'll see Dr. Pomeroy."

"If I have any more trouble, I'll go, but I'm feeling better now."

"So you'll rest at home today and Tyler will work with me. How's that?"

"Fine. Now go."

I'd returned to the store and worked with a surprisingly agreeable Tyler the rest of the day. He was a quick study, not only understanding procedures the first time I explained them, but offering good suggestions.

I'd meant to call Laurence last evening to tell him how well his grandson had done but I'd been sidetracked by Bianca's excited call. She couldn't wait to tell me that Sheriff Kraft had closed the investigation without accounting for the videotape from Vanessa's recorder. The camcorder had bounced three hundred feet down a cliff and the videotape was probably lying, broken, in a patch of sagebrush, but Bianca was sure that the tape would provide a vital clue, which she intended to find.

Now, all I heard was the recorded message at Laurence's house. I hoped he was sitting outside in the shade, resting.

ELEVEN

I SPENT THE NEXT MORNING at home on Laurence's orders. I'd finally reached him by phone the evening before, and he'd assured me he was feeling much better. He had quite a lilt to his voice when he told me he and Tyler would take care of the store together this morning. I certainly didn't want to get in the way of this new development in their relationship, so I spent my time tending some neglected raspberry vines in my back yard. I'd hoped that gardening in this peaceful setting would distract me from thinking about Bianca, but it hadn't worked.

Unfortunately, I was practically vibrating from the effort to keep myself from calling Bianca immediately to tell her what I thought of *Prove It, Puppy!* but I knew it was better not to say anything until tonight's meeting, when I'd have Minnie and Alix to back me up. I was reasonably sure that the lovestruck Tyler wouldn't be able to bring himself to criticize Bianca's choice of a book.

As I approached Thornton's at noon, the window display—"beach candy" books for summer reading—caught my eye. My garden wasn't the only thing that had been neglected recently. The window display hadn't been touched since July, and August was already half gone. Laurence wouldn't ever think to work on the window, even though he hadn't much cared for my choices for this one. If left to him, the window would contain only dusty, rare books, which didn't make the most electrifying visual presentation. I'd have to come up with something soon because a place called simply Thornton's Books needed all the marketing help it could get. If only we could get Bianca down to earth, maybe I'd be able to get back to the routine work entailed in running the bookstore.

In anticipation of finding grandfather and grandson working together at the store for the first time, I smiled as I opened the door. Laurence and Tyler confronted each other across the counter, their strained faces telling me everything I needed to know about the day.

"I wasn't even driving," Tyler protested.

"That's beside the point," Laurence said.

"Well, it is a point."

"Don't get smart with me, young man."

"Look, we didn't hurt your stupid car. It's no big deal—"

"Not to you, apparently." Laurence noticed me standing frozen in the doorway. "Jane, maybe you can explain to this young punk just why it's wrong to steal cars."

"Oh, that's good," Tyler said. "Steal? Your car's fine."

"My car," Laurence shot back. "So you acknowledge that the car does indeed belong to me. I wasn't sure you understood that elementary fact."

Tyler muttered, "I needed it."

"You don't even have a license," I said.

"I wasn't driving." Tyler looked at the floor, saying nothing more, and my heart sank. I knew who must have been at the wheel of Laurence's car.

Infuriated at Tyler's attitude, Laurence burst out, "Never thought I'd have to lock the car keys away from my own grandson. Maybe I'd better check the cash register—"

"If you think that…" Tyler went first white, then fiery red, "…then you can just go…" He pushed past me and out the door, banging it closed behind him.

"Oh, Laurence, you don't think he'd steal from you…"

"Don't tell me what I think. That kid's just like his parents—no sense of responsibility."

"You don't mean that," I said. The thunderous look on his face caused me to hedge. "Okay, maybe you do mean it right this minute, but I don't think he was lying about driving the car. It was probably Bianca."

"Bianca? What the—" The telephone shrilled at his elbow, but he only glared at it. "Doesn't matter anyway. I'm going home." He ostentatiously pulled a crumpled pack of Camels from his breast pocket as he passed me on the way out.

The caller was Marian McKee, with her usual incoherent book order. Unsure of the title, author, or publisher of the book she sought, she was nevertheless sure I'd be able to find it. "It was a beautiful book about birds of prey, and the author was from Australia—or maybe New Zealand. I saw it at the gift shop in the Honolulu Airport about five years ago. It had lots of pictures, and the cover was red."

"Well, Marian," I began, "it's like this…"

With Laurence and Tyler at each other's throats, Marian on the phone, and the Murder of the Month Book Club meeting tonight, it was likely to be a long time before I got around to thinking up a scintillating new display for the front window.

BIANCA WAS THE FIRST of the book club members to arrive that evening for the meeting. I made a conscious decision not to mention Laurence's car or the presence of the ever-faithful Wendell. Things would get unpleasant soon enough.

While I was on the phone taking an order a few minutes later, Minnie and Alix arrived simultaneously. At the look on Minnie's face, I clapped one hand over the mouthpiece and said, "Please don't start 'til I get up there."

"Were you able to get all the way through that dreadful book?" Minnie asked.

I nodded and gestured toward the phone, my hand covering the receiver. "Be right up," I whispered.

"Don't be long," said Alix. "This ought to be some discussion."

I soon locked the store and made my way upstairs, pausing outside the meeting room to gauge the tone of the conversation in progress. Bianca's voice floated out to me. She seemed to be talking about cooking, so I dared to enter.

"Strawberry-zucchini quiche—with a whole-wheat crust, and extra wheat germ added, of course. I had it on the counter, but…" Bianca's sideways glance at Wendell completed the thought. "I didn't know he could reach that high. But then I realized we shouldn't be sitting here eating snacks when there's work to do anyway."

Alix asked, "Since when has any snack ever made it past Wendell? I haven't seen any, have you, Minnie?"

Minnie seemed preoccupied. "Strawberry-zucchini quiche?"

"The green of the zucchini provided a nice contrast to the red of the strawberries," Bianca explained.

"Red and green."

"I didn't think of that, but it did look festive," Bianca responded.

Minnie was still having trouble with the concept. "And Wendell ate all of this…whole-wheat strawberry-zucchini healthful…thing?"

"Every scrap. I hope Ty won't be too disappointed. He's always hungry, and he probably doesn't think to add extra fruits and vegetables to his diet."

"Tyler probably won't be here tonight," I answered. "He's got something going on…with Laurence."

"Too bad," Bianca said. "He was a big help today. Wasn't that nice of Laurence? I thought he might be grumpy about letting us use his car. I didn't think we had time to bike all the way to the Crooked River Gorge. Borrowing the car was Ty's idea, but taking the pictures was mine."

"Pictures of what?" Minnie asked. "Rocks?"

"Don't be silly. Pictures of Vanessa's murder. You've all read *Prove it Puppy!* by now so you can guess what I did."

Alix said, "I'll take a crack at it. After those brilliant corgis tipped her off, Miss Pittimore sent Bernard an anonymous message."

Minnie said, "That's silly. No one would do that."

"Well, of course not." Bianca sounded so indignant that I thought maybe she recognized how foolish the plot was. Then she blasted my hope with her next words. "Not at first anyway. I had to lay the groundwork, to make Gil sweat."

"So you invited him to speak to our book club next week," I said, holding out the letter to her.

"Right." She passed the letter to Minnie. "How'd you get it, Mom?"

"Harley asked me to talk to you about it."

"Aha! Gil's worried. It's already working."

Minnie looked up from her reading. "The Murder of the Month Book Club. I do like that name. It sounds so official."

Alix took the letter from Minnie and pretended to read: "'Please come and tell us in vivid detail how you killed your wife. Snacks provided, if Wendell doesn't get them first.' You did offer snacks, I hope?"

"Very funny, Alix," Bianca said. "Yes, I mentioned refreshments, which you'll see if you read to the bottom of the note. After all, I had to make the meeting sound normal."

"When has anything been normal about our meetings?" Alix asked. "But thanks for clarifying the proper etiquette for entertaining a murder suspect. A book club is supposed to read about murders, not discover them."

"And after this case is closed, we will," Bianca agreed, "but we can't ignore a murder right in our midst."

"There was no murder," I said, for what felt like the hundredth time. I spoke slowly and distinctly. "We are sorry that Vanessa fell, and we are sorry she is dead. However, according to the official investigation, as well as the pure weight of common sense, she was not murdered."

Bianca lifted her chin and challenged me, just as she had done when she was two years old and didn't want to wear her coat outside to play in the snow. "Then why is Gil nervous about my letter? Tell me that!"

"He's not nervous," I said. "He's upset because his wife has died. He doesn't need extra problems right now."

"Then he shouldn't have killed her," Bianca said calmly.

Every rule that Raymond Morris ever devised wasn't going to help me tonight. I opened my mouth to say something I'd probably regret later, and only Minnie's timid comment prevented it.

"He might not be interested in coming, but I don't think he'd be nervous about getting an invitation to talk to our little group. After all, he is the district attorney, so he has a natural interest in crime and the law. I move that we just let him come. It would be less embarrassing than withdrawing the invitation at this point."

"I second that motion," Alix said. "This could be fascinating."

"All in favor?" asked Minnie. I seemed to be the only one in the room who was opposed. Hardly pausing to hear the chorus of ayes, Minnie said, "Oh, good. It's all settled."

"Except that Gil doesn't want to come," I said.

"Well, that's up to him. We'll just move right on to the second part of my plan, the anonymous letter. As I told you, I didn't send it at first. The letter inviting him to speak to our book club was first, just to soften him up."

I pursued the question while fearing the answer. "But

'at first' seems to imply that at some point...oh, Bianca, you didn't!"

Bianca said triumphantly, "I did! I even used the exact wording from the note sent to Bernard in *Prove It, Puppy!* The note said: 'I KNOW WHAT YOU DID!'"

"Well, that's it," Alix said. "After reading that cleverly worded message, Gil will confess immediately. Case closed. End of story. Time for healthful refreshments."

"No," Bianca said. "I'm pretty sure Gil's smarter than Bernard."

"This coffee table is smarter than Bernard," Alix assured her.

Bianca ignored the dig. "Anyway, that was just the second step. Don't forget that it took a while for Bernard to believe someone had really seen him murder Caroletta."

"Of course," I said. I was inclined to agree with Alix on the relative intelligence of the coffee table and Bernard. Then there was the question of the ability of an author who named characters "Bernard" and "Caroletta," but that was a discussion for another day.

Needing to know the worst, I pressed on. "And your third step was...?"

Bianca brightened at this chance to show off her cleverness. "Well, this one wasn't from the book. As I said, I thought it up myself after Ty offered to borrow Laurence's car."

"To gather evidence?" Minnie said nervously.

"Exactly," Bianca said, "and to manufacture some if necessary. Pictures can be faked, you know. What if I showed him some fuzzy pictures of Vanessa getting pushed?"

Alix rolled her eyes and strolled over to the window, opening it wide before she lit a cigarette. I watched enviously. Though I'd never smoked, I now realized for the first time what a handy activity it provided in times of stress.

"Oh, dear," said Minnie. "This is getting serious. The invitation was one thing, but anonymous letters and fake pictures? Oh, dear."

"Cheer up, Minnie," Alix said from across the room. "I'm sure Bianca can make fuzzy pictures, but I doubt she can make fuzzy pictures of a murder than never happened."

"What if he connects the anonymous letter with us?" Minnie asked.

"We'll pretend we don't know anything about it, pass it off as somebody's bad joke," Alix said.

"Which it is," I added.

"But I want him to connect the two," Bianca offered. "And as for the fake pictures, I wanted to see for myself how he reacted to the pictures."

"Speaking of pictures," Alix said, "I'm sorry I couldn't be at Vanessa's funeral. Minnie was just telling me about the useful, surreptitious pictures you took there."

Bianca defended herself. "The FBI sometimes takes pictures at funerals—"

"Mob funerals, Bianca. You were taking pictures of people we all know," I said.

"There were a few strangers—"

"Like Vanessa's parents?" Minnie asked.

"Well, it was just an idea," Bianca said. "I'm learning as I go. I found out today that faking pictures is tougher than I thought. I really wanted pictures of Gil pushing Vanessa over the cliff, but it didn't work out very well."

I sat down. "How…how…?"

"Ty was a big help. We were going to rig a dummy to look like Vanessa and then put it on a rope, so we could take pictures without having to climb up and down the canyon wall after every shot…and blur the pictures to make it hard to tell exactly what was going on."

"But you didn't," I said. "Tell me you didn't."

"We tried, but after we messed around with it a little bit,

we decided it wasn't going to work. Too bad. Anyway, Gil should be looking at a note by now telling about the pictures."

"The non-existent ones?" Alix asked.

"Right. The anonymous note promised that pictures would follow later, but now I think we should concentrate on finding the missing videotape instead."

I tried another approach. "But if you're using the book's plot as a pattern, you must know that there was no reason for Gil to kill Vanessa. Bernard needed his wife's fortune to buy the tropical island. Vanessa didn't have a fortune, and Gil already had access to her money."

"I didn't say I have everything worked out. Maybe she knew too much."

"About what?" Minnie asked. "What could she possibly know?"

"I don't know yet, but that happens a lot in mysteries."

Alix asked, "Does it matter to you at all that Gil has an airtight alibi? Jenna Lang, the Realtor in charge of the open house, swears he was there the whole time, and other people saw him there, too."

"I already said I haven't worked out a couple of the details yet. All I know for sure is that Gil murdered Vanessa. Now, can we get to work? You've all read the book. The plot shows that sometimes you have to pay attention to evidence that others dismiss. Minnie, doesn't your church teach you to have faith?"

"Yes, of course, but I have faith in the goodness of human nature, and I think you're completely wrong about Gil," Minnie answered. "I'm sorry, Bianca, but I can't and won't help you harass that poor man any further."

"I wouldn't mind harassing Gil in general," said Alix, "but this is a bit much, even for my warped sense of humor. Count me out, too. You don't need us. Wendell will probably solve the whole thing for you in a couple of days."

"Mom?" Bianca turned to me at last. Where was Raymond Morris when I needed him? I wanted to support my daughter, I didn't want to leave her humiliated and alienated from the group, but what could I do? Her idea was just plain crazy. Unfortunately, the determination on her face told me there was nothing I could do to change her mind.

"I'm sorry, Bianca," I said.

"I should have known." Bianca's color was high. "I can't believe... Oh, never mind. Come on, Wendell. We're on our own."

TWELVE

HAD THE PHONE BEEN ringing only in my dreams? The silence that greeted me when I picked up the receiver made me wonder. A stifled sob on the other end of the line sent a sudden ice cube down my spine. It was two-forty-three a.m. Like all mothers, I did a rapid, panicky inventory of the whereabouts of my children. Heart thudding, I sat bolt upright. "Hello?"

"Jane, it's Grandpa...he's...it's awful." I barely recognized Tyler's voice. He spoke briefly to someone in the background. "I gotta go. We're on our way to the hospital."

"I'll be there in ten minutes."

"Jane...could you hurry?" Again the quaver in his voice.

"Eight minutes."

Though Juniper's population had exploded in the past few years, the streets were still deserted at this time of night, reminding me of the days when our part of town consisted of open fields, not cookie cutter housing communities with artificial names. I shot past Rambling Ridge and Forever Sage before slowing briefly at the intersection of Custer Street and Highway 28 to check for cross-traffic. Seeing none, I ran the red light and roared past the garish Central Oregon Shopping Center toward my destination half a mile beyond.

High Desert Community Hospital had long been the tallest building in Juniper, and at night its eight stories of lighted windows resembled a solitary cruise ship navigating the night. To assuage my guilt for running the red light, I slowed to the required ten mph as I wound along the asphalt road through the sagebrush and juniper to the emergency entrance.

My headlights picked out the bright red letters on the ambulance at the curb as I made the final turn, but the attendants pulling the gurney from the back didn't look up from their work. After parking crookedly in the nearest slot, I ran to Tyler's side at the back of the ambulance. In the instant before he unexpectedly hurtled into my arms, I noted that Tyler was still wearing the clothes he had worn yesterday afternoon when he'd stormed out of the bookstore. No trace of yesterday's defiant expression remained on his face though. The sullen mask had been replaced by the wide-eyed stare of someone in shock.

He clung to me. "It's all my fault. I stayed out in the lawn swing last night to make him worry. You know, make him sorry for accusing me—"

"Never mind that now." I patted his back. "Just tell me what happened."

"Well, I couldn't get comfortable, so I was sort of awake, and then I heard him call out, or I thought I did, so I sneaked in the back door to listen. He was making sounds, like maybe he was dreaming. Anyway, then he started groaning something awful. I ran in and he was clutching his chest before he slumped over."

"Oh, Tyler!"

"Then I called 911 and started CPR, or as much as I could remember from our dumb health class. It's a lot harder on a real person. I was afraid I'd hurt him, so I was real glad when the paramedics took over. That's when I called you."

I continued to hold the shaking boy, feeling the slimness of his frame and marveling that this scared kid had done all the right things. "Tyler, you're terrific! You know that?"

The gurney carrying Laurence swept through the automatic doors and made straight for the area marked "No Unauthorized Personnel." Tyler turned his stricken gaze to me. "He's not gonna—"

"Of course not," I said. "They'll fix him up in no time. I'll just park my car so I'm not taking up three spaces and then we'll get the paperwork done."

At the admitting desk a few minutes later, Tyler flopped into a chair and I stood behind him, keeping one hand reassuringly on his bony shoulder. The RN on duty took one look at Tyler and directed her questions to me. It wasn't long before she was asking for information I didn't have.

"What's your grandfather's date of birth, Tyler?" I asked him.

"I don't know," he answered, "but there's probably something here." He produced a battered black wallet from the pocket of his oversized jeans. "I grabbed it on the way out the door. Thought it might come in handy."

"Remind me to sign you up if I ever recruit people for an emergency response team," I said. For the first time a smile flickered across his pale face, and I made a mental note to praise him whenever I could find the slightest excuse to do so. The admitting nurse asked Tyler the rest of the questions. Maybe it was my imagination, but I thought he sat up a little straighter in the chair from then on.

Once the formalities were completed, we took chairs in the adjacent waiting room and settled down to wait. Apparently, Juniper was experiencing a calm night because we had the place to ourselves except for one pajama-clad man who had been pressed into taxi service, according to what we overheard, when his wife had dropped a vodka bottle on her foot, possibly breaking a toe in the process. After checking her in, the man joined us, his collar askew and his eyes red-rimmed. He huddled in the corner, his neck craned at an awkward angle as he strained to catch the baseball scores being presented on the wall-mounted television set. I assumed he found watching the day's home run tally more relaxing than thinking about his wife clutching a vodka bottle at two-thirty in the morning.

Two hours later "Toe Woman" limped out of the hospital, complaining as she made her slow way to the parking lot, trailed by her reluctant husband. No wonder he preferred TV sports to everyday life. Listening to that voice would drive me to watch anything that would drown it out.

Whenever the doors to the emergency room swung open, Tyler and I looked hopefully in that direction. We watched as two uniformed police officers from the City of Juniper escorted a handcuffed young man to a patrol car parked outside. Later, several hospital employees checked out, laughing and cradling paper coffee containers in their hands. Finally, a doctor who looked too young to have finished college, let alone medical school, made his weary way toward us.

"You're here for Mr. Thornton?" He was looking at me. "I'm Dr. Blair. He's your…?"

"…grandfather," Tyler supplied. "He's my grandfather. I'm Tyler and Jane is our friend."

Dr. Blair shifted his gaze to Tyler. "Okay, Tyler. Well, your grandfather is stable and resting comfortably."

"Will he be all right?" Tyler asked.

"I hope so. The next few hours should tell us more."

"It was a heart attack?" I asked.

"Yes, a major episode. It's a good thing that you brought him in right away."

"Not me. Tyler's the one who called 911…and did CPR until the ambulance arrived."

I had the sensation that the doctor was starting to look past Tyler's baggy pants and the Smashing Pumpkins teeshirt he wore. So was I.

"Really," he said. "That was fine work. If your grandfather makes it through this—and I have every hope that he will—it will be in large part because of your quick thinking. Where'd you learn CPR?"

"School."

The doctor smiled and clapped him on the arm. "Well, well. Our tax dollars paying off at last."

"Can I see him?" Tyler muttered, looking down. "Just to make sure..."

"Maybe later. I'll let you know."

By the time the early morning light penetrated the waiting room, we had digested the previous day's sports scores, the details of a catastrophic earthquake in central Turkey, and the contents of the tattered copies of *Reader's Digest* and *Automotive Week* scattered around. The uncomfortable chairs didn't encourage sleep, so we finally just watched the fish swim around and around in the greenish wall tank. Eventually I levered myself to a standing position and approached the admitting nurse once again.

"Are you sure there's no word yet?"

"These things take time," she responded. After a glance at Tyler across the room, she continued in a low voice, "And it depends on the patient's condition."

Tears stung my tired eyes. "So it's a good sign that we haven't heard anything yet? I mean, if the news were really bad, surely we'd know by now."

The nurse withdrew behind a professionally neutral expression. "That's certainly the best way to look at it." She returned her attention to the computer screen in front of her.

I sat next to Tyler again. "Should we call your mother?"

Tyler assumed the guarded look I had come to associate with any mention of his mother. "What for?" he asked bluntly. "She can't do anything."

"She'll want to know."

"It would just set her off again. Nah, they wouldn't even put a call through to her at this stage of rehab."

"I don't know much about—"

"I know enough for both of us," Tyler said flatly.

I'll just bet you do, I thought. Aloud I said, "Okay, what about your dad?"

"Out of touch until next week."

"But Laurence must have some way to get through to him in an emergency. That's only prudent…"

Again Tyler's look silenced me. I struggled to contain my fury at Tyler's parents and their cavalier attitude toward their son. One of them in rehab and the other somewhere in Australia shooting a movie. All this after dumping their son with a grandfather he hardly knew, a grandfather who was now lying helpless in a hospital bed. By default, I was the closest thing to a relative that Tyler had right now. I only hoped that Susannah didn't decide to give birth in the next day or two. Then there was the still unsettled matter of Bianca's mischief. For someone with a supposedly empty nest, I had no lack of baby birds to tend.

"You up for some breakfast?" I asked. "The cafeteria's upstairs."

"Shouldn't we stay here? Just in case?"

"I'll tell the nurse where we'll be."

"Okay." He rose stiffly and stretched. "Man, I'm ready to get out of that chair for a while."

We made our way to the sweeping staircase and followed signs to the cafeteria on the second floor. Tyler was deep in his own thoughts, and I was too tired to manufacture encouraging comments.

As I sipped my third cup of coffee a few minutes later, I marveled at the volume of food that Tyler had been able to consume in the midst of this crisis, putting away every bit of the double-sized breakfast platter he had chosen. He popped the last bite of biscuit into his mouth and sat back at last.

"Do you always eat this much breakfast?" I asked.

"I missed dinner."

"Oh, yes." The blowup between Laurence and Tyler yesterday seemed like ancient history.

Tyler began slowly, "About the car..."

"You don't have to explain."

"I want to. It didn't seem so terrible at the time." He looked at me with haunted eyes that belonged in the face of a much older person. After a pause, he came out with what was bothering him. "But I keep thinking...if I hadn't taken the car, this wouldn't have happened."

I was careful not to touch him, not to sound patronizing. His bravery in owning up to his actions was remarkable. Making my voice as matter of fact as possible I said, "You are absolutely wrong about that."

"But I did take his car, and you saw how mad that made him—"

"People get upset all the time, and they don't all have heart attacks. If you want to blame something for bringing this on, blame those cigarettes he smokes. Smoking was—is—your grandfather's choice, and now he's paying the price. I know about your reasons for taking the car. You can shoulder the blame for that little stunt, but don't beat yourself up over the heart attack, because it's been brewing for a long time. Just be glad you were there when he needed you. You saved his life."

"You think so?" he asked.

"I certainly do, and Dr. Blair said the same thing."

"He did, didn't he?" Tyler scrubbed at his eyes with the heels of his hands, looking for all the world like a kid waking from a nap. Unfortunately, his grandfather's heart attack meant that Tyler was facing a real-life nightmare.

"Now that we have that straight, Hero," I said, "if you want to talk about the car, go ahead."

"I just wanted to... I didn't think it would matter. He doesn't drive it much anyway—"

"Why didn't you ask him?"

"I don't know. It seemed like such a kid thing to do. 'Please, Grandpa, may I borrow the car?' but he just went ballistic…"

So that was it. Tyler hadn't wanted to look like a kid in the eyes of the enchanting Bianca. Not so surprising. Ah, Laurence, your grandson is no delinquent, just a lovestruck boy.

"Bianca has a license—I asked her—so I figured it'd be okay. We drove to the gorge and came straight back. It wasn't like we went joyriding."

"Oh, Tyler, you read Bianca's book. That plot is founded on nothing. You can't use it as the basis for accusing someone of murder, can you?" Tyler remained silent. He was so young, and so vulnerable to anyone who would pay attention to him. Besides, what adolescent boy would want to believe that Vanessa's death had been an accident when he could have a murder served up to him, practically in his back yard? Especially if he and a gorgeous blonde could work together against the odds to solve the crime? I tried another tack. "You didn't find any incriminating evidence. Doesn't that tell you something?"

He remained stubbornly loyal to Bianca. "Just because we haven't found the missing videotape yet doesn't mean that we won't."

As I struggled to think what to say next, I saw that Tyler's attention was now riveted on something over my right shoulder. I turned to see the nurse who had been on duty in the lobby making her way toward us. She wasn't smiling.

"Dr. Blair is looking for you."

"Is it…I mean, is Laurence…?"

"You'll have to ask the doctor."

Dr. Blair was nowhere in sight when we arrived at the reception desk and addressed the new nurse on duty. "We were told that Dr. Blair is looking for us? About Laurence Thornton?"

"Oh, yes. He'll be back in a minute."

While we waited, a whimpering young girl holding her hand over one eye was dragged through the emergency entrance by her disheveled and obviously rattled mother. Over the girl's cries, we could hear as the mother tried to explain the situation.

"Tressa just pulled that perfume sprayer thing right off the dresser. I told her a thousand times to stay away from it, but she always wants to fix herself up. I give her a little squirt now and then—you know how they like that—but this time she took hold of it and sprayed herself right in the eye. I wasn't gone more'n a few minutes—I'd crawled back in bed for just a wink of sleep—and the little stinker must've just ran for it. She knows better'n that. I told you a thousand times, didn't I, Tressa? Stay away from Mama's 'Midnight in Paris.'"

Mama was still yammering and Tressa still whimpering, neither of them paying the slightest attention to the other, when the attendants escorted them through the swinging doors of the emergency room while the nurse, her mouth pursed, entered the incident into her computer. The official version would presumably leave out any commentary about Mama's parenting skills, but I wondered how often little Tressa was left to fend for herself while Mama went back to bed for just a wink of sleep?

Dr. Blair appeared at last and ushered us over to a private corner of the waiting room. I stood close to Tyler in an attempt to give him what support I could.

This time the doctor addressed Tyler directly. "Your grandfather has made it through the first crucial hours, and that's all to the good."

"What are his chances?" Tyler asked in a firm voice. "I need to know the truth." I thought fleetingly that Laurence should hear his so-called delinquent grandson now.

"His condition has stabilized, and that's the important

thing for now. We'll do more tests and we'll put him on medication to see how he does. Later, there will be some adjustments of his diet and exercise, of course, and he'll have to quit smoking—"

"Don't worry," Tyler said grimly. "He will."

"Good. We are cautiously optimistic that he'll make a fine recovery. He has a long way to go, of course, but there's nothing more you can do right now, so I suggest you go home and get some sleep. Your grandfather might be able to see you late in the afternoon. He'll be in the Cardiac Care Unit and Dr. Fauchet will be the cardiologist handling the case. He's the one you'll want to talk to." Dr. Blair shook hands with Tyler. "Your grandfather must be very proud of you."

"I hope he will be," Tyler answered.

After Dr. Blair left, Tyler turned to me with a smile. "Whew! That's better."

"It sure is," I agreed. "What do you say I take you home now and pick you up again at four o'clock?"

With a trace of mischief in his voice, Tyler said, "Maybe I should just borrow Grandpa's car and drive myself."

I matched his buoyant tone. "Oh, yeah. That's a great idea!"

A note was fastened to Laurence's front door when we arrived. I waited, engine idling, while Tyler read it and then disappeared briefly into the cottage. He soon returned to the open passenger window of the Volvo and asked, "How does she do that? It's barely daylight." He handed the note to me.

> Tyler—
> So sorry to hear about your grandfather. You left the door unlocked so the meals are in the fridge. (Heat in oven at three-hundred-and-fifty degrees for twenty minutes.) Books on counter. Call me if you need anything else, and remember, 'The Lord will provide.'
> Minnie

"It's almost nine o'clock," I answered. "Plenty of time for her to swing into action. Well, if Minnie's been here, it's official. Everyone in town knows about your grandfather's heart attack."

"How does anybody keep a secret around here?"

"Mostly, they don't. People help when you need help, but they also find out things you might want to keep private. It's a mixed blessing of small-town life. Did Minnie leave *Paint Her Dead?*"

"Right on top, along with Ann Rule's *Heart Full of Lies,*" Tyler answered.

"Great. You can start reading immediately, but what I want is sleep. Your grandfather might fire me for not opening Thornton's today, but I'm too sleepy to care. See you later."

"Jane, I hope you know how much I appreciate—"

"Glad to do it." As I eased away from the curb, I said offhandedly, so as not to embarrass him, "Hey, Tyler, you done good."

My answering machine at home blinked a steady stream of messages. Though longing for bed, I punched the button to hear them. Jeremy from down the street wanted to know when he was supposed to mow my lawn. Minnie offered a choice of fried chicken or lasagna for dinner. Harley said he'd just missed me at the hospital and would come by later.

Next, Alix's crisp voice informed me that she would keep Thornton's open for business today. My eyes filled with tears at this unexpected kindness, even as my weary mind struggled to figure out how Alix would manage to get into the store.

Susannah wanted a punch recipe. "You know the one, Mom. It serves fifty and we used it for Emily's graduation party. I assume Louise has calmed down by now. Call me." She said nothing about going into labor.

Finally, the message I'd been waiting for. Bianca's voice,

sounding uncharacteristically subdued. "Mom, I'm really sorry to hear about Laurence, and I just want you to know that you don't have to worry about me. I have everything under control. I'll call you tomorrow after…after I finish something up."

I knew enough about my daughter to recognize that even though she was still angry, she had sent her message to reassure me. Of course, it had the opposite effect. Just what did she think she was going to "finish up" by tomorrow? I dialed her number right away, but she wasn't answering.

The rest of the messages could wait. Halfway through the living room, I decided the bedroom was too far away and fell onto the couch. Pulling the afghan over my face to block out the light, I realized that, for once, my kids wouldn't begrudge me a nap today. Despite my anxiety about both Bianca and Laurence, I slipped into a deep, dreamless sleep.

THIRTEEN

THOUGH TYLER HAD BEEN allowed to see his grandfather as soon as we returned to the hospital, it wasn't until evening that I tiptoed in to see Laurence for five minutes. Observing the motionless figure in the sterile bed, I struggled to keep an encouraging smile on my face. It was hard to avoid looking at the tubes that tethered him to various machines, and even harder to disregard the lights and repetitive beeps that monitored his condition.

"Hi, Laurence. How're you feeling?"

"Like hell," he mumbled. "What'd you expect?"

His tart answer cheered me. This was the gruff old man I had grown to love over the past year, not some anonymous invalid. His next comment encouraged me even further. "What're you doing here anyway? You're supposed to be at work. Can't make money with Thornton's closed." He tried to raise his arm, but the tubes prevented him from doing so.

"Alix has been filling in."

"Alix Boudreau? What does she know about books? She can't—"

"She's doing fine. Besides, the store is already closed for the night. I'll swing by there in the morning."

"Night already? Can't tell a damned thing from inside this cocoon. You go by there anyway, check that she locked the door. I'm not paying you to sit around here staring at me."

"Yes, sir!" I said, saluting smartly. "Alix will be so glad to hear how much you appreciate her efforts."

"Give me a break. I'm sick," he said.

I was feeling better by the minute about his condition. "Drop the act, you old fraud. You're just lying in that bed so you can order everyone around."

"Ever try ordering a nurse around?"

"Not really, but I'm sure you have."

"Complete waste of time." He shook his head. "Like getting you to tend to my bookstore. Are you—"

"I'm going, but first I want to tell you about Tyler. He's been—"

"Everyone has been telling me about Tyler," he interrupted. "Does he have some kind of fan club going?"

"If he does, I want to be its president. He was terrific last night. And about the car—"

"Sorry, time's up." A cheerful nurse with "Gayle" printed on her name tag spoke as she paused by Laurence's bed.

"Thanks for saving me," Laurence told her. "Jane was about to lecture me about my grandson."

"Tyler?" Gayle asked. "He's a great kid."

"What'd I tell you, Jane? Now get to the store and leave me in peace."

"Gladly." I left the Cardiac Care Unit with a lighter step. Things were looking up.

Tyler wasn't waiting in the hall where I had left him five minutes before, so I started for the cafeteria. On my way through the lobby I noticed that the volunteer usually posted at the information desk was with a crowd on the other side of the room, watching the television set. I was halfway up the staircase before I could see the face of Tina Marquette on the screen. From this distance, her make-up didn't look half bad. A glance at my watch confirmed that the evening news should have finished an hour ago. Sure enough, the banner snaking across the bottom of the screen proclaimed a "KPHD News Flash." Probably another noxious weed alert. Our homegrown station hadn't quite mastered the knack of gauging what constituted breaking news, so I continued upward.

Whatever was on the news didn't have anything to do with me, unless… I paused in mid-stride. Bianca! I hadn't yet been in touch with her today, and who was I kidding? The chance of her being featured on a news flash fell somewhere between likely and inevitable.

I retraced my steps to the lobby floor and joined the viewers in time to see an annoying commercial which consisted entirely of various people sneezing until the name of some miracle medication appeared in the last shot. As the crowd dispersed, I spotted a vaguely familiar woman and headed her off.

"What was that all about?" I asked her, waving a hand at the screen.

"Oh, hi," she said. "You work at Thornton's, don't you?"

"That's right." Now I remembered her. She had come in looking for astrology charts, which, of course, we didn't carry. Laurence had definite opinions on astrology and all things metaphysical. "Did you find your charts?"

"I certainly did. Thanks for telling me about Heavenly Bodies and Books. I didn't even know that store existed, but it's wonderful. I've been back several times."

"Glad to help." Finally, one of Bianca's strange bits of knowledge had come in handy. "What was that news flash?"

"Oh, poor Gil Fortune," she said. "After all he's been through. This afternoon he was actually attacked outside the courthouse!"

"Attacked?" My heart was in my shoes. "Physically?" On second thought, that didn't sound like Bianca's style.

"Yes. He came up just as Gil left the courthouse and hit him. A couple of deputies grabbed him right away."

"You said *he?*" Just then I saw Tyler enter the lobby with

Max Wendorf. Max turned toward the emergency room and Tyler came my way. This was starting to make sense.

"Yes, Kurt Wendorf. If people can't control their kids, they shouldn't blame the district attorney when their kids get in trouble."

"Uh, right," I said. It must be nice to have such certainty about how to manage your kids. "Well, I'd better go—"

"Me, too. Actually, I'm on my way to Heavenly Bodies and Books right now for a spiritual renewal session they're having tonight. You might—"

"Right." I smiled, nodded, and edged away.

"You won't believe what happened, Jane," Tyler said as soon as he came close enough.

"Max's dad attacked Gil," I said. "It's on the news."

"Wow! That was fast. It just happened. Look, Jane, Max is here because his dad got roughed up when the cops grabbed him. Can you come and talk to him?"

"What? I hardly know Max, or his dad."

"No, but you know me. I can vouch for Max and Max can vouch for his dad."

I was having a little trouble following his reasoning. No wonder this kid got along with Bianca.

"Please. Max doesn't have anyone else. You know what Bianca thinks of Gil. Well, she's not the only one. You need to know what Gil did to Max over that thing at school."

He waited while I thought this over. It seemed that everyone was turning to me this week, as various adults dropped out of the picture and left me responsible for their kids. "That thing, as you call it, wasn't a minor prank. Max set off a smoke bomb in a school." Didn't Tyler realize that perhaps Max and his dad caused their own trouble?

"But he didn't know it would cause so much damage. He just mixed up a teaspoon and a tablespoon. He isn't a delinquent." I gave him a look and he amended his statement. "Okay, so it was dumb, but please talk to him anyway."

"Oh, Tyler. What good will that do? At some point people have to behave reasonably. Max's father apparently hasn't learned that yet either. He's not setting a great example."

"But you don't know what Gil did to them. Max told me that Kurt went to him privately, and Gil promised he wouldn't use anything against Max that Kurt told him, but he did—even though he denies it. And then—"

"I get the point. You're saying there's more to the story."

"There sure is!"

"Okay, I'll talk to your friend Max, but not now. He's busy with his dad and I'm taking you home. This day has gone on way too long already."

FOURTEEN

THOUGH IT WAS LONG AFTER closing time when I pulled up in front of Thornton's, the door was wide open and the telephone ringing. By the time I threaded my way through the books piled all over the counter and the floor next to it, the ringing had stopped. Stunned at the disarray, I lifted and read a few of the notes in Alix's distinctive block printing that littered the counter. They all represented book orders, and far more of them than Thornton's had seen since Megabooks Plus! had opened its giant maw last fall and swallowed many of our customers. What was going on?

I edged past the wavering mountains and entered the office in the back room. "Alix?" No answer, but the outside door was ajar and I could hear voices beyond.

There I found Alix, cigarette in hand, lounging in a comfortable chair she had scrounged from somewhere. In front of her stood Minnie, waving a copy of *Prove It, Puppy!* and saying, "That part where the dogs climbed the cliff was outrageous. Corgis don't have the legs for… Oh, Jane, there you are. How is Laurence?"

"Cranky as ever, but the doctors think he's going to be okay."

"Thank the Lord!" Minnie said.

Alix smiled briefly before resuming her usual detached demeanor. "I hope that means you'll be coming back to work soon. I don't know how you keep everything straight in this madhouse. It's worse than planning a three-hanky wedding with twelve groomsmen."

I refrained from mentioning that one of my organizational tricks was to stay in the store, answering the phone and putting away books, rather than smoking cigarettes out back. After all, Alix had generously put aside her own business to fill in at Thornton's today. "Laurence especially wanted me to thank you for your help today. How did you do it? There are more orders sitting on the counter than we've seen in months."

"I didn't do much," Alix said. "When people heard Laurence was in the hospital, a lot of them called to check on him. As long as they were on the phone, I asked if they wanted to order books…and voila! Someone even ordered a book called *Forty-Seven Ways to Improve Your Memory with a Ball of String.* Do you ever just burst out laughing?"

"Sometimes it's hard not to," I answered.

"That book just might have some good ideas, Alix," Minnie interjected thoughtfully. "Goodness knows we all need more memory aids as we get older. Did you order any extra?"

Alix opened her mouth and closed it again without saying anything, struck speechless for once. She merely shook her head.

"Too bad," Minnie said. "Oh, well, we'd better deal with Bianca first anyway. No problem remembering that. Have you talked to her today, Jane?"

"No, but she left a message."

"Has she changed her mind?" asked Alix. "That book was the biggest load of crap I've ever seen."

"Of course it is," Minnie said, "but we can't say that to Bianca. As the Bible says, 'Blessed be the peacemakers, for they shall find peace.'"

"What's that mean?" Alix asked. "We're supposed to make peace with Bianca? Assure her that we just love her darling little book?"

"I'm trying to remind myself, Alix," Minnie answered, "that no matter how big a load of…that we need to pour oil on troubled waters, not stir them up. Why don't we give it another try? Talk to her one more time. Maybe a day of thinking about it has softened her up."

"I don't think she's changed her mind," I said.

"Oh, come on," Minnie urged. "Let's ask her to come over right now."

"If you're all fired up with Christian charity, Minnie, it's fine with me," Alix offered. "Of course a two-by-four might work better."

"Not a two-by-four, but firm words," Minnie said. "That's what we need, and a nice chicken salad for a late supper. Oh, wait, does she eat chicken?"

"Maybe you could tell her that Swami Rhami loves chicken salad," Alix suggested as we walked to the front of the store. "Won't matter anyway. If Wendell is nearby, he'll get it before anyone else can pick up a fork.

"I forgot to tell you, Jane, that Harley was looking for you today," Alix said. "He was in here twice, as a matter of fact. You're finally going to give him a chance?"

"What's all this?" Minnie was always on the lookout for romance. "Oh, Jane, that would be wonderful."

I dialed Bianca's number. "Don't get excited, you two." Bianca either wasn't home or wasn't answering her phone. Finally, I put the receiver back in its cradle. "She's not answering. I just hope she's not out stalking her prey."

"You're working late." Gil Fortune's distinctive voice came from the darkness outside the open front door. We all recognized it but, for a frozen minute, no one moved or spoke. Then he moved into the light and the room exploded into dusty chaos. Alix knocked a stack of books off one end of the counter with her elbow while Minnie dislodged another heap with her voluminous handbag. I just stood there with an idiotic smile plastered on my face, thinking that we looked like Larry, Curly, and Moe.

"Sorry, I didn't mean to startle you," Gil said.

"No, no, don't be silly," I said as the others started picking up the books. "We were just, just…juggling books—badly." I giggled, something I didn't normally do, and then trailed off, unable to think of anything the least bit plausible to say. I couldn't very well tell the truth, but I almost giggled again at the prospect of hearing what Gil would say if I told him they had been wondering how far Bianca had progressed in getting him to confess to the murder of his wife. Alix and Minnie continued to stack books as though it were the most important task they'd ever had, leaving a conversational gap big enough to drive a bookmobile through.

A small bandage on one cheek was the only sign of Gil's recent run-in with Kurt Wendorf. Kurt was a big guy, so Gil had probably lucked out by having a couple of muscular deputies nearby when Kurt attacked him.

I studied Gil in an effort to see him the way Bianca did. He was casually dressed in sport coat and slacks, tieless and with his shirt collar unbuttoned. His looks were the sort that often graced the pages of upscale magazines that catered to young entrepreneurs and community leaders. It was impossible to imagine him being dragged away in handcuffs. Prison stripes weren't at all his style.

Minnie, never long at a loss for words, recovered first and plunged into the conversational chasm. "Oh, I hope you don't think that…that is, I hope you didn't take it badly at such a sad, sad time that… We'll understand perfectly if you don't want to talk to our book club."

I finally gathered my wits about me. Oh, yes, Bianca's invitation. "It was just a whim…to ask you. I…I guess I wasn't thinking."

"Don't worry, Jane," he said. "Remember, I saw Bianca a lot when she and Vanessa were putting together that photo essay, so I can guess whose idea it was."

"It wasn't just Bianca," Minnie said gallantly. "It was sort of a joint whim. We all weren't thinking."

I interrupted Minnie before she could start talking about all for one and one for all. "I can't tell you how sorry I am, Gil. It was in the worst possible taste."

"I understand perfectly," he said, "and...well, let's just leave it at that." He looked steadily at each of us, one by one, and spoke in a low, determined voice. "Nothing is ever going to take away the pain I feel at losing Vanessa, but I must go on without her. Do you understand? I can't let myself get distracted by things that have no importance. I just can't, so let's consider the matter closed. That's what I came to tell you."

"Oh, you poor, brave man," Minnie said. "I hope you enjoyed the pot roast I sent over."

I was still absorbing Gil's words. While Minnie chattered on about spices and oven temperatures, I exulted that we were off the hook...so far. When I found Bianca, I was going to put masking tape over her mouth.

Gil took Minnie's hand and patted it. "Out of this world, the best I've ever eaten. I ate every bite of it. Thank you so much for caring."

Minnie's kind face turned pink. "What are neighbors for, if not to help in time of trouble?"

"If everyone reacted to trouble the way you do, Minnie, the world would be a far better place."

"Oh, you're too kind," Minnie said in a quivering voice. "Do you like lemon bars? I can make you some lemon bars, or chocolate éclairs, if you prefer."

Patting his flat stomach, Gil laughed. "You're really out to get me, aren't you? That's an idea though. You know who could use some help with food? Harley...for the class reunion."

"Why, of course, I'd be glad to help," Minnie said. "I don't suppose you'll be going. No, of course not."

"No, I just couldn't," Gil said. "You understand."

"We certainly do," Minnie answered. "I'll contact Harley to see what he still needs."

"Do that," he said. "That'd be great." He waved and left, closing the door behind him.

Minnie sighed. "Doesn't your heart just ache for him? Going home to that empty house."

"Don't worry about Gil. He won't be alone for long," Alix said.

"Why are you always so hard on him?" Minnie asked.

"Because I've known him since we were kids, and that means I know way too much about him. Meanwhile, it's good to know he's not holding a grudge against us for that stupid invitation."

"No," Minnie said. "He didn't look angry, just sad."

"You're right," I said. "But didn't he also seem a bit too…I don't know…too distraught about life without Vanessa, or too calm?"

"You can't have it both ways," Alix said. "Was he too upset or too calm?"

"I don't know…both, at different times. It was just a funny feeling. I'll try Bianca again. This nonsense has gone on long enough."

FIFTEEN

I GAVE UP ON SLEEP LONG before sunrise. Bianca hadn't answered her telephone last night or this morning, and I could hear the first whisper of fear in the back of my mind. Telling myself I was being foolish, I banged down the receiver once more and climbed into the shower. Ten minutes later, hair dripping wet in the early morning chill, I headed for the car. When I located Bianca, I knew I'd encounter scorn for fussing and being "such a mom" to someone of her advanced age and experience, but I didn't care.

Raymond Morris's Rule Number Six ought to work best: *Admit to your own weaknesses.* Bianca already knew about my over-developed capacity for worry, so I'd simply throw myself on her mercy. I was a mom, and I wanted to see my daughter, whether she was mad at me or not. I had replayed her message countless times. She'd said she would call me later, and she hadn't.

I streaked east on Highway 28 in the growing daylight. Only occasional traffic shared the road with me at this hour, and, uncharacteristically, I passed every car I overtook. My thoughts were far away from my driving and I was lucky that no deer ventured out in front of me.

Bianca's trailer looked even more forlorn than usual, perhaps reflecting my apprehension. No lights glowed from inside and Bianca's bicycle wasn't in sight. My careful scrutiny of the rise behind the trailer revealed no slender figure meditating, a sight I'd have welcomed today.

"Wendell! Here, boy!" I called as I approached. Nothing,

but I hadn't really expected to see him. Wherever Bianca was, Wendell would be, too. His food and water dishes stood empty.

I knocked briefly and then opened the trailer's cheap metal door, registering the fact that it was unlocked. "Bianca, are you here?"

I'd been reading too many mysteries. The open door merely suggested that Bianca trusted everyone—except Gil Fortune, of course. Still, I listened before stepping inside, trying without success to overcome the feeling that I wasn't alone. I cocked my head and listened harder. If there had been a sound, it wasn't repeated. The trailer was so small that I could see the entire living and kitchen area from the doorway, but the door beyond was closed. After a minute of indecision, I tiptoed across the matted shag carpet and threw open the door to the bedroom. Empty. So was the tiny closet.

All that remained was the bathroom at the far end of the room. Its door stood halfway open. I crossed the room and smashed the door hard against the wall. Poised to run at the slightest threat, I jumped back as a figure appeared before me. It took only a single, heart-stopping second to realize that I was looking at myself in the bathroom mirror.

Shaking, I entered the bathroom and leaned on the built-in vanity. I was alone, but the strained expression reflected in the mirror told me that I was almost out of control.

I splashed some cold water on my face and took stock. Bianca didn't view the world the way I did. Possibly she hadn't even realized that I was worried about her. Once she learned of my apprehension over her absence, she'd be incredulous, telling me to loosen up. She'd also chide me for my lack of faith in her ability to take care of herself. After all, she was nineteen years old.

Nineteen. I was never nineteen the way Bianca was, with a carefree nature and a desire to experience as much of the world as possible. By the time I was her age, I was already head over heels in love with Tony, planning our wedding and wanting to start a family as soon as possible. Well, I'd gotten what I wanted, and if my chosen path wasn't adventurous, at least it had led to a warm contentment that I had relished until Tony's death. Since then, I had been slowly rebuilding my world.

But now that Bianca had stirred things up, I seemed to be losing ground. I was in such a state this morning that I hardly recognized myself. Really, what were the chances that a killer would be hiding in Bianca's trailer waiting for someone to happen by? About as likely as the notion that Gil had killed Vanessa. I pictured the calm, self-assured man who had talked to us last night at Thornton's. Ludicrous to picture him as a killer! Bianca's whole premise was a fantasy, the product of her overactive imagination. I couldn't let myself get caught up in her world. It was my job, as always, to provide her with reason and perspective. But to do that, I needed to find her.

Somewhat self-consciously, I returned to the kitchen area and looked for clues that might tell me where she had gone. An extensive collection of Tazo herbal teas overflowed a basket on the counter. One label proclaimed that "Calm Herbal Infusion" was "the reincarnation of tea." If Bianca were to learn about my panicky search of her trailer, she'd prescribe a daily dose of this tea immediately.

The few treasures that adorned the trailer—feathers in a colorful bowl, a black and white photograph of a running horse, and a mound of smooth rocks artfully arranged in the middle of the floor—declared Bianca's personality, but didn't tell me where she was.

In the current mysteries I had scanned to familiarize myself with the stock at Thornton's, clues were sprinkled liberally throughout and the main characters immediately understood the significance of each of them. Apparently, I didn't have the knack. Pamphlets on the benefits of massage therapy and a half-written scenic postcard of nearby Broken Top addressed only to "Al" rested on the counter.

I retraced my steps to the bathroom. This time I noticed some photographic equipment stacked neatly in the corner of the shower stall. If I hadn't been so frightened earlier, I'd also have noticed the acrid odor of chemicals hanging in the air. Bianca had used her makeshift darkroom recently. Was this a clue? It was the best I could do, but I already knew about the fuzzy photos she took at the gorge, so it didn't seem too useful.

The hair on the back of my neck prickled as a wail issued from somewhere outside. The ancient, mournful sound was eerie, but my heart jumped at the thought that Wendell might be near. If he had arrived, Bianca would be here, too. I ran for the door, wondering whether retrievers were supposed to howl. Probably not, but then Wendell wasn't exactly a purebred.

I all but fell down the two steps leading from the trailer in my haste to scan the surrounding area. No sign of either Wendell or Bianca. Confused, I ran all the way around the trailer and was halfway through a second circuit when the howling began again. It was coming from the front. This time I looked into the blackness underneath the trailer. Once my eyes adjusted, I could make out the outline of a large black dog.

"Wendell, come out of there! Wendell!" The usually exuberant dog didn't move. "Come on, boy," I coaxed. Something was wrong. I scooped up his water dish and filled it from the kitchen tap. Slowly, Wendell emerged and lapped up the entire bowl of water before sinking onto his haunches in the dust. He wagged his tail slightly when I knelt to pet him, but out in the sunlight I could see that his one good eye looked dull, and he winced when I touched his right side. He put his head on his paws and looked at me.

After a final struggle, I let go once and for all of the very sensible idea that Bianca had just wandered off. She might be careless about leaving doors unlocked, but she would never have left Wendell hurt and without water.

I didn't know what was going on, but something very bad had happened to my daughter. The earlier whisper of fear had now become a scream. Where was Bianca?

Twenty-five minutes later Alix's cream-colored Saab convertible pulled up beside my Volvo. Before the occupants of the convertible were fully visible through the dust stirred up by their arrival, I identified Tyler as the lump of clothes in the back seat, Minnie by the fuchsia scarf swirling around her head, and Alix by her words.

"This had better be good. If we were dragged out here to eat Surprise Seaweed Soufflé, so help me—"

"Don't look at me," Minnie responded irritably from beneath the floating scarf. "You kidnapped me—and I don't know what the Knitwits are going to do for cable stitch instructions until I get back." Minnie tamed the scarf temporarily and heaved her bulk out of the car.

Alix rounded the front of the vehicle and stared at the dismal surroundings. "Does Bianca really live here? No wonder she prefers Swami Rhami's philosophy of searching for a higher reality. So would I if—"

"Really, Jane, was it necessary to interrupt my cable stitch session? Those Knitwits are all just sitting there in my house waiting for me. They can't do another thing until I get back."

"Minnie's knitting group," Alix contributed helpfully.

"Where's Bianca?" Tyler slid over the side of the car without bothering to open a door.

"She must be here somewhere," Alix said. "There's Wendell. She doesn't move an inch without him."

"She's not here," I said.

"She's probably inside, getting ready to spring some ground-up kelp juice and tofu on us," Alix said.

"I'm telling you, she's not here," I repeated.

"Then she's probably off…off…picketing Gil's office or something," Minnie said.

"Without Wendell?" I asked. "Alix just said that she never goes anywhere without him."

"I meant in general, "Alix said.

"That still doesn't make this an emergency," Minnie added reproachfully. "Cable stitch is hard enough to teach under the best of circumstances, but Alix said that you wanted us to come, so I came."

"What about the hospital?" Tyler suggested. "Maybe she went to visit Grandpa."

"I checked. Bianca didn't go visiting, or picketing, or anything else like that. And yes, Minnie, this is an emergency," I said. "Wendell was here alone, and he was out of food and water." I let that information sink in.

Minnie tried first. "Well, it's been very hot…" She trailed off, unable to sustain the fiction that the temperature of the day would explain things. "Are you sure?" she finally asked.

Even Alix looked uneasy. "That doesn't sound like Bianca."

"Wendell has already emptied his water bowl twice," I said, "and he wasn't interested in the food I gave him."

"Did you try frosted bran bars?" Alix attempted a joke, but she sounded worried.

"Besides," I continued, "there's something wrong with his side. He's been hurt somehow."

We all looked at Wendell as though waiting for him to explain what was going on. He had looked up briefly at the sound of his name, but now lay back down. The sight of Wendell ignoring a full food dish was frightening.

"An accident?" Alix asked.

"I'd have been notified. Besides, I checked."

"She left me a message," Tyler said slowly, "but she didn't want me to tell you about it."

"What message? When?" I was seized with a sudden burst of hope.

"Yesterday, when I was visiting Grandpa."

"Yesterday!" I grabbed his arm. "What did she say?"

He hesitated. "She was going to check out Gil's alibi by talking to Jenna Lang at her house."

"What else?"

"Well, remember how in the book Miss Pittimore sent a message to Bernard, hoping to rattle him?"

"She already sent Gil that message," I said. I noted irrelevantly that Tyler and I were exactly the same height as we stood facing each other.

Tyler nodded. "She was going to sort of follow up on it… with those dummy pictures, and maybe a dummy videotape."

"How?" Alix asked. "Just walk up and hand them to him, expecting a confession?"

"She didn't say," he mumbled.

"Maybe she's playing a joke on us…you know, paying us back for making fun of her ideas?" It was clear that Minnie didn't believe her own words.

"Crazy as it sounds, what if she discovered something incriminating?" Alix asked.

Though I ached to have Bianca float in here clutching a spray of desert wildflowers and offering herbal tea, the sick feeling I had in my stomach told me it wasn't going to happen. Everyone looked at me silently until I voiced our common thought. "Something's happened to her."

"I thought she'd be back by now," Tyler said miserably. "I should have—"

"It's okay, Tyler," I said. "You didn't know. We'll go to the police."

"They'll never believe us," Minnie said. "*I* don't even believe us, and I know we're right."

I was thinking furiously. "We don't have to accuse anyone of anything. We'll just tell them that Bianca has disappeared, and play it by ear."

"They'll never believe us," Minnie whimpered again.

"We have to try!" Alix said. "She left the dog hurt and without food and water. She might do a lot of fool things, but never that."

I mentally tallied a long list of sensible reasons for believing that Bianca was simply off somewhere being irresponsible. Then I balanced them against Wendell's condition. Was I prepared to go to the police based on an ill-defined hunch and a dog's empty water dish? Yes. No question about it.

"We'll drop Wendell at the vet's office on our way," I said. Tyler, the boy who had already demonstrated once this week that he could handle an emergency, gently picked up the injured dog and carried him to Alix's car. "Okay, Wendell. Here we go."

Yes, I thought. Here we go.

SIXTEEN

THE RUSSELL COUNTY Sheriff's Department had outgrown its cramped space in the basement of the county courthouse several years before. Its expanded reincarnation now sprawled in high-tech glory on the northern outskirts of town. It was all sharp angles and rows of shiny patrol vehicles lined up in the parking lot. Gone was the quaint country atmosphere of the department some ten years ago, when Russell County needed only a couple of patrol officers to stay ahead of crime in the rural community. As the county's population had exploded, the crime rate had risen as well, and the Russell County Sheriff's Department had evolved to meet the new circumstances.

When we arrived, the deputy on duty in the entry hall concentrated his attention on the metal detector we passed through, rather than our faces. At first we clustered just inside the entrance, but soon Alix led the way to the glassed-in window beyond. She said, "When you party as much as I did in high school, you get familiar with the general layout of law enforcement facilities, especially if you're not a fast runner." She added in a low voice, "Gil was a sprinter."

"Really?" Minnie said. "He was a…a little wild in high school?"

"Along with half the cops who work here now. Funny how the football players like Gil and Kurt never seemed to get caught. All those wind sprints paid off. Harley didn't play ball because his mama wouldn't let him, but he could always talk his way out of trouble. Vanessa and I got busted a lot."

I faced the middle-aged woman at the desk behind the

glass, but she was intent on her keyboard. After waiting in vain for her to recognize our presence, I tapped on the glass.

"Excuse me. We're here to report a missing person, or… well…to check on my daughter, who might be missing."

Looking up reluctantly from her work, the woman produced a mechanical half-smile. "Is she missing or not?"

Alix stepped around me and read the name from the picture ID clipped to the woman's collar. "Well, Ms. Peterson, if we knew for sure that she wasn't missing, we wouldn't be here now, would we? Could we talk to someone who might actually help us?"

Ms. Peterson apparently had been at her job long enough to recognize troublemakers. She gave Alix a sour look and said, "I'll see," before disappearing into a back room. She closed the door behind her with considerable force.

"No need to be rude, Alix," Minnie said.

"Oh, yes, there is," Alix said dismissively. "Officious twerps need discipline."

I noted Tyler's grin and wondered how many officious twerps he had already encountered in his short lifetime. "Please let me handle this, Alix," I said. "We need these people on our side."

Alix waved me forward. "Be my guest, but don't take any crap."

I stepped in front of her again. The officer who now emerged from the back room looked as though he had come to the department fresh from a stint with the U.S. Marines. I resisted the urge to salute. His stiff demeanor proclaimed that Ms. Peterson hadn't given him a favorable report about us, so I hoped that Alix would keep quiet.

Unfortunately, he looked over my shoulder at Alix and directed his opening comment to her. "Well, if it isn't the charming Ms. Boudreau."

"Deputy Kincaid." Alix's tone was no warmer than his.

"Taking a break from harassing the local business owners?" I made a mental note to leave Alix at home the next time diplomacy was called for, and especially to exclude her from any future dealings with the Russell County Sheriff's Department.

"Look we had a complaint and—"

"—and you always go by the book. Yes, you certainly did go by the book and I'm sure Sheriff Kraft was very proud of his little helper."

Kincaid flushed an unhealthy brick color. Fortunately, Minnie chose that moment to step around Alix and speak up. "We'd like to file a missing person's report, please."

Deputy Kincaid gave Alix a look that would have boded ill for her had she been a subordinate in his platoon. His flush now extended all the way down his thick neck to his collar line. Ostentatiously, he turned his attention to Minnie and snapped an official-looking form onto a clipboard. "Yes, Ma'am. Who's missing?"

I had my doubts about the wisdom of letting Minnie speak for us, but at least she wouldn't insult anyone. As a further precaution, I placed my elbow on the window ledge squarely in front of Alix. By this time I'd ceased to care that we all looked as though we were jockeying for good starting position at the Preakness.

Minnie spoke clearly. "Jane's daughter, Bianca Serrano, is missing...we think."

Kincaid paused with his pen in mid-air. "You think?"

"We're almost certain," Minnie said. "We haven't actually seen her since Wednesday afternoon, though she left several messages yesterday."

"How old is your daughter, Ma'am?" he asked me.

"Nineteen," I said.

He put down the clipboard. "Nineteen? She can go wherever she wants. Does she have a roommate we can check with?"

"Yes, but that's just it," Minnie said earnestly. "That's what makes us so certain something is wrong."

"Okay." He picked up the clipboard again. "Her roommate gave you some information?"

"Wendell? Oh, my, no." Minnie chuckled at the notion. "He wouldn't...actually he couldn't..."

The bewildered Deputy Kincaid didn't see what Minnie found so amusing. "Do you want us to talk to this Wendell guy or not?"

"That's absurd. You can't do that."

"Is Wendell missing, too?" He was totally confused now, but I thought that his confusion was preferable to the reaction he'd have as soon as he understood this conversation better.

"Well, no, but he was out of food and water," Minnie explained helpfully, "and his side was hurt."

"Out of—"

"Wendell is Bianca's dog," I said. "Look, Deputy, I know it sounds odd, but Bianca is very attached to him, and she would never have left him that way."

"I see," he said, stepping back and looking at our group clustered around the glass like goldfish waiting for food. I had the uncomfortable feeling that he had already assigned us the reasoning capacity of goldfish as well. Alix, whom he already knew and disliked, was accompanied by several people who made no sense whatsoever. This distinguished delegation was wasting his valuable time with talk of some teenager most likely guilty only of neglecting her dog. "I don't suppose you have any evidence—"

"If you mean a bloody knife on the counter, a ransom note, or something like that, not really," Minnie said regretfully, "but we have a theory—"

"An accident." I interrupted loudly before Minnie could mention Gil and further erode our already negligible credibility. "We thought maybe someone had reported an accident."

"I don't think so, but I'll check." With another look at Alix, he said, "I guess I have time to do that before I get back to harassing the local business owners." He, too, closed the door to the back room more forcefully than necessary.

I turned on Alix. "Is there anyone in this station you haven't offended yet?"

Alix made a rude sound. "That jerk! Look, it was just a simple mix-up and he—"

"Oh, it doesn't matter," I said wearily. "I'm sorry I cut you off, Minnie, but we agreed to keep quiet about you-know-who for now."

"You're right. You're absolutely right, Jane. I forgot. My goodness, Alix, he seemed very cross with you. What did you do to him?"

"Mr. Macho doesn't like having his authority questioned."

"Another twerp, Alix?" Tyler asked.

"Yep. He and Ms. Peterson have a lot in common."

Minnie said, "Maybe I should bring them some of my cinnamon pull-aparts."

"Do you start cooking every time there's a problem in this town?" Alix sounded genuinely puzzled.

"Well, not every time, but you'd be surprised at how often food helps to defuse a tense situation."

Alix nodded. "Throwing a cream pie at Kincaid's face might make me less tense, all right."

"Oh, that wasn't what I meant at all," Minnie said, "and of course being hit with one of my pull-aparts might cause real harm. They're quite large—and sticky."

Laughter erupted from behind the closed door and a moment later Kincaid reappeared. I was relieved to see that his color had returned to normal.

"No accidents reported since yesterday, Ma'am, but is your daughter about five feet seven inches tall, with long blond hair?"

"You've found her?"

"Well, yes and no."

"Is she all right?" Minnie asked.

"Far's we know." He jerked a thumb toward the back room. "Deputy Maxwell saw somebody coulda been her yesterday south of town." He almost succeeded in keeping the smile off his broad face as he continued. "She was sitting cross-legged on a rock."

"Yoga," Tyler said.

"She was all right?" I asked. "Did he say when this was?"

"From what he could tell, she was fine. Course he was just driving by. Said it was mid-morning."

"Was her dog with her?" I asked. "A big, black dog?"

"That's what I asked. Matter of fact, he was. She probably took off and left him."

"I'm sure you're right and she'll turn up any time now," I said hastily. This oaf was no help and I didn't want to stir his interest in us any further.

"She wouldn't do that! She'd never abandon Wendell," Tyler burst out. "Besides, how did he get back to her trailer? It's way out of town the other direction."

"We were probably overreacting," I babbled.

"Are you going to let us file a missing person's report or not, Kincaid?" Alix asked.

"Tell you what. Why don't you come back when you got something more'n a dog's empty water dish."

"We'll be going now. Thank you for your time," I said desperately. I gestured urgently for the others to follow me out of the building before someone made another insulting remark. Once outside, I said, "She was on her way to Jenna's house, or Gil's. They're both south of town."

As Minnie comprehended the meaning of my words, her face drained of blood so fast that I had to catch her arm to keep her from falling. Tyler grabbed her other arm and we escorted her to a nearby bench.

"Put your head between your knees," I commanded.

"I think…I'm fine," Minnie replied faintly.

"Just stay there," I said.

"What now?" Tyler asked over Minnie's bowed head.

After weathering the results of the last, disastrous few minutes, I figured I'd be better off proceeding on my own. "We don't do anything," I said. "I appreciate all you've done so far, really. You've been great, but I can handle it from here. Tyler, you need to get back to the hospital, and you have a business to run, Alix."

"I can help," Minnie said, raising her still-pale face.

"And you, Minnie, need to go home and rest. We're probably getting worked up for nothing." I tried to pump some sincerity into my lie. "You know Bianca. She'll probably show up—"

"And I'm the Tooth Fairy," Alix said.

"Me, too," Tyler and Minnie said in unison.

"You're not leaving me out," Minnie continued as she struggled to her feet. "I'm fine, and I'll drive my own car so we can fan out and do…whatever it is we decide to do. That way, it will be harder to trace us."

"Why would anyone be tracing us?" Tyler asked.

"Goodness, Tyler, I'm sure I don't know right now, but I'm trying to think ahead," Minnie said. "We're going to search for clues, aren't we? Well, then, if we fan out to do that, and anyone tries to follow us, they'll have a hard time doing it!"

"You know, Minnie," Alix said, "you are something else. I can't follow your logic, even when I already know what you mean to say! If the instructions you give the Knitwits for cable stitching—whatever that is—aren't any clearer than this, they must turn out some interesting projects."

"My land!" Minnie said. "I forgot all about the Knitwits.

They're still waiting at my house. I'd better tell them to go home." She started for the nearby phone booth, and then turned back. "By the way, Alix, you were right about the cinnamon pull-aparts."

"What'd I say?" Alix looked confused.

"Well, actually you said something about Deputy Kincaid and Ms. Peterson. I believe that 'a soft answer turneth away wrath,' and I try to keep a Christian attitude, but you were right about those people. They were very, very rude to us. We needed help, and they not only turned us away...they mocked us. You were right. They don't deserve cinnamon pull-aparts...and you know what? They're not getting any!"

Alix recognized the magnitude of Minnie's declaration. "That's positively revolutionary. Cutting off someone's supply of cinnamon pull-aparts is an act of war!"

"Exactly," Minnie responded.

Alix said, "Okay, Jane, you can skip the flimflam. We all know Bianca isn't going to show up on her own, and we're not going to waltz out of here and leave you to look for her by yourself."

Tyler and Minnie nodded in agreement. The three of them stood shoulder to shoulder facing me like an amateur modern version of *The Three Musketeers.* They might lack finesse, but they were gutsy and loyal. Besides, they were all I had.

SEVENTEEN

TWENTY MINUTES LATER I settled onto my living room couch and emptied my mind of everything but the next step. If and when I finally worked up the courage to punch in the number of the Russell County District Attorney's office, I didn't want any trace of anxiety to sound in my voice. I breathed in and out deeply several times, making use of the relaxation techniques Bianca was always urging on me.

I had insisted that my co-conspirators remain out of earshot in the kitchen while I made the call. The smell of fresh-brewed coffee now told me that Minnie would keep Tyler and Alix occupied by serving the coffee with the snickerdoodles she had thoughtfully tucked into her oversized knitting bag this morning. No, probably she would insist that Tyler drink a big glass of milk instead. She seemed to think it quite normal to bake cookies before breakfast so they'd be fresh for her meeting. Not only had the Knitwits lost their cable stitch instructor, they had also lost their snickerdoodles.

Dragging my chaotic thoughts back to the task at hand, I closed my eyes and tried to think like a con artist. Nothing came to me. Then I tried to think like the most cynical person I knew: Alix. That did it. I knew just how to proceed, so I placed the call. Waiting for Gil's secretary to answer, I counted the rings to distract me from the nagging of my conscience. I promised myself I'd return to my usual law-abiding tendencies after I found my daughter.

"Good morning," I said briskly. "This is Sandra Samuels calling Gilbert Fortune from the Oregon Department of

Justice, Fraud and Abuse Division. To whom am I speaking, please?"

"Frances Norris, Mr. Fortune's secretary."

"Thank you," I said. "That matches our information. We're doing a routine check of time management and—"

"Do you wish to speak with Mr. Fortune?"

"That won't be necessary," I said, as my heart rate jumped. "I'm sure you can give me the answers just as well."

"Oh, good, because he's attending a noon Rotary meeting in Sisters."

I checked my watch. Perfect. We had plenty of time. I continued with my cover story. "You are Mr. Fortune's confidential secretary? You manage his schedule?"

"Yes, of course. Look, Ms. Samuels, is there something wrong? Maybe I'd better check with Mr. Fortune—"

I forced a laugh through my rapidly constricting windpipe. "No, nothing wrong, at least not in Russell County. It's just that…and I'm sure I can rely on your discretion in this matter…some district attorneys have been using work time to conduct personal business and—"

"Mr. Fortune is absolutely scrupulous about separating his work from his personal activities."

"Exactly. That's our information, too, but you understand that we have to check with all the counties before issuing—"

"You're talking about the Grant County D.A., aren't you?"

"I really can't say," I murmured, "and I must ask you to keep this call to yourself, at least until the news breaks."

"Of course. You be sure to check out Phil Tanaway in Harney County, too, while you're at it." Apparently Gil's loyal secretary wasn't above a little gossip.

"Sorry, I can't say more, but…very soon." I rustled the pages of yesterday's *Juniper Journal* for effect. If I didn't redirect this conversation fast, Ms. Norris's fertile imagination would indict half the district attorneys in the state. "Tell me about...oh...let me pick a day at random, Ms. Norris—"

"Call me Frances."

"Frances, then, thank you." This was going better than expected. Maybe I had an unexpected flair for deception. "Well, Frances, how about Wednesday, August eighth?"

Frances gasped. "That was the day Gil's wife died."

"Oh, what an unfortunate choice, but it will do just fine for our spot check. Our records show that Mr. Fortune was out of the office on personal business for most of the day. Is that correct?"

"Yes, it is. He used his own car, signed out for the hours he planned to be gone, everything."

"He sets a fine example."

"He's wonderful. We're hoping he's going to be the next Attorney General of Oregon, you know."

"Sounds as though he already has your endorsement. So, Frances, let's just get the details and I'll let you get back to work. With all the recent growth in Russell County, you must be pretty busy."

"We certainly are." Frances lowered her voice. "I really don't know how Gil's kept going, in spite of everything. With the news coverage and all, I guess everyone in the state knows—"

"Yes, such a sad situation. The poor man must be devastated. Now, about that day—"

"Let's see. He left here about ten, signed out for a Realtor's open house on a place that he and his wife were thinking of buying. Isn't that sad? He was there when he heard the news of her death. Naturally, he didn't return to the office, so that's about all I can tell you. Will that help?"

"More than you know," I said sincerely. Now that I knew Gil's whereabouts, all I wanted was to end this conversation.

"Thanks again for everything, Frances. Remember, mum's the word."

"It's Jim Farber in Gilliam County, too, right?"

"Frances, you're a shrewd one," I said, and hung up.

EIGHTEEN

AS THE OTHERS CLAMBERED out of my Volvo, parked on the far side of the field behind Gil's house, I sat for a moment behind the steering wheel. Just how crazy were we to be here?

Tyler appeared at my window. "Are you all right?"

I managed an imitation smile. "Fine." I climbed out of the car and pulled on a pair of black gloves that were way too hot for this summer day.

"You look kinda green."

"Nope. I'm fine."

"Are you sure I—"

"We already settled this, Tyler." I didn't intend to add a charge of corrupting a minor to my already-overburdened conscience. It was bad enough that he was even here. For the first time, I was glad that Laurence was in the hospital so I wouldn't have to face him. To soften the blow to Tyler's sense of manliness at being left behind, I repeated my strongest argument. "Your grandfather doesn't need the emotional stress of having you commit a felony, or whatever this is. Remember though, you're our lookout."

"Your daughters wouldn't approve of what you're doing either," he grumbled.

"That's right," I agreed. "They probably wouldn't even bail me out."

"Do you suppose the Knitwits would bail Minnie out?" he asked.

"Depends on how desperate they are to learn that cable

stitch. Just do your job and nobody will have to bail anybody out."

The waving crop of alfalfa didn't provide much cover, but it smelled good. No other houses were near enough to make detection by a curious neighbor a problem.

Minnie had underscored the seriousness of our venture by discarding her trademark floppy hat in favor of a black knit watch cap from my hall closet. A muted paisley scarf was slung over one shoulder. Alix was her usual elegant self in a sleek black tank top and matching capri pants. Just what was the proper attire for housebreaking? Tyler and I looked remarkably nondescript in shorts and tee-shirts next to the other two.

"You didn't tell Gil's secretary who you were, did you?" Minnie was having second thoughts.

Alix said, "She even asked Gil's permission to search his house."

"You didn't!" Minnie's mouth dropped open. "That'll spoil everything."

"She's joking," I said.

Minnie clapped a hand over her heart. "My stars! Don't do that, not at a time like this."

I started across the field, with Alix and Tyler beside me. Minnie hung back.

"Shouldn't we crawl?" she asked.

"You can if you want," Alix said over her shoulder, "but Gil's not home, so I'm walking."

"It doesn't seem right," Minnie mumbled as she fell into step beside Tyler. "Where are you going to be?" she asked him.

"Somewhere I can watch both the driveway and the road in front. That's where the cops'll come from if there's an alarm or something."

"An alarm. I hadn't thought of that. How can we tell, Jane?"

I shrugged. "Have to get up close and look, I guess."

"Oh, dear. I don't like the idea of an alarm."

"Didn't you bring your bolt cutters, Minnie?" Alix asked.

"I did," announced Tyler, holding up a wicked looking implement.

Minnie was shocked. "We're not common vandals."

I stopped and faced her. "Look, the truth is that we might have to do some damage to get into the house."

"Did you think Gil would leave the key under the welcome mat for us?" Alix asked.

"Well, no," Minnie said, "but—"

"Stay out here if you want," I said. "At this point I'm not going to worry about breaking a pane of glass." I turned on my heel and marched toward the house.

"For heaven's sake, Jane, let me finish." Minnie trotted along behind me as fast as she could, catching up just as I reached the back door. "That's not what I meant at all. I simply don't see the need for violence."

She pulled a crochet hook out of her pocket. Bending to the lock, she inserted the pointed end and twisted. The door swung open. "See?"

"Cool!" Tyler breathed. "Where'd you learn that?"

"After I locked myself out of the house a time or two, I figured it out."

"Why don't you just hide a spare key to your house?" Tyler wanted to know.

"Why, bless your heart. That's a good idea," Minnie said, "but not nearly as much fun."

"I know what you mean," Alix said, pulling a slim black implement out of her pocket and holding it up for inspection. "Not *all* of my encounters with the police have been unproductive."

"Wow!" Tyler exclaimed. "What's that?"

"Picklock," Alix said. "A detective I once dated gave me

this instead of flowers." Her sly smile indicated that he had made a wise choice. "Showed me how to use it, too."

Minnie and Tyler crowded close. Minnie showed a professional interest in the slightly different shapes of their respective housebreaking implements, and Tyler was fascinated. I'd certainly led a sheltered life. How had I gotten mixed up with these people?

"C'mon. Let's get this done," I urged. "Tyler, let us know if you hear anything, but don't come inside."

The cool interior of the house stood in stark contrast to the heat of the summer afternoon. Our stealthy footsteps provided the only sound as we tiptoed into the back entry hall and on through the kitchen. I surveyed with surprise the sleek granite counter tops, the glass-fronted cupboards filled with crystal, and the oversized gas range. How could Gil afford all this on his salary? Tony's career as a civil engineer had provided us with a comfortable standard of living, but our blue and white farm kitchen was more suited to toasted cheese sandwiches served on paper towels than the elegant dinner parties that went with this set-up.

Poor Vanessa. Her state-of-the-art kitchen hadn't done her much good. I felt a twinge of guilt that I had all but forgotten about her death in the confusion following Bianca's disappearance. Now, surrounded by the emptiness of what had so recently been a showcase home for the seemingly ideal couple, I felt a renewed sense of sadness for Vanessa. Had she been murdered? If so, would we ever be able to prove it? Only Bianca had even thought to raise the question.

I caught my breath at the sudden fear that Bianca might disappear with just as much ambiguity. No. That wasn't going to happen. I would find her.

I wandered around the kitchen, wondering what to look for. The clues unearthed by the dog detectives in *Prove It,*

Puppy! were totally unrealistic. Besides, all I had in real life was poor one-eyed Wendell, who was presently recuperating at the High Desert Animal Clinic. Even had he been here, I suspected he'd be more interested in the shiny metal kitchen garbage container than anything else. On a whim, I stepped on the foot pedal and glanced at the sack inside, but found only the remains of a T-bone steak dinner. In the midst of his supposed grief, Gil was eating well.

Leaving Minnie to explore the kitchen further, Alix and I went through the living room and into the bedroom wing. While Alix checked out the spare rooms, I ventured into the master bedroom and to the bath beyond, opening cupboards at random, but finding nothing of interest.

Apparently Alix and Minnie were having the same experience. We all arrived simultaneously in the living room and turned, as one, to gaze at the professional portrait of Vanessa on the wall. Serene and lovely, she looked out at us from a rose garden. The picture must have been painted elsewhere, since the roses didn't appear frostbitten. Juniper's capricious summer night-time temperatures played havoc with gardens.

"Anything?" I asked.

"Nothing on the answering machine," Alix said, "but, of course, he could have erased it by now. I see he has caller ID though, so if Bianca tried to call him anonymously…"

"…he'd have known exactly who was on the line. She might not have realized that."

"Of course she wouldn't, poor thing," said Minnie. "Caller ID costs extra. I certainly wouldn't pay for something that frivolous."

"It's not frivolous when you have a couple of ex-husbands you don't want to talk to," Alix volunteered.

"More than one?" Minnie asked. She seemed to be distracted by something, only half paying attention to the conversation.

"Did you find something, Minnie?" I interjected. This wasn't the time for a rehash of Alix's love life. "You didn't find…?"

"Oh, no, nothing like that, dear. Sorry, I didn't mean to scare you. I didn't find Bianca, but I did find a very distressing clue." Minnie's chin quivered as she continued. "Remember when Gil told us the other day how much he'd enjoyed my special pot roast? Well, I just looked in the refrigerator. He hasn't touched it. It's sitting there, rotting away."

"Why is that a clue?" Alix asked the question before I could.

"If you can't trust him about this, you can't trust him about anything. He lied about it. I didn't go to all that work just to watch my good food go to waste. I have half a mind to take it home with me today."

"Wouldn't that sort of tip him off to the fact that someone was in his house today?" Alix asked.

But Minnie wasn't so easily dissuaded. "If he even noticed it was gone! He deserves to have somebody rifling his house if this is the way he treats a perfectly good pot roast. Do you know what one costs?"

"No," said Alix, "but I'm sure you can tell me."

"Please," I said, "can we—?"

Though I didn't hear his approach, Tyler now burst into the room. "We're screwed!" he announced.

"Tyler, stay outside!" I said sternly. "We don't—"

"He's coming…Gil's coming!"

"But he's in Sisters," Minnie sputtered.

"That's what you think," Tyler said.

"Quick! Out the kitchen door!" I said, grabbing Minnie's arm.

Tyler blocked our path with outstretched arms. "He's coming that way."

"Front?" Alix asked.

"He can see that door from where he is," Tyler said.

"Bedroom window," I decided, heading for the master bedroom with Minnie in tow.

"I can't climb out a window," she wailed.

"Sure you can," Alix assured her. "It's all in the wrists."

I urged everyone down the thickly carpeted hallway and into the master bedroom. Racing toward the windows on the far side of the room, I heard the distant click of the back door opening. I put my finger to my lips. From the way the others had frozen in place, it was clear that they too had heard the sound.

One louvered closet door wasn't quite closed, so I eased it open further and pointed inside. The gardenia-scented hangers and the flowing dresses inside indicated that this closet had been Vanessa's. Alix and Minnie crowded inside, followed by Tyler. There wasn't enough room left for me, so I squeezed under the king-sized bed.

Over the hammering of my heart, I could barely make out the sounds of footsteps coming down the hall and into the room. I heard a dresser drawer open, then close. The footsteps approached the wall of closets. I could see Gil's highly polished loafers as he passed beyond the closet where the others hid. He opened the door to another closet and I heard the rattle of a hanger.

Finally, after I had aged about ten years, Gil's closet door closed once more, his loafers recrossed my line of vision, and his footsteps retreated down the hall. I didn't move until I identified the sounds of the back door closing and the engine of his car starting up.

Then I crawled out from my hiding place. After one incredulous glance at the closet door, I swung it wide open. "Quick! We have to get out of here!"

"Whew! That was close," Minnie said, as she untangled

herself from a green chiffon tea dress that seemed determined to come with her.

"You can say that again," Tyler said. "That was creepy."

"Get moving," I ordered. "Minnie's scarf was sticking out of the closet door. Gil couldn't have missed seeing it."

"Then why—" Alix began.

"Why didn't he call the cops?" I asked. "I'm sure that's exactly what he's doing from his cell phone right now."

NINETEEN

"FREEZE! POLICE!" The command came simultaneously from authoritative voices on each side of us.

Alix stifled a laugh and muttered out of the side of her mouth, "I thought they only said that in the movies."

"Don't shoot!" Minnie squeaked, shifting from foot to foot in the iris bed.

"We have no intention of shooting, Ma'am. Just stay put."

Getting Minnie through that bedroom window had been no small task. In the future, I'd recruit only accomplices as lithe as Alix and Tyler. I glanced around, but Tyler was nowhere in sight. He had probably sprinted into the alfalfa. That was fine with me. One less person to explain. Now I could concentrate on manufacturing a plausible reason for having my gloved hands inside the open window of Gil's bedroom. There was also the matter of explaining the actions of my companions, who were currently making mush of the flower bed.

"Turn around slowly, all of you, hands over your heads."

I mustered all the heartiness I could. "You really scared us. What a silly mistake." I attempted a small laugh to match my words, but it died in my throat at the expressions on the two deputies' faces. They advanced shoulder to shoulder, ready to defend Truth, Justice, and the American Way—but not to laugh off this situation. Both were now close enough to allow me to read their name tags: Charles Quigley and John Weems. They looked so official and serious that I wanted to tell them to lighten up—they weren't facing Al Capone here—but they weren't in a joking mood.

"Somebody made a mistake all right," said Deputy Weems. His words might have sounded more menacing had I not been distracted by a cowlick which caused his brown hair to stand straight up at the back of his head.

Alix spoke up. "We can explain everything."

"Oh, my, yes," Minnie added in an unnatural voice. "We certainly can. Go ahead, Jane."

"You'll get your chance, Ma'am," said Deputy Quigley, "but first we need to see some identification."

"I'm Jane Serrano and this is Minnie Salter and Alix Boudreau. Anyone in town can vouch for us. You must be very new to the department or you'd recognize us."

"Identification, please."

"I don't have any with me, but—"

"You work with Brady Newman, don't you?" Minnie asked. "He used to cut through my yard on his way to and from school when he was a youngster, and I was his Sunday school teacher. Brady can tell you that we're perfectly respectable."

"Uh huh," said Deputy Weems. "Why were you climbing in this window?"

It wouldn't help our cause if I mentioned that we were climbing out of the window, not into it, so I just skipped that part. "Look," I improvised, "it's all perfectly innocent. We were trying to help our friend Gil—District Attorney Gilbert Fortune, that is—with…uh…well, men are so helpless around the house, you know. We thought the poor man probably needed help…with the housework."

"Uh huh. And the gloves?"

Alix came through. "Did you ever try to keep a manicure in decent shape? No, of course not." She stripped off the gloves and held up her delicate hands for inspection. "You simply can't do housework without gloves and hope to keep your nails from breaking."

"Did Mr. Fortune ask you to do his housework?" asked Deputy Quigley.

"Of course not. It was to be a surprise, and now you've ruined it," Minnie said. She was rallying nicely.

"Uh huh," said Deputy Weems again. His conversation needed a little punching up and I was becoming annoyed with his attitude. He didn't believe a thing we said.

Meanwhile, Deputy Quigley was looking at the mess we'd made of the garden. "He'll be surprised at the way those flowers look, that's for sure. Come with us, please."

"Where?" Minnie asked.

"To the station, where you can be reunited with your old friend Brady," Deputy Weems said.

"That would be a big waste of time," Alix said.

"Uh huh." Weems returned to his favorite rejoinder.

"But I've explained the situation to you," I argued.

"Yes, Ma'am, but you'll have to do it again down there," Quigley said politely.

"Can't you call Brady?" Minnie asked. "He'll tell you."

"Yes, Ma'am. He can do that at the station."

As we made our way to the patrol car parked in the driveway, I looked around for Tyler, but he was keeping himself well out of sight. While Deputy Quigley settled us into the back seat, Deputy Weems radioed ahead. "Tell Gil we got 'em, but it wasn't who he thought. No sign of Kurt."

We exchanged looks. Gil had known very well who was in his house when he called in the alarm, unless Kurt had recently taken to wearing paisley scarves. He had simply wanted to humiliate us.

"You won't put the siren on, will you?" Minnie wanted to know.

"No need for that," said Deputy Quigley as he settled himself behind the wheel. I had the feeling that if Deputy

Weems had been in charge, we'd have ridden through town with siren blaring.

As we drove back to the sheriff's department, which we had left only a few short hours before, we stuffed our gloves into our pockets. No need to highlight them. Someone there with a suspicious mind might be tempted to think the gloves were something housebreakers might wear. We arrived all too soon. This time we drove around to the back of the building, where Deputy Quigley wheeled the patrol car into place with a flourish before escorting us inside.

Gil was waiting for us, his campaign smile at the ready. "Ladies, what's this all about? I assumed it was that fool Kurt acting up again—or maybe his delinquent son."

"They *claimed* they were there to help you with the housework," Weems volunteered.

"Yes, since you have a lot on your mind right now," I said. I launched into our bogus explanation as sincerely as possible, but it sounded ridiculous, even to me. "You probably aren't used to taking care of the house by yourself."

Gil appeared puzzled. "You thought Vanessa's closet needed cleaning? I don't understand."

"You don't?" Minnie's voice came out as a monotone, very different from her usual cheerful prattle. "Actually, we thought you might need more food, since you enjoyed my pot roast so much."

Gil walked right into it. "Well, you certainly know the way to my heart, Minnie. You have an unorthodox way of offering help with the house, but your cooking makes up for everything. That pot roast was all that kept me going last week."

"Well, now, if this is all cleared up, maybe we can go," I said cheerfully. It was a last desperate try at staving off disaster. Minnie's voice remained level, but I could sense that the volcano was about to blow.

"You don't know how glad I am to hear you say that," Minnie replied. "Were you able to finish it?"

"Every bite. It was delicious."

I closed my eyes, helpless. Here it came.

"What have you done with Bianca?" Minnie roared. "Where is she?"

"What?" Gil's smile slipped.

"That pot roast wasn't touched! We know all about...everything! We know what you did!"

"What are you talking about?" Gil was incredulous at Minnie's words, as well he might be.

"A man who will lie about pot roast will lie about anything," Minnie insisted.

"We know Bianca went to see you, and now she's disappeared," Alix said. "And what did you do to her dog?"

"Where's Bianca?" Minnie thundered.

Gil threw up his hands. "I've tried to be patient, but this has gone far enough. I didn't see your daughter and I didn't do anything to her dog." He turned to the waiting deputies. "Please escort these ladies from the building."

"I'm not going anywhere until you tell me where she is," I said.

"Now!" Gil ordered. "I don't have the time or the energy to go through this nonsense again. Get them out of here."

"But, Gil, they're threatening you." Deputy Weems was itching to use his shiny handcuffs.

"They're crazy. No charges. I just want them gone." Gil strode from the room. The two young officers faced us, arms folded.

"Hiding behind your deputies won't work, Gil!" I shouted at his retreating back. He kept going.

TWENTY

MY EYES BURNED FROM lack of sleep. I hadn't been able to settle down after the fiasco at the sheriff's department yesterday, but I had done a lot of thinking about how to proceed. Unfortunately, I now had a ringing in my head that I knew well from the months after Tony died. Too little sleep and too much tension were a bad combination, but there was no help for it. I was running on pure adrenaline.

I picked up the revolver from the passenger seat of the Volvo. Its unfamiliar weight sat awkwardly in my hand. I looked toward Gil's house. His car was in the driveway so I knew he was home. The paths we had made only yesterday through the alfalfa were still visible, but today was a new day. Gil was going to tell me what I needed to know.

I fumbled with the tape recorder at my belt, making sure I could activate it without looking. The sonorous tones of Gil's voice should carry clearly through the lightweight sweater I had thrown on for concealment. I'd have to get near him, but not close enough for him to grab the gun. Ridiculous to wear a sweater on an August morning, but no more ridiculous than my whole plan. Goading Gil into revealing anything about Bianca by threatening him with a gun—especially a gun without a firing pin—was pathetic. I'd be more likely to catch a burst of Gil's laughter on tape than any useful information about Bianca. Still, what choice did I have?

Once more I fought down the sick feeling that came over me whenever my mind strayed to the specific question about what Gil had done to Bianca. Perhaps my obvious agitation would convince Gil that I wasn't bluffing. Any information I could squeeze out of him would be worth whatever penalties it cost me. Susannah and Emily would just have to understand.

For the thousandth time, I wished Tony were here. For one thing, he'd have been more convincing with the gun. Of that I was sure. I had no previous experience with firearms and had, in fact, been uneasy about even having this family heirloom in our home. Though its lack of a firing pin rendered it harmless, I'd insisted Tony keep it in a locked cabinet.

But Tony wasn't here. Minnie, Alix, and Tyler would be eager to help, but I didn't want to involve them further. The sheriff's department saw no reason to look for Bianca. They'd made that clear. Harley kept offering assistance, but he was Gil's best friend, so that made him off-limits for this particular task. Laurence was in the hospital. I even considered calling Nick, but he'd left a message yesterday informing me that he was fishing on the Crooked River and would call when he returned. I was on my own.

As I made my way across the field, I thought back to last night's conversation with Tyler and Max Wendorf. I had dragged home from the encounter at the sheriff's department to find them waiting for me, literally lurking in the shrubbery flanking my front door. While I had been glad to see that Tyler had escaped from Gil's property undetected, Max's presence reminded me that I had promised to talk to him. After observing yesterday's encounter with the police outside Gil's house, Tyler might find it hard to recommend me to Max as a model of adult authority, and neither of them knew about my ineffectual outburst at the sheriff's department. Following that episode, I understood better how Kurt Wendorf could have been goaded to fury by Gil's supercilious attitude. Max's first words told me that I needn't have worried about him condemning me for our escapade at Gil's house.

"Cool idea, Ms. Serrano. Even if you did get busted, you

threw a scare into him." Max and Tyler were at opposite extremes physically. While Tyler was wiry and blond, Max looked like a shaggy brown bear. If he'd taken up high school football instead of setting off smoke bombs, he'd have been a formidable obstacle.

"I don't know, Max," I said. "It didn't seem to scare him all that much. I'm glad you got away, Tyler."

"Didn't see any reason for all of us to get hauled in."

"Let's go inside. No sense advertising that we're in contact more than necessary." I led them into the living room and plopped wearily onto the couch. They perched on the edges of the armchairs facing me, avid to hear the details.

"Don't get too excited. It was a mess. Gil didn't buy our cover story."

"I wasn't close enough to hear what you said."

"We told them we were there as friends to help Gil with the housework."

Not surprisingly, they both snickered. Tyler said, "That wouldn't explain the dive out the bedroom window."

"Not unless Gil's a real moron," Max contributed.

"Well, he's not, and it didn't," I replied. "Besides, Minnie was mad that he hadn't eaten her pot roast."

Max looked totally lost, so I said, "Don't bother trying to make sense of it. The point is that everything is out in the open now."

"So how come you're not in jail? My dad was held overnight after he went after Gil," Max said.

"Probably because your dad seemed like a credible threat, Max. Everyone there just laughed at us. After making sure everyone knew how stupid we were, Gil graciously agreed to let us go."

"That's the same thing he did with Dad, except for the letting go part," Max said. "It's like Gil has some kind of invisible shield. Nobody sees what he's really like."

"You couldn't expect him to give your dad a medal for hitting him," I said.

"No, but he could've kept his mouth shut about me. He promised Dad he would."

"Maybe, as D.A., he didn't have that option once he knew—"

"But he wouldn't have known who set off the smoke bomb if Max's dad hadn't told him," Tyler said.

"You weren't caught, Max?"

"No," Max said. "Nobody knew who'd stunk up that locker until Dad figured it out. He was plenty mad at me, but he wanted to do the right thing, so he went to his old friend for help. Gil swore he wouldn't say a thing to anyone, but next thing we knew, he was on TV and I was charged with arson. Yeah, I screwed up. I knew that right away, but he could have given me a warning, or charged me with criminal mischief or something. Instead, he picked the heaviest charge he could find. Now I've got an arson rap on my record. Great."

"It's great for Gil's career," Tyler said. "The way he told it on camera, it sounded like Max was trying to burn down the school. Then when his dad tried to tell everybody what really happened, Gil denied it and nobody believed Kurt's story."

"See?" Max said. "It's the same with Bianca. She saw through him—"

"Exactly," I said, "and now we do, too."

"How about a private investigator?" Max offered. "Are there any in Juniper?"

Tyler bounded from his chair and started flipping through the phone book. "Here they are, under 'Investigators,' a whole bunch of them." He looked up eagerly. "Or maybe we should go through Gil's house again. It'd be faster."

I started to nod my agreement, then pulled myself back to reality. What was I thinking, involving these two kids further?

I was supposed to be a responsible adult. "I'll call a private investigator first thing in the morning."

"But—" Tyler said.

I forced a smile. "I don't know about you, but I need some sleep before I do another thing."

They both stood and moved reluctantly toward the door. Their slumped shoulders made an eloquent protest against the wasting of all the adrenaline their young bodies were pumping. I searched for a task to keep them busy for a few hours.

"How about writing down exactly what happened to you and your dad, Max?"

"What good will that do? Nobody believes us anyway."

"Not yet, but it's important to get the details down before they get hazy. As we gather more evidence, it would be good to have this information ready to use. Tyler, you can help. It gives more clarity when someone from the outside looks at things."

"Okay." They looked considerably more cheerful as they made their way out the door. "We'll check back with you tomorrow morning."

"How about noon?" I suggested. "You can stop by the hospital to see your grandfather on the way."

"Oh, yeah. I'll do that." Tyler looked abashed. Obviously, now that Laurence had passed the crisis stage, Tyler found it more exciting to chase a crook than to sit by a hospital bed.

AS I REACHED THE FLAGSTONE patio behind Gil's house for the second time in two days, my head felt strangely detached from my body. This was like being in a play and watching myself disguised as someone else playing out this scene. Even as I proceeded, I doubted that I could really do this.

The back door opened at my touch. No need for yesterday's assorted tools for breaking and entering. Maybe this easy entry was a portent that everything today would go smoothly. I'd find Gil and Bianca sitting in the armchairs that flanked the picture of Vanessa over the fireplace, and they'd rise up to greet me with smiles, saying, "Surprise! This was all a big joke."

I shook my head and tried to rid myself of the floating sensation that had come over me. The kitchen was in perfect order, just as it was yesterday. The workmanlike hum of the Amana refrigerator was reassuringly normal. Had Minnie's pot roast made it to the dining room table yet or had Gil thrown it away, now that his deception had been uncovered? If you led a double life, would you bother with such mundane chores as cleaning out the refrigerator?

Gingerly, I poked the nose of the gun into the back of my belt, under my sweater. That ploy was to be saved until needed. Before moving further into the room, I slid the bolt closed on the back door. I didn't want anyone surprising me from the rear.

A low voice came from another room. Was Gil talking to someone? There had been no other cars in front. Maybe he was on the phone. I crept across the tile floor and crouched behind the counter to peer into the empty dining room. Now another voice sounded, followed by the familiar tones announcing CNN's "Headline News."

My feet moved forward of their own volition and my hand went to the switch of the concealed tape recorder. Again I had the peculiar feeling of being an outside observer of my own actions. Was this what it felt like to go crazy? Over the hammering of my heart, I registered the solid thud of the front door closing. Foot suspended in mid-air, I waited. Had someone entered?

Surely if someone had come into the living room, I'd hear conversation by now. I lowered my foot and continued my stealthy approach, composing myself for the anticipated confrontation. I wanted to appear calm, rational, and implacable.

I'd start by confronting Gil with my new-found knowledge of his betrayal of Kurt and Max. If that didn't elicit a response, I'd move on to the idiotic "I know what you did" approach Bianca had chosen. If all else failed, I'd attempt to scare him with the gun, assuming I could stay far enough away so that he wouldn't recognize it as inoperable.

This was like some Grade B movie from the nineteen forties, with me trying to convince him that I had him dead to rights…with nothing to back it up. He might not even believe me when I told him the truth, that I'd mailed a letter today to Nick, detailing my actions and my suspicions and asking him to take it to the Oregon State Police in the event of my death or disappearance. I could hardly look like more of a fool than I already did in the eyes of the law. Since Nick was an attorney as well as a new friend, he wouldn't let the matter slide.

I rehearsed again my opening remarks. Everything sounded melodramatic: "Okay, where is she?" or "What have you done with my daughter?" Most likely, Gil would show the same scorn that he had yesterday, brush aside my useless gun, and usher me out the door.

As I entered the living room, I announced in a loud voice, "Okay, Gil. It's…" I was talking to myself. CNN continued to give the headlines, but Gil was nowhere in sight. The former neatness of the room had been erased. Chairs were overturned, a coffee cup spilled liquid onto the luxurious carpet, and Vanessa's picture above the mantle had a diagonal slash through it. The international chaos showing on CNN had nothing on the chaos in this room.

I recalled the sound of the front door closing. Had Gil just left? Maybe he was outside right now, calling the police again. I turned to retrace my steps just as the phone began to ring. I stood paralyzed, unable to think what to do next.

Four rings and the answering machine picked up. I recognized Harley's voice. "Hey, Gil, where are you? If you're hearing this, you're in the wrong place. I'll wait at McNulty's a while longer, but I'm getting hungry." He clicked off.

Maybe it hadn't been Gil who had just left here. Gil was probably pulling into a parking spot outside the popular downtown restaurant at this very minute. Involuntarily, my thoughts turned to Kurt and his attack on Gil the other night. The deputies had dragged him away in handcuffs, a humiliating situation made worse by Gil's perceived betrayal. Kurt could have done this. The desecration of Vanessa's picture and the ransacking of the living room seemed too personal for a random burglary. Had Tyler and Max relayed to Kurt our conversation last night? If so, it might have stirred him up again. Kurt's fiery temper had already caused him plenty of grief this week, but surely I didn't have anything to fear from him, or did I? The violence of the destruction here might indicate that he'd lost all control.

Suddenly the house seemed very large and quiet. I couldn't decide whether to go out the back door and run for my car or lock myself in and call the police. Calling the police from inside Gil's house seemed like a really bad idea, given the events of the day before. But my car now seemed far distant across the field, so I put off the decision, opting to creep across the living room and lock the front door first. So far, so good. Now Kurt—or whoever it was that might be outside—couldn't burst in. Carefully, I peered through the decorative glass door panels. Gil's car was still in the driveway. In my consternation at seeing the condition of the living room, I had forgotten all about seeing it there earlier. Clearly, Gil hadn't left to meet Harley for breakfast, unless he'd driven Vanessa's car.

Maybe Gil was still hiding somewhere in the house. He might even mistake the noise I was making for that of the earlier intruder. I raised my voice in a tentative question. "Gil?" No answer. "Whoever vandalized your house is gone now." Nuts. I'd have to go through the house room by room to make sure he wasn't here. As long as I was at it, I'd search again for Bianca as well, even though we'd found no trace of her presence yesterday.

I took two steps back toward the bedroom wing and gasped. I wouldn't have to search for the house's owner after all. He lay sprawled motionless on his side behind the couch, a gag in his mouth.

My hands fumbled at the knot holding the gag, a brightly patterned scarf, while my mind registered the fact that I had seen this material before. When the gag finally came loose, it didn't help. This man wasn't going to talk to me, or to anyone else, ever again. Taking a deep breath, I grasped his shoulder and rolled him onto his back. His arm flopped without resistance and his sightless eyes stared at the ceiling. The coffee spilled in the middle of the straw-colored carpet had already left a dark brown stain. The blood oozing from his chest now added a rusty pool. Even though the colors went well together, it had been an all-around bad day for that rug.

I retched at the sickly sweet odor of blood. With the aid of the couch, I stood up and backed away, still clutching the gag, and held it up, trying to make sense of its presence here. My daughter had been wearing it as a belt the last time I saw her. The bright fabric had provided a startling splash of color against her white shorts.

I couldn't even begin to make sense of my discovery, and I didn't try as I jammed the scarf into my pocket and made my unsteady way to the back door. No matter who waited outside, I had to get out of here. With the hem of my sweater, I rubbed my fingerprints from the back door lock and prepared to twist the knob. Just in time, I remembered that I had also touched the lock on the front door, so I raced to the living room to repeat the process there.

Another peek out the front window revealed the same quiet scene. I fled back through the house. The only sounds were

CNN's continued commentary and my own ragged breathing. I pounded across the patio and into the field, stumbling and almost falling when I risked a glance behind me.

No one followed me. Still, I didn't slacken my pace until I flung myself into the front seat and reached for the ignition switch. No keys. Where had I put them? I patted my pants pocket and felt only the softness of the scarf I had removed from around Gil's head. Keys, keys. Oh, yes. Out of the car again to fumble under the front seat. Stupid place to leave them. Should have left them in the ignition.

I was still outside the car when the two patrol cars screeched to a stop in a confusion of noise and dust around me. Instinctively, I drew the scarf from my pocket and crammed it down behind the driver's seat.

"Stay right where you are," commanded a familiar voice. Deputy Weems again, the person I least wanted to see. Why didn't they put Brady Newman out on patrol? "Don't move! Russell County Sheriff's Department. Okay, now raise your hands very slowly and put them on top of thc car."

I did as instructed, thankful I no longer held the scarf.

"What's the matter?" I asked as innocently as possible.

"What are you doing here, Ms. Serrano?"

"Last time I looked, this was a public road," I answered. A good offense was supposed to be the best defense.

"Last time I looked, you were breaking into Gil's Fortune's house yesterday," he answered. "Maybe you should find yourself another hobby."

"And maybe you should watch your manner, Deputy," I replied. Where had that come from? Tony wouldn't even recognize the cheeky scofflaw I had become.

"Sorry, Ma'am," he answered, sounding not the least bit sincere. "Could you please tell us what you're doing here?"

"I don't believe I am required to answer you." I hoped I

was right about that because I certainly needed some time to prepare a plausible answer.

"We had a report of a crime at Mr. Fortune's house. So far, you're the only one we see on the premises."

"I'm not on the premises."

"Near enough."

"After what happened yesterday, do you think I'd be stupid enough to go back?"

"Could be. Have you been inside that house today? That's the question."

"That's insulting." I hoped he wouldn't realize that I hadn't answered his question.

He seemed willing to let my answer go unchallenged. "I think we'll just wait here until we see what Brady turns up inside."

The blood was pounding in my head. I didn't want that scarf found. Putting as much annoyance into my voice as possible, I said, "Well, I need to open Thornton's in exactly ten minutes. Since you know who I am and where I'm going, I suggest you just contact me if you need anything further." I swung into the driver's seat and attempted to close the door.

Weems's meaty hand closed over the top of the door and stopped it from moving. "No. You'll wait here. Thornton's will manage without you."

"But I'm the only one working there today. Laurence Thornton is still in the hospital and he depends—"

"You're staying put, Ms. Serrano, until we figure out what's going on. If and when Gil gives Brady the all-clear, there'll be time enough for you to get to work."

I knew Gil wouldn't be giving anyone the all-clear, but I didn't want to annoy the deputy further, so I subsided. I did not want to give the police any extra incentive to search my car.

TWENTY-ONE

"DON'T GO ANYWHERE," Deputy Weems warned me. "We're not done here yet."

"Fine," I answered. I tried for a look of bored resignation, rather than the panic I felt. He sauntered back to his patrol car, presumably to polish his holster or something. If I had to choose someone to pass the time of day with, it wouldn't have been Weems. He didn't appear eager for my company either.

Sitting in the driver's seat of the Volvo and ostentatiously looking at my watch periodically, I considered Bianca's scarf. Was it less likely to be discovered in its hiding place behind the front seat or should I try to drop it out the car door, hoping no one would notice? On the other hand, what could be more natural than to have my daughter's scarf in my car? I decided to leave it where it was.

The police radio crackled to life at the same time I saw uniformed figures coming our way from around both ends of Gil's house. I didn't need Weems's report to tell me that Gil's body had been found. I prepared to be shocked.

"Is it still your story that you didn't enter that house today?" he asked.

"My story?" I repeated. "That's an odd way to phrase it. Look, Deputy Weems, I've humored you long enough. I have a job to do. Now, may I please get to work?"

"Just answer the question."

"I don't care for your tone at all, so I don't think I will."

"Then we're going back to the department."

"Don't you have anything better to do than harass me?"

"So you don't know anything about..." He trailed off, obviously remembering some page in the manual that governed the questioning of suspects. His hunger to get me to say something incriminating was in conflict with his desire to avoid a blunder at this exciting moment in his budding career. He was probably already visualizing tomorrow's headlines and interviews. So was I, even before he escorted me into the all-too-familiar back seat of his patrol car. As I climbed in, I glanced back at my car in time to see distinctive yellow tape being staked around it. So much for my hope of drawing attention away from Bianca's scarf.

LYING HAS NEVER BEEN my best skill. Other than this situation, when I was trying to protect my daughter, I didn't have much use for it. The next two hours were excruciating, to say the least, especially when Deputies Weems and Quigley were joined by Sheriff Kraft himself to interrogate me.

When I decided I needed an attorney, I had to think hard about whom to call. The only time I'd needed one before today was during the settling of Tony's estate. That had been handled by old Cecil Kellogg, who had since retired to Flagstaff.

Finally, I called Nick Constantine, the only other attorney I could think of in my agitated state. He picked up the receiver, sounding out of breath.

"Nick, thank goodness you're back."

"Jane? Well, hello to you, too. You caught me coming in the door, and have I got fish! How about dinner tonight? Bring almonds, if you—"

"You're licensed to practice law in Oregon, right?"

"What?"

"Nick, please. I don't need dinner. I need a lawyer. Can you help?"

My questions stopped him in mid-menu. "This is about

your daughter? They aren't going to charge her for mouthing off, Jane."

"No, no, that's not it. You're licensed in Oregon?" I could hear my voice rising and knew that he could hear it, too. At least I had his full attention.

"Yes, but—"

"Will you represent me? It's not Bianca they're charging. It's me. I'm afraid they're going to charge me."

"With what? Defending your daughter's right to make a fool of herself?"

"No. With murder. Gil Fortune's been shot, and the only other lawyer I know lives in Arizona." I had a belated thought. "You do know about criminal stuff?"

He sounded amused. "Yes, I know about criminal 'stuff' as you put it, but—"

"And you'll represent me?"

"Yes, of course, but slow down. Why are you involved?"

"Well, first, they caught me yesterday breaking into Gil's house, and today they found me there again right after he was shot."

He whistled. "Breaking into his house?"

"I didn't kill him, if that's what you're wondering."

"It wasn't." He sounded reassuringly calm. "But I do wonder just what the hell you were thinking?"

"Can I explain in person? I'm at the Russell County Sheriff's Department, north of town."

"I can hardly wait. Be there as soon as I grab a quick shower."

"Please don't wait for that. Just come now!"

"I smell like fish."

"Please?"

"Okay, Jane. I'll be right there. Meanwhile, don't say anything to anyone."

"Don't worry, I won't."

Ten minutes later, I was still mentally sifting through the shocking events of the morning when Deputy Kincaid arrived at the interrogation room where I'd been told to wait. "You can go," he said, looking somewhere over my head as he spoke.

"Now?" I asked, surprised. I hadn't seen Nick yet. "Did my attorney come?"

Kincaid looked as though he wanted to cry and I didn't think it was because of sadness at my departure. "Sheriff Kraft just told me you could leave. We'll be talking to you again, so don't leave town. Your car stays here."

"But I need it." More to the point, I needed to retrieve that scarf.

"You can get it tomorrow."

I didn't want to call attention to the car by further protest, so I merely asked, "How do you expect me to get to work?"

"Oh, I don't think that'll be a problem. Those *friends* of yours are outside." From his tone, I knew which friends he meant.

"How did they know I was here?"

"Ask them yourself."

Without another word he led me through the maze of corridors that opened at last into the lobby. Once he had safely delivered me to the public area, he turned and disappeared down another hallway, surprising me again with his abruptness. He must have an appointment to chew nails or something.

"Jane, you're free!" Minnie's glad voice echoed through the lobby. "Praise the Lord! We were just about to raise another ruckus."

Another ruckus? No wonder Deputy Kincaid had beaten a hasty retreat.

"Are you okay?" asked Alix in a low voice. Behind her, Tyler grinned, but said nothing.

"Yes, I'm fine," I said. "What are you doing here?"

"Did you think we'd let you rot in this hole?" Minnie asked.

This brand-new complex of buildings could hardly be described as a hole, but that detail didn't seem to trouble Minnie. She was ready to do battle.

"How did you know I was here?" Things were moving too fast. I had barely adjusted to the prospect of being locked up and charged with obstructing justice, or worse, when I was tossed back onto the street.

Alix steered me toward the door. "Let's talk about this outside, okay?"

"Okay." My escorts propelled me out the door so fast that we nearly ran into Nick coming in. He still wore his stained and dirty clothes, so a fishy smell preceded him.

"What are you doing out here?" he asked.

"They let me go," I told him. "This wasn't your doing?" To the others I explained, "Nick's my attorney. He just got back from fishing."

"Cool," breathed Tyler.

"No, I haven't talked to anyone yet," Nick said.

"They told me to go and I wasn't about to argue."

"That's strange," he said. "I'll go see what I can find out."

"I think maybe it was because of us," Minnie announced proudly. "We threatened to stage a sit-in. We'd have done it, too, and they knew it."

Nick and I just stared at them. Tyler and Alix were nodding their heads as though to say, yes, that's what happened, and, yes, it made perfect sense.

Then Nick shook his head. The frown on his face wasn't reassuring. "This doesn't add up. Even if you were wonderfully persuasive, and I'm sure you were, that's not enough reason for them to let you go." He added, "Not if what you told me was accurate."

"It was accurate as far as it went. But I haven't told you everything—"

He put up a hand to stop me. “Well, don’t. Not right now. Why don’t you go home and let me find out what happened here. I’ll be over in a few minutes.”

TWENTY-TWO

THE PHONE WAS RINGING as we walked in the front door of my house. I grabbed it.

"Bianca? Where are you?"

An unfamiliar female voice responded. "I must have the wrong number. This is Hilde from High Desert Community Hospital, trying to reach Jane Serrano."

"I'm Jane Serrano. Sorry. I thought you were someone else."

"Obviously," came the amused voice. "I don't know where Bianca is, but I was given your number to call on behalf of Laurence Thornton."

"Is Laurence all right?"

"Perfectly all right physically, but he's probably getting more agitated than he should be and he suggested…well, to be honest, he demanded…that I call you and find out, as he so delicately put it, 'what the hell's going on.' Apparently he's had some trouble trying to reach—"

"Yes, I can imagine. Could you please tell him that something came up?"

"Maybe you'd like to explain it yourself. It's really not good for him to get so upset."

"How about if I send his grandson over to see him right away?"

"If you mean Tyler, then yes, that should help. He's been asking rather forcefully for him, too."

"I'll bet. Please tell him Tyler is on his way, and thank you."

I hung up and turned to the expectant group facing me.

"Laurence must be feeling better if he's giving the nurses a bad time. Tyler, could you please go there and tell him…"

"…that Thornton's wasn't open today because you were in jail. Sure."

"Maybe not that, but I'm sure you'll think of something. Minnie, could you take him?"

"Why me?" complained Minnie. "I want to help find Bianca."

"Because," Alix drawled, "a visit from me wouldn't help Laurence's peace of mind. You can take him some of your scones."

"He does love my scones." Minnie brightened at the thought. "Maybe some soup, too. But we get to help as soon as we get back."

"Right," I said.

"What can I do?" Alix asked.

I needed time to think things out before this group further muddied the waters, so I improvised. "Someone needs to pick up Wendell from the vet."

"Okay," she said. "I can do that."

"All right then," I said briskly. "Let's get going."

Nobody moved.

"Aren't you forgetting something, Jane?" Alix asked.

"Yeah," Tyler said, "like telling us what's going on?"

"We don't mean to pry, dear," said Minnie, "but we *did* pick you up from jail."

"Oh, that," I said. They were all watching me as intently as Wendell watched his food dish. "Well, that was an unfortunate misunderstanding. Deputy Weems found me on the road behind Gil's house again." Seeing their accusatory looks, I explained further. "I didn't call you because I thought Gil would be more likely to talk about Bianca if we were alone. I didn't kill him though! He was already dead when I got there."

"Well, of course you didn't," Minnie said with just a trace of relief in her voice, "but you must admit—"

"Any idea what happened?" Alix asked.

With difficulty, I pushed away the image of Bianca's scarf. I shook my head.

"What about Bianca?" Minnie asked.

Had Minnie been reading my mind? "She had nothing to do with this," I declared.

"Are you sure?" Alix asked. "She was chasing him and now he's dead. What do you know that you're not telling us?"

I hesitated. On the one hand, these people were ready to believe and support me. On the other hand, their previous efforts hadn't exactly helped the situation. I wanted to keep them out of it, but things were getting complicated.

"You can trust us," Minnie said gently.

"I know that," I answered automatically, and then suddenly, as I looked into their earnest faces, I meant it. After all, they'd already risked going to jail to help me. They wouldn't let me down and they deserved the truth. "Okay, I'll tell you. I found Bianca's scarf at Gil's house. Remember the bright one she was wearing for a belt at the last book club? I found it wrapped around Gil's head, used as a gag."

Everyone took a sudden interest in studying the carpet. After a long, silent moment, Tyler said, "Well, it wasn't Bianca who did that. We know that much."

"Right," Alix agreed.

Minnie was the last to speak. Using the same take-charge voice with which she organized church potlucks, she summed things up. "So, what we need to do is figure out who took Bianca's scarf and killed Gil."

Tyler nodded as though this seemed perfectly sensible to him.

"That's all?" Alix asked. "We ought to be able to finish up in a couple of hours. But maybe we should find Bianca first. If that scarf is at the house, it probably means she's hiding nearby."

"The scarf isn't exactly at the house right now," I said. "I took it with me when I ran."

For once, even Minnie was speechless. She waved her hands around in front of her in jerky, random gestures before finally clasping them together in a prayerful gesture.

"Look, I wasn't thinking. I recognized the scarf and…at that point I thought Gil might still be alive, so I untied it to let him breathe and then…" I trailed off as the scene came rushing back to me in all its horror. "And then, I saw that it…didn't matter."

Goose bumps pimpled my arms and I attempted to rub away the sudden chill. "But you know what? Right now I really don't care what happened to Gil. I just want my daughter back."

"It all must be related," Tyler said. "Vanessa's death, too."

"Tyler's right," Alix said. "People here wouldn't just start disappearing and dying all of a sudden unless there was a connection."

"It was Gil!" Minnie squealed in excitement. "Gil was the connection—"

"—but he's not talking," Tyler said.

My brain was finally starting to thaw. "Yes, of course he was the connection, but he didn't shoot himself. We need to take another look at Vanessa's death. Crazy as it sounds, I think Bianca must have stirred something up with her so-called investigation."

"Maybe Gil really did kill Vanessa," Alix said.

"But he had an alibi," Minnie reminded her. "People at the open house saw him."

"But Jenna Lang was one of the people Bianca was planning to question, so that's something to follow up," I said. "As Bianca said, people mill around at crowded events and no one pays attention to exactly when they saw someone. Here's something else to think about. Assuming that there is only one murderer currently on the loose in Juniper, and assuming that Gil didn't shoot himself, then maybe Gil didn't kill Vanessa either. So, who did?"

"Aha!" Minnie said. "We need to figure out who knew both Gil and Vanessa."

"That's easy: everybody in town," Alix said. "Do you suppose it's worth looking at the alibis of both Jenna and Gil? What if they were fooling around? That would give Jenna a special reason to get rid of Vanessa."

"But what about Gil?" Minnie asked. "If you're right, and I'm not saying you are, Jenna certainly wouldn't want to kill him."

"Maybe things went bad between them. It's happened before," Alix suggested.

"Could be," I agreed. "Also—sorry, Tyler, but we have to consider it—there's Kurt Wendorf. He's known both Gil and Vanessa for years, and he had a spectacular grudge against Gil. Maybe he didn't like Vanessa either."

"Max's dad didn't have anything to do with this," Tyler insisted.

"Probably not, Tyler," I assured him, "but we have to check out everything."

"So how do we get someone to confess?" Minnie asked.

"We start by doing just what we decided before," I said. "You and Tyler go to the hospital to calm Laurence down, Alix will get Wendell, and I'll monitor the phone here in case Bianca calls. After that, we'll decide what to do next."

"But how is all this going to help us find Bianca?" Minnie asked.

"I don't know," I said, "but we have to start somewhere, and the police certainly aren't going to help us."

As soon as they drove away on their respective missions, I

was out the door and on my way to the garage out back. The police still had my Volvo, but Tony's Ford Explorer fired up on the first try. I felt that I had the best chance of catching Jenna Lang off guard if I went alone. Of course, that's what I'd thought about going to see Gil this morning. I hoped this interview would go better.

TWENTY-THREE

I WAS FORCED TO NEGOTIATE a number of annoying speed bumps while searching for Jenna Lang's townhouse in the midst of the numerous cul-de-sacs that made up the trendy Misty Mountain Meadow complex. The teeth-rattling obstacles and maddening roads to nowhere were designed to deter gawkers, and I could guarantee that I wouldn't be coming here again voluntarily, in spite of the stunning views of the Deschutes River.

All the townhouses featured tiny golf-course-perfect lawns and low-maintenance greenery planted precisely in identical window boxes. Everything must have been part of the original package. No humble snapdragons and petunias need apply. No need for an owner to spend a moment keeping up the place either. Plenty of time for Caribbean cruises, power meetings, and gala real estate events that provided good alibis.

As I waited for Jenna Lang to open her front door, I noted that even the chimes for Number Sixteen Misty Mountain Way sounded expensive. I knew her only from her glossy ads in the *Juniper Journal* and the feature story the paper had done about her triumphant return a year ago to invigorate the family business, Lang Realty and Interior Design. She'd spent the previous five years making an extended study of upscale developments from Bangkok to Buenos Aires. She'd come a long way, baby, and was now ready to shake up stodgy old Juniper, Oregon. I just hoped I could shake her up.

The person who opened the door resembled only slightly the confident young beauty pictured in the Lang Realty ads.

Her red-rimmed eyes told me that she had already heard the news about Gil, and her scowl told me that she knew who I was. So much for the element of surprise.

"You've heard," I ventured.

She nodded. "Why are you here? You're not going to pretend to be sorry he's dead, are you?"

"No."

"So...?" The question hung in the air while somewhere behind me the motor of a sports car roared to life. I hoped no one was watching, but I didn't turn around to check. This was a conversation best conducted in private.

"May I come in?" I started forward, as though taking her permission for granted.

She put one hand across the open space and gripped the edge of the door, effectively blocking my path. "No. We have nothing to talk about." She attempted to push the door closed, but, without thinking, I slapped the flat of my hand against its surface to prevent it from moving.

"We do, Jenna. You know why I'm here. It's way past time for you to tell the truth...if not to me, then to the police."

She startled me with a short bark of laughter. "Okay, then I choose the police."

She tried again to close the door, but I resisted her efforts. We struggled silently for a few seconds until she suddenly let go and turned away, retreating into the dim room behind her. The door banged against the wall before I could catch it, but the noise didn't seem to bother her. I followed cautiously as she sank onto a peach-colored velvet loveseat that probably cost more than all the furniture I'd ever owned. She'd decided against physical resistance, but she picked up a portable phone—peach-colored, to match the couch, of course—and looked challengingly at me. "Will you leave or do you want to explain your presence to the police?"

I'd already had enough chances this week to explain to the

police my presence in various places, so I turned conciliatory. "Okay, I'll go, but…don't you want to know who killed Gil?"

"I assume it was your daughter, and so do you, or you wouldn't be here."

"No! That's not true!" With considerable effort, I lowered my voice. "Bianca couldn't possibly have used violence against another human being. She doesn't even kill flies, just wraps them in a dishtowel and puts them out the door." I wasn't getting through to her, so I tried something different.

"You think I'm defending her just because she's my daughter, but she hardly knew Gil. She had no reason to kill him. If you look at it that way, and take Bianca completely out of the picture, doesn't it make better sense that someone else killed both Gil and Vanessa?"

"Vanessa's death was an accident—"

"No, it wasn't. I'm almost sure of that now, and if somebody killed her, the chances are about a million to one that the same person who murdered Vanessa shot Gil. It wasn't my daughter. Please, please help me." I waited, unsure from her silence whether I had touched a chord with my somewhat shaky argument.

"Anyway, why should I talk to you?" she asked. "Maybe your daughter killed both of them. Why don't you ask her?"

"Because I don't know where she is. No one has seen her since Wednesday night. She was going to come and talk to you sometime after that. Did you see her?"

When she finally answered me, her voice was flat. "I didn't see her and I can't help you. I really can't. Go away and leave me alone."

What other lever could I pull? "I know you lied about Gil's alibi," I bluffed. "If you help me now, no one else will ever have to know you did that."

Jenna looked up abruptly and narrowed her eyes. "You don't know what you're talking about. I've said all I'm going to say." Without waiting for my reaction, she stretched out on the loveseat and put one arm across her face. Our conversation was over.

"All right. I'm going, but I'll be back. Think about what I said."

Brave words to Jenna, but what more could I do? I returned to my empty house, out of ideas and out of hope. When the phone rang, I didn't even reach for it. It would just be something else I couldn't deal with.

Once I recognized Jenna's hesitant voice, I jumped to cut off the answering machine. "Hello? Hello?"

"Oh, you're there," Jenna said. "Okay, come back and I'll tell—"

"I'll be there in five minutes," I said, and I was, running yellow lights without a second thought and ignoring the speed bumps in her development.

This time, she opened the door to me without an argument. She looked somehow smaller than she had just a few minutes ago. Maybe it was the slumped shoulders. She led the way inside without a word and then turned to face me.

"Okay, I'll tell you what I know." Her quiet start shifted quickly to belligerence with her very next words. "But I'm warning you right now that I'll deny everything if you blab it to the police."

"Believe me, I have even less interest in talking to the police than you do," I assured her. I waited in silence for her to continue. Without knowing what had changed her mind, I didn't want to say anything that would upset her. Her vacillation between cooperation and belligerence told me that she was still ambivalent about talking to me.

To distract myself while I waited for her to decide how much to divulge, I studied the tasteful furnishings. She had several Cascade Festival of Music prints on the walls and an enormous free-form bronze filling the lighted niche in the twelve-foot-high wall between this area and whatever palatial rooms lay beyond it. I looked in vain for a stray sock or a pile of newspapers beside a comfortable chair. Even the framed pictures sitting on various polished surfaces looked as though they had come as a color-coordinated set. No snapshots of Jenna laughing while holding up a fish or standing proudly atop South Sister with her family.

My rough estimate told me that either Jenna was the most successful interior designer in the state, or she had gained access to her family trust funds immediately upon reaching adulthood. Either way, her life probably wasn't exactly going according to plan. By the time I had completed my survey of the room, she was ready to talk.

"Their marriage was a sham," she stated, "and Gil was going to divorce her. He'd outgrown her provincialism years ago, and he and I were in love. Nobody else knew."

Even though she'd grown up in Juniper, Jenna apparently didn't understand how the small-town grapevine worked. If Alix's assertions about Gil's general philandering were true, Jenna didn't know much about him either.

"I know for a fact that he didn't kill her. That's why I said he was at the open house the whole time."

"But you can't be sure of the exact time she fell. Just because you loved him doesn't mean he ”

"I'll spell it out for you," Jenna said impatiently. "We saw her fall. Gil and I were together down in the gorge. She must have been trying to catch us on camera and she fell, right near us."

"You were there!" My thoughts spun. No wonder Jenna had given him an alibi. She knew he hadn't killed Vanessa, but she didn't want the whole community to learn about their affair.

"You actually saw…?"

"She didn't make a sound, just…dropped out of the sky like a rock."

"Did you see anyone else?"

She shook her head. "It didn't occur to me. I was looking at her…and then Gil figured out what she must have been doing. He told me to get back to the open house, so I just ran. We had separate cars, of course. He said he'd see what he could do for Vanessa and no one would know I'd been there. I didn't see the harm."

"I'm sure you didn't," I said soothingly.

"Besides, I thought it was an accident." She looked pleadingly at me. "I really did…until I heard about Gil. Now I don't know what to think."

"But you knew all this when I talked to you a few minutes ago. What made you change your mind about talking to me?"

"I turned on the TV after you left," she said. "Of course they're talking about Gil's murder and a lot of background, including the day Vanessa died, about how she didn't die right away. I didn't know that. Somehow I'd missed it before."

"The end was the same," I said. "Does it matter so much?"

"Yes, it matters! When Gil got to the open house, he told me that the fall had killed Vanessa instantly. On the news they said she lived for at least half an hour. She even tried to crawl. She must have been in terrible pain, and he just left her there to die. I didn't know. Really, I didn't."

Now I understood. Jenna had believed in Gil, believed everything he'd told her, but now she was seeing him in a new light.

"And another thing," she said. "They said the camcorder was smashed, but it wasn't, not when she fell. When I left, it was fine. It seemed ironic that she was all smashed up, but it wasn't."

"So you think Gil took the tape?"

"Could he have done that?" Jenna asked in wonder. "It's so calculating."

"I can understand why you don't want to talk to the police,"

I said. "If they learn about your relationship with Gil, they might even think you had something to do with his death. Maybe he broke up with you, or maybe you were the one who pushed Vanessa. Nobody can corroborate your version, now that Gil is dead."

"It was nothing like that! I've told you the truth about what happened!" Jenna cried.

"I believe you," I said. "I'm just pointing out how things might look to the police. We each have our reasons for wanting to know what happened this week. It's a fact that Gil was murdered. I believe that Vanessa was also murdered, probably by the same person. I need your help to prove that that person wasn't my daughter."

"I've told you everything I know," Jenna said. "I didn't even see your daughter this week."

I needed to press her further and now I had a lever. She didn't want her reputation destroyed if she could avoid it. "Maybe if we work together, no one will ever have to know that you lied about Gil's alibi. That might not be possible, but it's the best chance you have."

Jenna was convinced. "What do you want to know?"

"You were here all day yesterday?"

"Gil came over mid-morning and we left for a while. I worked at the office in the afternoon."

"Weren't you nervous about being seen together? I mean—"

"I know what you mean. We had a system. He'd call on his cell phone when he was getting close and I'd walk down the road to the cul-de-sac by the woods there. It's right at the edge of the developed area, out of the way. That's what he did yesterday. We drove around and talked for a while about our future, what we should do next…and then he brought me back. That was the last time I saw him. We were trying not to see each other too openly for a while. We thought we had plenty of time."

Don't react, I told myself, willing my face to remain neutral. Jenna had been horrified to find that Gil had been a cold, calculating person, but she should take a look at herself. Still, Jenna was talking, focused on yesterday, and that was the important thing. "What about later?"

"He called last night about nine."

"Had he seen Bianca?"

"No. I'm sure he'd have mentioned that."

"How about today?"

"He was going to meet Harley downtown for breakfast. That was a regular thing."

"Anyone else ever join them?"

"Vanessa sometimes insisted on going." Her face closed again.

Oops. She'd be more likely to cooperate if the topic was Gil's murder rather than his marriage. "Can you think of anyone who might have wanted Gil dead?"

"Kurt Wendorf, maybe. He hated Gil, I guess, for prosecuting his rotten kid."

I let her subjective interpretation of Max go by. Jenna had been thoroughly indoctrinated by Gil on the necessity for maintaining the safety and moral fiber of the community—so long at it didn't interrupt their affair. "Did Gil feel Kurt was dangerous?"

"He thought Kurt was making a fool of himself."

That made sense. And Kurt was even stupid enough to do it publicly, giving Gil free publicity and enhancing his glow as the aggrieved community hero. His political future would have been a slam dunk, if only he had lived long enough to cash in. I wondered again whether Kurt had an alibi for the time Gil was shot. And where he had been the day Vanessa died. “Do you know of anything Kurt had against Vanessa? Maybe something going way back?”

Jenna shrugged. “He probably was in love with her in high school. I hear everybody was.” The look on her face showed that she couldn’t quite see why. She probably had trouble imagining that Vanessa, in her late thirties, had ever been attractive. The eternal arrogance of youth. Bianca had it, too, as well as the knockout figure and long blond hair. I sincerely hoped that that was where the similarity between Bianca and Jenna stopped.

Jenna might not have seen Bianca yesterday, but perhaps Bianca had seen her. “You said Gil parked at the end of the road. Could you show me where?”

Jenna was eager to get me out of her townhouse and I was eager to go. Leading me back onto the tiny front porch, she indicated a clump of aspens that was just barely visible from here as the road curved. We didn’t bother with cordial good-byes.

The cul-de-sac Jenna indicated had obviously been the designated location for workers’ cars and cigarette breaks during the latest building phase. They hadn’t yet spruced up the area. There had been too much traffic through here to distinguish footprints, so I brushed aside branches and walked a few yards further into the trees. Jenna’s townhouse was visible from here, so Bianca might have found this an ideal place to lie in wait for her. Thinking like Bianca was tough, but I had to try.

Just then I spotted light bouncing off something metallic, something that didn’t belong in the woods. It was too high off the ground to be a stray beer can. An old washing machine illegally dumped? I moved cautiously toward it. Lying on its side and half-covered with branches was Bianca’s bicycle. I didn’t touch it.

“Bianca!” I shouted. No sound but the rush of nearby traffic. I looked wildly around and called several more times. Nothing. She had been here, but she wasn't here now. How and when did she leave? Someone—and I could only hope it was Bianca—had attempted to hide the bicycle. The police needed to know about this right away, but first, I had another question for Jenna.

Back on her front porch, I kept my finger steadily on the chimes until she opened the door. Still out of breath from my run up the street, I asked, "When you met Gil at the end of the road, did you get right into the car?"

"What possible difference—"

"Please, it's important."

"We walked back into the woods for a couple of minutes—so we wouldn't be seen—to talk over what we should do."

"But you didn't see Bianca?"

"In the woods? No, of course not." Then Jenna's face, already pale, lost all color. "Oh, no. You didn't… Is she…?"

No one could fake that reaction. I was sure of it. This development was a surprise to her.

"Bianca's bicycle was hidden in the trees. Did Gil get there before you?"

"No, he called as he was driving and we arrived at the same time."

"What happened after you and Gil talked?"

"I told you. We got into his car and drove around for a while. And then he brought me back here and left."

At last I had a small piece of the puzzle. Bianca had been near this place sometime after Wednesday night. It might not be much, but it was a start.

"You're not going to tell the police about me, are you?" Jenna asked.

I dodged a direct answer. "Right now I'm going home." I wanted to check again to see whether Bianca had finally showed up. After that, I didn't know what I'd do. I'd keep

Jenna's name private if I possibly could, but her chances of coming out of this situation with her reputation intact were looking worse by the minute.

TWENTY-FOUR

MY HOUSE *APPEARED EMPTY,* just the way I had left it, but I called out anyway, "Bianca? It's okay. I'm alone." I listened intently for any sound of her presence, but there was nothing other than the steady ticking of the mantel clock. Today its sound reminded me of how much time had gone by without any word from Bianca.

Outside, a car door slammed and I raced to see who had arrived. Nick was coming up the walk slowly, head down. He looked up as I opened the door, and the expression he wore caused the blood to drain from my face.

"Bianca?" I asked faintly. "Is it Bianca?"

"You'd better sit down."

I didn't really plan to sit down, but my legs gave way, so I did. "Tell me!"

"Well, she's sort of okay."

"She's hurt?"

"No, not the way you mean it, but she's been arrested for Gil's murder. That's the reason they let you go."

"That's preposterous. Just because she accused him—"

"It's based on a little more than that."

"Okay, just because she was at Gil's house—"

He looked sharply at me. "How did you know that?"

I wasn't sure whether he was going to end up being my lawyer or Bianca's, so I didn't want to tell him anything he might be forced to reveal later. "Tell me first. Is she really all right? Where was she?"

"Give me a chance," he said. "Yes, she's all right. They

found her hiding in the woods, near a gun that might be the murder weapon."

"Well, there you go. Bianca doesn't believe in guns," I retorted. "She wouldn't have the faintest idea how to use one."

"You can tell that to the sheriff. Of course, they'll do tests to confirm whether it's the right gun and whether she fired it, but meanwhile, they're holding her. Your turn."

"I need to see Bianca for myself. I'll tell you what I know as we drive."

Minnie's ten-year-old Buick Regal eased up to the curb, dwarfing Nick's Jeep. Tyler jumped out first while Minnie levered herself from under the wheel.

"Any word?" Minnie asked. "We hurried as fast as we could, but it took some time to convince Laurence that everything was all right. Where are you two going?"

Before I could answer, Alix's convertible screeched to a halt just inches behind Minnie's bumper. She emerged in one fluid motion. "What's going on? Has something happened?" As she spoke, she rounded the front of the car and opened the passenger door to let Wendell make his slow way out onto the grass. Tyler took the leash from her.

"She's been found!" I explained, trying to make my way past the sudden crowd forming around me. "Bianca's all right. I'm going to—"

"But where is she?" Minnie asked, trotting after me.

Tyler could see that Wendell wasn't going anywhere, so he dropped the leash and followed us. "How come she's not here?"

"She's not here?" Alix crowded me from the other side.

I edged toward the passenger side of the Jeep. "Nick's taking me to see her. We'll be right back."

"Going where?" Alix blocked my way.

"What's going on?" Tyler now stood with Alix between me and the car door.

"Please," Minnie murmured, the softness of her word belied by the working of her sharp elbows as she made her way to the center of the group. "Remember, we're a team."

Some team. Even Wendell had started to make his laborious way toward us. Well, every team needs a mascot, I thought.

"Bianca's been arrested," I said.

"Arrested!" Alix repeated.

"That's crazy—" Tyler said.

"Does Brady know?" Minnie asked. "I'm going to have a talk with that young man."

Their comments tumbled predictably over each other as they digested the news. I tried again. "Nick and I are going to see her now. We'll be back as soon as possible." In the silence that followed my announcement, I gently edged my way to Nick's Jeep and climbed up onto the high front seat.

"Let's go, Nick, and make it fast, before they think of anything else to say."

"Okay," Nick said, as he put the Jeep in gear, "but it's not going to work. Look behind us."

I turned and saw that Tyler was helping Wendell into the back seat of Alix's convertible beside him, while Alix jerked open the driver's door and Minnie scrambled into the passenger seat. We had a head start, but with Alix at the wheel, I doubted that we'd get to the sheriff's department first.

TWENTY-FIVE

AS WE DROVE, I FILLED Nick in about what I knew and what I had done. He listened silently, though he tightened his hands on the steering wheel when I mentioned the gun and tape recorder, both of which were currently in police custody. He swerved slightly when I told him I had taken Bianca's scarf from Gil's body. When I finally ran out of useful information, his expression conveyed total incredulity.

"Well," I concluded, "maybe you had to be there."

As predicted, we didn't beat the others to the Russell County Sheriff's Department. Not only were they already there, but they were inside, leaving our mascot to guard the front door. Wendell wagged his tail when he saw me.

I should have known that Alix's convertible would be programmed to swoop along the bypass at speeds considerably higher than the law allowed. Nick, being new to town, didn't know the tricks that would have allowed us to navigate Juniper's traffic nightmare with maximum efficiency, and I was too preoccupied to direct him. I could hardly have found my own driveway today, so I wasn't really up to thinking about traffic patterns. Even the roundabouts which had recently sprung up all over town were too much for me today.

I had other things on my mind. For example, I now had no doubt that both Vanessa and Gil had been murdered. Probably even slow-witted Arnie was finally ready to agree with me on this point.

Like most law-abiding citizens, I don't usually pay much attention to the Russell County Sheriff's Department, but now it occurred to me to wonder why Arnie was still running it. While he might have been able to handle the job as it existed in the county's early days, recently law enforcement had become complex enough that he was out of his league. Gil had actively campaigned for Arnie's election. Why would such an ambitious man support a sub-standard chief law-enforcement officer? They had been high school friends and teammates, but Gil had shown himself quite able to jettison old friendships when it suited his purpose. He had turned on Kurt without a qualm, so why was Arnie treated differently? Did Arnie's dullness allow Gil to run the county with a free hand?

I'd ask Alix what she remembered about Gil's early relationship with our sheriff, if I could tear her away from her probable current preparations to help Minnie and Tyler break Bianca out of jail. At the thought, I quickened my pace, pulling open the massive door before Nick could reach for it.

"Slow down," he said, "and let me do the talking."

"I'll do whatever you say if it will get me in to see my daughter."

"I think it will…if we aren't too late to intercept your friends. Your job is to keep them out of the sheriff's face."

"Easy for you to say," I answered.

I heard Minnie's voice first. She was standing at the same glassed-in window we had tried before. "You absolutely can't treat us this way. This is America!"

Alix was right in there swinging. "Kincaid, we demand—"

Oh, no, not Kincaid. Was he always on duty, or just when we came in? Nick uttered a low moan and urged me forward.

"You demand, eh?" Kincaid said.

"Damn right we do." Alix might as well have waved a red flag in front of him. I was moving toward the counter as fast as I could, expecting Kincaid to start pawing the ground. "What kind of chicken—"

"Please." Tyler wisely interrupted Alix before she could

really get going. I noted once again how much common sense this skinny kid had. He even managed a pleasant tone of voice. "Just a few minutes?"

Kincaid looked down at him. "You hang out with that Wendorf kid, don't you? Better pick your friends more carefully in—"

Minnie squawked and flew at the window like an angry hen, actually causing the large man to step back a pace. "Now, you just—"

"My daughter's lawyer is here to see his client," I said breathlessly.

"If it's all right with you, Deputy," Nick said smoothly, stepping up to the window beside me.

"I thought you said before that you were *her* lawyer," Kincaid said, stabbing a thick finger in my direction.

"I represent both of them. In fact, I'd like Ms. Serrano to accompany me to see her daughter now."

"Well, I don't know..."

"It's legal, I assure you."

"Well, maybe it is and maybe it isn't. Either way, I don't know as I need to let her go in there with you."

"That's a judgment call, isn't it?" Nick said. "I'm sure you have the authority to decide that." He moved closer to the window and gave Kincaid a significant look. "If she goes in with me, the others won't have any reason to stay. Otherwise, they'll probably wait here until I'm done."

Nick's quiet voice and unruffled approach was having the desired effect, even though I wasn't too sure of his logic. I willed everyone to keep quiet while Kincaid weighed his options. He wouldn't want to do me any favors, but he wasn't sure of the rules and he didn't want to seem like a child who had to ask permission from Arnie to make a decision. Most telling of all, he didn't want our quarrelsome group cluttering up his orderly reception area.

He completed his calculations at length. Once more he spoke directly to Nick, as though to an ally. "Okay, the two of you can go in, but only for fifteen minutes, and the rest of them have to go away."

I turned to the others and mouthed, "Please," with as much urgency as possible. They got the message. Minnie patted my arm, Tyler gave a wan smile, and Alix contented herself with merely the faintest of sneers before they made their way outside. It wasn't until the doors had swung closed behind them that I let out my breath.

"Fifteen minutes," Kincaid said.

"That'll be plenty. She'll probably be going home soon anyway," I answered.

Nick shot me a warning look. He didn't want me to provoke Kincaid, even now.

"Don't count on it," Kincaid said.

The institutional blandness of the jail area couldn't detract from the relief I felt at knowing Bianca was safe. I hardly comprehended the instructions Kincaid gave us or minded the brief search he insisted we undergo. We moved through yet another metal detector into the holding area for prisoners. My search was done by a female officer whom I had last seen at Thornton's buying a best-selling book called *Lifeline for Your Marriage*. The tightness around her mouth as she patted me down told me that probably her life hadn't improved since then. When I overheard her tell Kincaid that'd she'd be coming home late from work tonight, I sympathized. Life with Kincaid would be like permanent boot camp.

The heavy metal door to the interview room swung open and Bianca entered. She'd pulled her long hair back into a pony tail and wore the drab coveralls of a prisoner. Even with a bruise on one cheek and no make-up, she looked beautiful. We hugged for a long time while I patted her back repeatedly and murmured, "It's okay, it's okay. Don't worry."

Meaningless phrases under the circumstances, but I was in "mom" mode.

Nick cleared his throat, reminding me that we didn't have much time. I stood back, but still held Bianca's hands in mine.

Before I could speak, she burst out, "Is Wendell okay? I was worried—"

"Yes, he's outside. Please, Bianca, we don't have much time. Tell us what happened. This is Nick Constantine. He's going to represent you."

Bianca looked startled. "They're not going to let me go? But I didn't do anything. Why would I need a lawyer? No offense—"

"It's just procedure," I improvised. "We needed a lawyer so we could get in to see you. There are still a few loose ends." That was the understatement of the year.

"I didn't do it, Mom!"

"Of course. I never thought for a minute—"

"It was awful and I didn't know what to do and—"

"Can you just tell us what happened?" Nick asked.

"After you went to talk to Jenna Lang," I said. "Start there. You did go to see her?"

"Tyler told you? That seems like a long time ago. Yes, I was going to get her to tell me what really happened the day Gil killed Vanessa—"

"But you didn't talk to her," I prompted. We needed to speed this up. "Why not?"

"It was the funniest thing. Wendell and I were hiding at the little turnaround place at the end of Jenna's street, and Gil drove right up beside us in Vanessa's Audi. Can you believe it? At first I thought he'd seen us, but then Jenna came down the sidewalk to meet him, so I knew he hadn't. They walked off into the woods together, and it seemed like too good a chance to miss, so I popped the trunk and we jumped inside."

"We?" Nick asked. "You and your dog got into the trunk of Gil's car?"

"I was afraid Wendell would give me away if I tried to leave him. I left the trunk open a little for air, if that's what you're wondering."

I didn't think that was what Nick was wondering, but I could hardly blame him for being dumbfounded. I'd known Bianca longer than he had. I nodded to show her that I was following her logic.

"We almost got caught right then. They came back just a couple of minutes later and off we went. I couldn't hear much from the trunk, just muffled voices. Besides, I was busy trying to hold the trunk closed. I could see enough to know that we were driving away from town, so the next time we came to a stop sign, I let Wendell out and told him to go home. And he did, didn't he?" she said proudly.

"Just like Lassie," I responded. I didn't mention that Wendell had had a rough journey.

"I was afraid that Gil would hurt him if he found us. Remember, Wendell was the one who growled at him."

"Weren't you worried about yourself?" Nick asked.

"Well, sure, but I had to find out what he was up to."

"And did you?" I asked.

"First, I found out that you can't tell much from the inside of a trunk. He dropped Jenna off after a while and went home. Trouble was, once we got into his garage he noticed the trunk was unlatched and he slammed it shut. Good thing he didn't look inside right then. I didn't know what to do after that, so I just stayed put.

"Then the weirdest thing happened. The trunk popped open again. I thought for sure I'd been caught, but no one came. I heard a big commotion and then it got quiet again. I didn't know what was going on."

Maybe Bianca didn't, but I could figure it out. While Tyler

was supposed to be outside Gil's house on guard duty, he must have come into the garage to do a little investigating on his own. That's the reason I hadn't heard the back door open when he had come to warn us that Gil was on his way. Too bad he hadn't had time to check the trunk before the deputies arrived, but it had been nice of him to unlatch it for Bianca.

"After a long, long time, I sneaked into the house and hid in the front coat closet with the door open a little bit. He talked on the phone a couple of times during the evening, but I couldn't hear what he was saying. At first I was scared that he'd realize I was there because of my scarf, but I guess he never noticed it."

"What about your scarf?" I asked.

"A bee was trapped in the closet with me and I used my scarf to wrap it up and put it safely back outside. The scarf snagged on the window ledge, so I had to leave it there when I heard Gil coming and ran back to the closet.

"Anyway, I got really excited one time when he looked through a bunch of videotapes and laid one out separate from the others. I just knew it had to be the missing tape from Vanessa's camcorder! Once he was asleep, I ran out and got it. I was so sure it was the right tape that I made the sheriff watch it today."

"What did it show?" I asked.

"Nothing. It was a tape of some boring trial."

"Why didn't you call us?" I asked. "We've been so worried."

"Were you?" Bianca sounded surprised and pleased. When I remembered the skeptical reception we had given her ideas earlier in the week, I could see why she hadn't been anxious to tell us what she was doing. "I did think about calling Ty to ask about Wendell, but I didn't have a chance. Besides, I knew Wendell would find his way home and you'd take care of him."

She looked at me with the trust of someone who had always found the world a good place, a place where dogs found their way home safely and people lived happily ever after. I hated to go over the next part of her story, but we had to know what had happened. But before I could bring myself to ask about the next morning, Bianca started telling us about it, almost as though she were reliving it.

"I was still in the closet when someone came in the front door. Gil said, 'What are you doing here?' in an unfriendly way, but this person didn't answer. Then Gil asked, 'What's going on? Yes, she's… Wait a minute! You can't…' and then I heard shots."

I put my arms around Bianca then, but she was so caught up in her story that she jumped in fright. Her eyes were wide and unfocused at first, but gradually she returned to the present. Once she actually saw me instead of the scene in her mind, she relaxed, just as she used to after a nightmare. After a moment, she continued.

"It was awful. I kept smelling the wool of the coats around me and thinking that it was too warm for wool and those coats should have been put away somewhere for the summer."

"Oh, Bianca," I said through the tears that were now running down my cheeks, "I'm so sorry you had to go through this."

Nick had been taking notes. "Are you sure about Gil's words?"

"Not exactly, but it was something like that."

"And how many shots did you hear?"

"Two. I kept waiting for more, but they never came. Next thing I heard was something—or someone—falling. Then something banged up against the closet door. I figured someone out there must know I was inside, so I thought I was a goner. Instead, there were all kinds of crashing sounds.

Finally everything stopped and I heard the front door open and close. It was weird, after all that noise."

"Footsteps? Anything like that?" Nick probed. "Could you tell whether you were hearing a man or a woman?"

"No, just…crashing and then the silence. I finally tried the closet door, but it was blocked. After a while I got panicky and started beating on the door until it came open. A chair had been half-wedged under the doorknob, but it wasn't stuck in there tight enough to hold when I really hit the door. The room was a mess. Things were smashed, and then I saw Gil. He was behind the couch, and there was a gun on the floor beside him." She made a vague gesture toward her waist.

"Your scarf." I said. It wasn't a question, of course.

"Yes, I sometimes use it as a belt, but it was tied…over his mouth like a gag. I tried to loosen it to help him breathe, but his eyes were wide open." She shuddered and lapsed into silence.

I prompted her. "And then…?" I gently shook her. "Bianca? What happened next?"

"Someone came in the back door. I thought it must be the murderer—you know how the murderer is always supposed to return to the scene of the crime?—so I picked up the gun and ran out the front door."

"You picked up the gun that was lying beside Gil's body," Nick said wearily.

"For protection," Bianca said.

"Do you know how to use a gun?" he asked.

"I've seen lots of movies. How hard could it be? Anyway, that's why I shot it into the air later. For practice, in case I had to use it. It sure was loud."

"For practice." Nick had stopped taking notes and was staring at Bianca.

"But then I thought it wasn't smart for me to have it in my

possession, so I wiped off my fingerprints and got rid of it. That was harder than you'd think. I didn't want kids to find it and get hurt, or any little animals, but I knew the police would want it. It was evidence, you know."

"I know," Nick repeated. "Where did you put it?"

"In a juniper tree, inside a plastic sack I found. Those twisty trees are hard to climb, but I got high enough to find a good branch and tied the sack to it. It was out of sight and would have been a great place, except—"

"You were afraid a bird would find it and shoot itself by accident?" Nick asked.

Bianca missed his sarcasm. "No bird could have reached the sack," she answered. "That was the beauty of it. It was hanging too far below the branch. No, the problem was that the police arrived before I got all the way back down the tree. That sort of messed up my plan."

"Your plan?" Nick said. He turned to me. "That was her plan, Jane."

I shrugged.

"Time's up." Kincaid was back in person to make sure we left on time.

"Mom, when can I come home?" Bianca asked.

"As soon as possible," I answered, "but it might not be today."

A sound from Kincaid caused Bianca to address him directly. "You don't really think I killed him, do you? This is all—"

"Don't say anything more, Bianca," Nick warned her. "You are not, under any circumstances, to talk to anyone here when I'm not present."

"But I can explain—"

"That's what I'm trying to avoid."

"Mom, I'm really sorry about this."

"It'll be okay. Just do what Nick says." I forced a smile onto my face and hugged her once more. "I'll take care of everything."

And I would, though right now I didn't have the faintest idea how.

TWENTY-SIX

"I'M WARNING YOU," Kincaid said as we neared the lobby, "you have five minutes to get them out of here." I assumed he was just being his usual unpleasant self until I heard the sound of chanting from outside.

The sound soon resolved itself into two words: "Free Bianca!" One look at the half-concealed smirks on the faces of the uniformed officers present told me that I was hearing it right. Reluctantly, I crossed the lobby, opened the front door, and looked at the scene outside. I closed my eyes in disbelief and then looked again.

Unfortunately, the view remained the same. Minnie carried a handmade sign lettered in her trademark fire-engine red lipstick. It read, "We demand justice," while Tyler's scrawled placard offered the emphatic comment, "No way!" As they marched past the entrance, I could see that the back side of the posters advertised the Wedding Belle. Alix lounged against the side of her Saab, smoking. She had no doubt supplied the poster board from the trunk of her car, though apparently she herself had opted out of the *ad hoc* demonstration. All three of them appeared to be having the time of their lives.

"Can we pretend we don't know them?" Nick asked plaintively.

"My thought exactly. We have to get them out of here before Kincaid either turns the fire hose on them or records their activities on camera as evidence for a future trial."

I approached the marchers and kept my voice conspiratorially low. "Let's get back to my house quick. We need to plot strategy." I was sure the word *plot* would get their attention, and it did.

"How is Bianca?" Alix asked. She stubbed out her cigarette and moved around to the driver's seat of her car.

"Is she okay?" Tyler wanted to know.

"We can talk later," Minnie said. She handed her sign to Tyler and bounced into the passenger seat. "Hit it, Alix!"

Tyler and the signs tumbled into the back with Wendell just as Alix gunned the motor. They were halfway down the street before Nick and I even reached his Jeep. We looked at each other in wonder.

"Good job," he said.

"Don't talk. Drive. We'd better get home before they call the governor."

Nick didn't turn off the engine when we pulled up in front of my house. "I'm not coming in," he said. Alix, Minnie, and Tyler were lined up on the porch, waiting for us. "You go right ahead and tame the lions. Try to keep them from…well, at least try to avoid more charges of breaking and entering."

"Very funny. We had a good reason—"

"Just kidding," he said. "Look, Jane, I need to do some preparation, find out what we're up against. You want me to get your daughter out of jail, don't you?"

"Oh, sorry. Of course I do." I scrubbed my hands over my face. "I'm just not thinking too clearly right now. This is all so…so strange."

"And I came here thinking Juniper was a quiet little place."

"Not since Bianca came back. You *do* think you can get her out?"

"Well, she had motive and opportunity, and there was that stunt with the gun." He held up a hand to forestall my rebuttal. "I know. She didn't kill him. I believe you—"

"But Arnie doesn't," I said, "so he's not even going to look for the real killer. Somebody killed Gil and probably Vanessa, and it wasn't Bianca."

"Would you please let me see what I can do *legally* before you do anything else? There's a real killer out there somewhere and you could be putting yourself in danger if you get too close to that person's identity. This isn't some silly mystery novel, even if the other members of your book club seem determined to make it one."

"I'm not going to sit on my hands while they charge my daughter with something she didn't do. I want to talk to Linda Sanchez, for one thing. She didn't seem too enthused about Gil."

"Really. Why don't you let me talk to her? Maybe she can give me a picture of the internal politics in the D.A.'s office. I can talk 'criminal stuff,' as you call it, with her, so just give me a chance, will you?" He gestured out the window at the others. "It would help if you could slow them down, too. Keep them out of the sheriff's way and I think we stand a better chance of getting whatever sympathy he might have."

The door handle was wrenched out of my hand and Minnie poked her head into the car. "If you're coming in to talk, let's get to it. If not, how about if we take our demonstration downtown—lots of people there on a Saturday afternoon—and call KPHD?"

"I'm coming, Minnie," I told her. Turning back to Nick, I said in a low voice, "I see your point." I jumped out and slammed the door.

"Call you later," he said through the open window.

I shook my head in weariness as I considered the position my daughter had put herself in. Only someone as naive as Bianca could pick up a murder weapon and fire it without realizing how it would look later in a court of law. And that didn't even take into consideration her other activities, like writing anonymous notes, hiding in the trunk of Gil's car, and sending her dog for help.

I contemplated my assembled pseudo-detectives. Clearing Bianca was going to be hard enough without extra problems. Alix could help, except for the fact that she antagonized the sheriff's department with every word she uttered. Then there was Tyler. He was plenty smart, but I was the only responsible adult in his life at the moment so I probably ought to keep him out of jail. And Minnie. Oh, yes, Minnie, whose heart was in the right place, but who—to coin a phrase—was one tortilla short of a taco.

"Let's go inside," I said, mostly because I needed more time to think. Rational explanations didn't go anywhere with this group. If I told them the truth—that Bianca was in a real mess and I had no idea how to get her out of it—within twenty minutes they'd be gathering ropes and horses for a jailbreak like something out of an old Gene Autry movie. And that would be only the first step. I didn't even want to think about what else they'd dream up after they'd had more time to organize. They were practically vibrating with excitement at the prospect of action. All I knew for sure was that whatever action they decided on would complicate things.

"Let's call the governor!" Tyler suggested.

"The hell with him," Alix snorted. "He's a Republican."

"Besides, he's too far away," Minnie said. "We need to get ourselves on TV right here, with bigger signs—"

"—and a megaphone," Tyler added.

There was only way to slow this crazy train before it went off the tracks. I forced a huge smile onto my face and lied my head off.

"No need for that! Everything's under control. All we have to do is…is lie low."

"What's changed?" Alix sounded suspicious.

Tyler asked, "They're going to release her?"

"They should have told us about this at the jail," Minnie complained, "before I ruined my favorite lipstick."

I made my fake smile even bigger and added a wink for good measure. "The less you know, the better. You'll be able to keep a straight face until everything is settled."

"Is Bianca going to be released or not?" Alix demanded. "And who killed Gil?"

"Of course she'll be released," I answered confidently. My affirmations sounded great, though they were based on nothing. Swami Rhami would be proud of me. "Do you think I'd be sitting here if I didn't believe that?"

"Well, no," she said after a minute's consideration, "but what about the rest of it?"

"Gil's killer? That's the part I can't tell you right now. I want you to act natural until the sheriff makes an arrest. Okay?" I hoped I wasn't sweating clear through my clothes. I'd lied more this week than I had in my entire life. It was hard work.

"Then it's somebody we know?" Minnie asked. "Oh, my, I hope it's not someone coming to the church potluck tonight. That would certainly be a bad way to attract new parishioners. I mean, who wants to—"

"You absolutely should go to that potluck." I tried to sound mysterious.

"Really?" Minnie was obviously thrilled with her assignment.

"Yes, really," I answered, "and don't you have a wedding reception tonight, Alix?"

"Well, yes, but—"

"You have to go," I said fervently. "Nothing's going to happen until tomorrow anyway. And Tyler, your grandfather must be getting frantic for company by now."

"What are you going to do now?" Tyler asked. He sounded unconvinced.

"Me? I'm going to catch up on a few things at Thornton's. I might as well spend a little time there as long as we can't do anything until tomorrow anyway. It might relieve Laurence's mind if you tell him that when you visit him." My explanation sounded so phony that I couldn't believe they'd go for it, but apparently my proposed trip to the bookstore was a clear indication that the army could stand down for the night. I herded them toward the door.

"What about Wendell?" Tyler asked. "The vet said he's going to be okay. His ribs are just bruised, but I don't want to leave him alone."

"I'll take him with me," I said.

Alix was still suspicious. "And everything will be settled by tomorrow morning?"

"Even if Arnie hasn't made the announcement by then, I'll fill you in."

"I'll bring breakfast here at nine o'clock sharp," Minnie said.

"Great," I said. Our little caravan moved at Wendell's halting pace down the sidewalk. The rest of them waited until I had helped him into my car before they finally left me.

"I'll have Grandpa call you from the hospital so you can give him an update, okay?" Tylcr gave Wendell a last pat on his head.

"Good idea," I said. After I watched the others roar off on their various errands, I dropped my fake smile and turned to the dog sitting quietly on the front seat beside me. "I hope you've been thinking about how to clear Bianca. I'm sure you're a better detective than Bipsy and Mr. Potts put together." Wendell regarded me steadily with his one good eye, but apparently he was too modest to reply.

TWENTY-SEVEN

THE STILL UNCHANGED window display rebuked me as I approached Thornton's. I wasn't watching my step as I felt around in my bag for the keys, so I half-tripped over a hose stretched across the front doorway, a hose I'd asked Tyler to move several days ago. Obviously, he hadn't. Would I ever get back to such mundane tasks as moving hoses and changing window displays again? Right now it was hard to imagine.

Piled in front of the door were several bulging cardboard boxes, which I reached around with difficulty to unlock the front door. The stale heat of the room provided mute evidence that no one had been tending the store for several days. I left the door open and switched on the counter fan. The slanting rays of the sun highlighted the dust in the air. I sighed as I pictured poor Laurence, lying in his hospital bed, worrying about his health and his store, and wondering why his usually reliable employee couldn't seem to find the time to open Thornton's for business. The telephone rang and I glanced at my watch before picking it up. Past seven o'clock already.

"Why didn't you tell me what's been going on?" Laurence said without preamble. "You've had a rough week." Tyler must have arrived and filled him in on the story. I hoped it had been an edited version.

"Not as rough as yours was," I said. "Look, about Thornton's—"

"Never mind the bookstore, Jane. I'm just glad that beautiful, long-legged daughter of yours is going to be released. Ridiculous to hold her in the first place."

Beautiful? Long-legged? Laurence's health must have improved since the last time I'd seen him, if he was starting to think about pretty girls again. "Uh, yes. That's what I thought."

"So, who killed Gil? You're not going to make a sick old man wait until tomorrow for the news, are you? I might not last that long."

"You don't sound all that sick to me," I said. "Sorry, you're out of luck until tomorrow, unless you can get Arnie to tell you something."

"Huh! If Arnie Kraft is able to track down a murderer, I'll eat the flowers right here in this vase. By the way, thanks."

"I didn't send flowers." No need to explain that I was busy breaking into Gil's house during the time I might have thought to do it.

"It says right on the card that they're from the Murder of the Month Book Club, in lieu of a casserole, whatever the hell that means."

"That means Minnie's been busy." How had she managed this thoughtful gesture in between bouts with the police? I was impressed.

"Waste of money," he said gruffly.

"Right, no sense doing something nice for a cranky old man."

"Never mind that," he answered. "What's the bottom line at the store? Has anybody sold a single, solitary book since I left?"

"Your store has been doing just fine." I let my gaze wander to the boxes of books yet to be unpacked, the accumulation of messages on the counter, the blinking answering machine light on the phone. "Everything is under control."

It was easy enough to sort through the notes and determine their origin. Alix's stark printing matched her caustic commentary on the literary taste of our customers, while Tyler's cramped writing pointed out glaring errors in the inventory, such as the absence of Howard Zinn's work. Minnie concentrated on non-literary matters in her looping scrawl: "How can you work in a place without a proper coffeemaker?" and "Curtains would brighten the back room."

I was contemplating Minnie's suggestions when Laurence asked, "Jane, are you there?"

"Just reading some notes. Didn't Tyler tell you? He's been working at the store, and Minnie and Alix have pitched in, too."

"Good God! You haven't let Minnie near the cash register!"

"Oh, please. First you complain that no one is selling books and then you fuss if someone has. Ever heard of looking a gift horse in the mouth?"

"Bah!"

"You're impossible, Laurence. It's a good thing I have work to do now or I'd tell you what I really think." Now that everyone was safely out of the way for the night, I wanted to get off the phone and do some thinking.

"Work," Laurence said. "That has a nice ring to it. You go right ahead… Oh, I almost forgot. Tyler, hand me that pad. We've been talking about some ideas. This boy has a good head for business, you know." Apparently Laurence and Tyler had made peace over the borrowed car incident. "I have a couple of things I'd like you to check right now, Jane. Won't take a minute."

I heard a feminine voice in the background and then Laurence came on the line again, "They want to do some fool procedure. Call you right back."

His voice was replaced by the dial tone. Casting my eye around for something simple to do while I waited for him to call back, I spied the boxes outside the door.

"Too bad you're not a sled dog, Wendell," I said. "You could make yourself useful hauling these boxes." Wendell thumped his tail on the floor, raising more dust motes to dance in the waning sunlight.

Someone had scribbled a few words in pencil on the flap of the top box. The letters were half-formed, obviously written in haste: "Family emergency in Boise. Pls. keep 'til reunion resched. Or give to Harley. Thanks. Helen ('Sassy') Bartells."

Just what we need here, more junk, I thought irritably. We'd allowed the committee to hold meetings upstairs, but why leave their boxes here now that the reunion had been postponed indefinitely? There must have been some better place. And couldn't they have found sturdier boxes? With difficulty, I carried two of the three tattered masses of buckling cardboard inside and set them beside the counter. Unfortunately, the third box disintegrated midway across the room. Photos, notebooks, blue and gold streamers, and even one scuffed red high-top tennis shoe cascaded in all directions.

The noise startled Wendell, who jumped up to sniff at the debris.

Unexpectedly, I burst into tears. This mess on the floor was the last straw. I sank down beside it and gave way at last to the despair that had been building for days. The box of Kleenex we kept under the counter was half-gone before I calmed down enough to think again.

Sitting here crying wouldn't get Bianca out of jail. Now that I had vented some pent-up emotion, I felt better, but I was also restless, itching to do something productive. I wished Laurence would hurry up and call back so I could get going, even if I didn't know which direction to go.

I regarded the jumble strewn around me and decided to let it sit. I couldn't even begin to work up the energy necessary to care about it. Sassy might have her own set of personal problems, but so did I.

I leaned against the counter and emptied my mind of everything but my conversation with Bianca. Her description of what she had heard from inside the closet would surely yield some clues if only I could order my thoughts. Still sitting on the floor, I reached under the counter for a legal-sized pad of yellow paper and started making notes on what she had said.

First, Gil had seemed surprised to see the person who entered his house, but if Bianca's report was correct, his words—"What are you doing here? Oh, I see"—sounded more annoyed than scared. Was the intruder someone he knew?

Second, the person had come carrying a gun, though it probably wasn't in view at first. Gil's murder was premeditated.

Third, what had Gil meant by saying, "Oh, I see"? What did he see or know? That Bianca was in the closet listening? Supposing Gil and the intruder both knew that Bianca was present, why would that person then kill Gil, knowing that there would be a witness to the crime? Then it came to me. No, not a witness. Bianca would be a suspect. Everyone knew that Bianca detested Gil. She could have been being set up to take the fall for his murder.

Yes, this was making more sense by the minute. The chair that had held the closet door closed hadn't been tightly wedged under the door handle, but maybe that wasn't just a mistake. The chair would have held Bianca captive long enough for the killer to escape without being seen, but once she made a determined attempt to get the door open, she'd have had no trouble getting out. The killer couldn't have counted on her to do anything so stupid as to pick up the gun and carry it away. That had been a stroke of pure luck.

While mulling these ideas, I had absently begun collecting the papers and folders from the floor. A 1984 Juniper High School yearbook caught my eye and I leafed through it, looking for the pictures of the kids who were this year supposed to be celebrating their twentieth high school reunion.

Their smiles reflected a youthful happiness that they thought would last forever. I flipped to the inside of the front cover. In gaudy pink ink, a feminine hand had claimed it: "Vanessa Mae Farmer, Class of '84." I checked her senior picture and, sure enough, there was the younger version of the person I'd known. No doubt Vanessa Mae Farmer thought she had it made when she became Vanessa Fortune. When she and Gil had volunteered to co-chair the reunion, did they ever suspect that neither of them would live long enough to attend?

Next to Vanessa, Gil beamed from his picture, supremely confident and handsome. A large pink heart encircled the two pictures. How convenient that their last names had placed them together in the annual. Together in life; together in death. Were they murdered by the same person? This apparently successful couple wasn't so lucky after all. I slapped the book closed. No wonder Sassy wanted to get these ghosts out of her house.

"Are you all right, Jane?" asked a soft voice.

I jumped, banging my hand on the shelf under the counter and upsetting a box of tacks in the process. "Harley! I didn't hear you."

I scrambled from my dusty place on the floor, brushing the remaining half-dried tears from my cheeks with the back of my hand. Was Harley here to accuse my daughter of murdering his best friend? He'd have to stand in line for that duty, behind the police. Well, why not? He had more reason than most to be upset. "I…uh…I'm sorry—"

"Oh, Jane," he said with a sad smile, "did you think I came to berate you for supporting your daughter? You don't have to pretend. I know what you thought of Gil, what Bianca thought of him." He bent to pet Wendell, who agreeably flopped onto his back for a stomach rub.

Since Harley had brought the controversy into the open,

I figured I might as well skip right to the point. "She didn't kill him, Harley."

"I agree." He straightened up and approached the counter. "That's the reason I'm here."

"You do?" I stepped back carefully from the tacks littering the floor. I'd clean them up later.

"Don't you think I know that no daughter of yours could do such a terrible thing?"

"I can't tell you how relieved I am to hear you say that. Honestly, I didn't know what you'd think. After all, Gil was your friend—"

"Well, now you know. And you must also have guessed by now how I feel about you, Jane, so you can count on me to do everything in my power to help you clear Bianca. When I heard they'd taken her into custody, I couldn't believe it."

"Tell that to Arnie. He doesn't have any trouble with the idea."

"The fact that she apparently went to Gil's house doesn't look good, but I'll talk to him tomorrow, see what I can do. I wanted to see you first though and offer my full support."

"I do appreciate your help," I said. "This is all so crazy. I just want it to be over so I can have my daughter back. I know how insensitive it is of me to be going on like this when it won't ever really be over for you, losing two close friends—"

"No, don't apologize for being honest. It's one of the things I admire about you. Yes, I still have to come to terms with my own loss, but I'm hoping that we'll be able to help each other through this trying time."

I appreciated Harley's help, as a friend, but I knew we were on tricky ground now. Agreeing to go to the reunion with him had merely given him false hope. Thank goodness the event had been cancelled. I hesitated, and then said simply, "I'll do whatever I can to help you." This was not the right time to tell him that there would never be anything more between us than friendship.

He started to move around the counter, looking steadily into my eyes, and I was suddenly on alert, knowing that he was going to try to take me into his arms. I didn't want to hurt his feelings, especially tonight after everything he'd been through, but I wasn't going to lead him on any further. I stepped back in what I hoped was an inconspicuous way.

"Could you help me pick up this stuff?" I improvised, gesturing at the mess on the floor.

He blinked, and after a moment looked down slowly at the papers spread across the floor as though seeing them for the first time. "What's all this?"

"Ask Sassy. She left it here."

"Sassy? Why?"

"The reunion committee material. You want it?"

"With Gil and Vanessa gone, I suppose I'll be the one in charge of reunions from now on. There will be others, I guess, eventually."

Was I determined to rub salt in his wound? What a topic to bring up. I watched in helpless silence as he slowly bent to retrieve a pile of yearbooks.

"On second thought, never mind that now," I said. "I can do it tomorrow."

He didn't seem to hear me as he opened the yearbook I'd been looking at. He leafed through the glossy pages, pausing at the colorful double-page devoted to the senior prom. Naturally, Gil and Vanessa were featured front and center, caught with broad smiles as they were crowned king and queen. "On Our Way to the Stars" read the crooked blue and gold banner behind them. I recognized an adolescent version of Alix laughing and clapping as she stood beside Kurt Wendorf. Kurt was watching the coronation, too, looking anything but happy.

I pointed to his picture. "What was that scowl about? If looks could kill…"

Harley looked at me but said nothing.

"Did Gil's trouble with Kurt start that long ago? I thought they were friends."

"Well, they were on the football team together, but…well, they did have some trouble over Vanessa."

"Kurt was interested in her, too?"

"She was irresistible back then, and she knew it. She took up with Kurt several times, after she and Gil had had a fight or something, but she always went back to Gil. Kurt never learned, never took Vanessa's rejection very well. Kurt even put his fist through the wall one time—"

"So he could have harbored a grudge against both of them," I said doubtfully. "I haven't been able to put the two murders together—"

"—*if* Vanessa was murdered," he interrupted.

"—oh, I'm sure now that she was, but maybe—"

Harley nodded. "Kurt's always been a hothead, about his son and everything else—"

"I know, but somehow he doesn't quite seem like the type," I said.

"What type is that? Surely you agree that Kurt's been out of control recently."

"Yes, but I'm starting to think that Gil's murder was done by someone who planned it carefully. That doesn't sound much like Kurt. Still, it has to be checked out." I pushed away the memory of Max's youthful certainty about his father's innocence. Any son would think that, and Max probably didn't even know about his father's high school crush on Vanessa. What father, wanting to impress his son, would tell him stories about how he got dumped for a more successful man, especially if it had happened more than once? "The first thing is to find out where Kurt was this morning," I continued.

"You know what? I'm not going to wait until tomorrow. I'm calling Arnie right now. He won't want to listen, but maybe with your help—"

"You've got that, Jane."

"Thanks." I smiled at him as I reached for the telephone book under the counter.

"But don't get your hopes up too high," he warned. "Arnie seems convinced that Bianca did it, and you have to admit that the gun and the scarf are difficult to explain."

I ran down the listings under Russell County until I found the numbers for the sheriff. I started to punch in the non-emergency number. Only half-listening to Harley's words, grateful for his support, I was halfway through the task when my brain belatedly processed what he had been saying. Had I heard him right?

His words echoed over and over to the drumming of my heart. He'd said, "the gun and the scarf," only he couldn't have known about the scarf. Bianca said she hadn't told anyone about it except Nick and me, and I had removed it before the deputies arrived on the scene. Other than the members of the book club, only one other person could have known about the scarf, and that was Gil's murderer. He was standing in front of me.

TWENTY-EIGHT

THE RECEIVER DROPPED from my suddenly nerveless hand. I kept my face turned away from Harley as I trapped the swinging receiver and hung it up. If I looked at him, he'd know in an instant what I had just figured out.

Before I could redial, the phone rang. I snatched up the receiver on the first ring, certain that it was Laurence calling from the hospital. My brain whirled as I tried to think how to let him know what was happening.

"I've checked. There's nobody suspicious at the potluck," came Minnie's muffled voice. She must have been covering the receiver with her hand to deaden the sound. "Are you sure Gil's killer is here?"

"Definitely not, Minnie," I said. "Good idea to ask. Harley is here with me right now."

"How nice that you have someone to keep you company," she said. Minnie didn't get the hint. She chattered on, apparently not noticing that my responses were little more than monosyllabic grunts. My throat was so constricted that I wasn't sure I could form real words, but I had to keep the conversation going. This telephone was my lifeline and dear, oblivious Minnie was my only hope.

I reached for a pad of paper and busily scrawled notes, keeping the paper shielded from Harley waiting quietly on the other side of the counter. My thoughts scrabbled around like the proverbial rats escaping a sinking ship and I didn't think my shaking knees were going to hold me up much longer. I longed to sit down on the stool fastened to the stairwell behind me, but I had to remain poised for action.

I held one hand up, palm facing Harley, as though listening to something of importance, but I didn't dare look at him. I wasn't that good an actress. Meanwhile, the counter, which had always seemed so substantial, now appeared as flimsy as balsa wood, and as easily breached. I'd never noticed before this moment that someone on the other side of it was actually standing close enough to reach my throat.

"Well," Minnie said, "I'd better get back to the potluck. My chicken enchilada casserole is about to come out of the oven and—"

"Bianca's favorite!" I broke in, practically shouting it into the phone. I had to stop her from hanging up.

"It is? I'm surprised. I thought she preferred vegetarian dishes."

"That's right. No doubt about that," I answered, trying to put an ominous note into my voice. "Your pot roast tops the list, way above everything else."

"Really? Then why did you just say chicken enchilada casserole was her favorite dish?" I now had Minnie's attention, but I wasn't getting through to her. I wasn't surprised. These clues wouldn't win any prizes for clarity.

"Yep, that's the question, Minnie." I forced a laugh that sounded like a croak. "Maybe we could discuss it at book club."

"Book club? Why would we discuss enchiladas at book club?"

"You said it! And let's go for your book next."

"But you didn't think that *Paint Her Dead* belonged in a mystery book club because it was about a real-life murder—"

"Exactly, and I haven't changed my mind." I let that sink in for a minute before I continued deliberately, "Your book is precisely the one we should discuss—"

"I don't understand—"

"And you've already made the refreshments? The ones we had the night Wendell upset the table? That's terrific—"

"Frosted bran bars?" Minnie sounded horrified. "I would never make frosted bran bars."

"Alix loved them so much—"

"She hated them! Don't you remember how dreadful that night was, with Bianca accusing Gil of murder and everyone arguing that there hadn't really been a murder and—"

"Yes, I remember. We need more of that."

"More? But it was awful!"

I said nothing, hoping that mental telepathy worked.

The silence lengthened and then I heard Minnie ask, "What's going on?" Good old Minnie. She'd finally figured it out. I held my silence and continued to scribble on the pad with white-knuckled intensity. Then Minnie's laugh came through loud and clear. "You won't believe this, Jane, but they're chanting for my casserole in the other room. I'll call you back later."

Just like that, she was gone. Stunned, I gripped the receiver hard. Talking to the dial tone made about as much sense as talking to Minnie, so the fake answers I came up with to Minnie's supposed comments were fairly easy for a few seconds before raucous beeps announced that the phone was off the hook.

Over the racket, Harley told me what we both already knew. "Your call is over, Jane."

I looked up. He had moved to the end of the counter and the gun he was pointing at me removed any doubt about what was going on. Did he have an endless supply of guns? Bianca had already taken one of them.

"You just couldn't leave it alone," he said. "Too bad."

I agreed wholeheartedly. If I'd been asked at that moment whether I'd be willing to return to selling books, leaving murder investigations to others, I'd have said an emphatic yes. But no one seemed to be asking.

"I don't know what you're talking about," I stammered.

"Don't insult my intelligence, Jane," Harley said. "You'd be a very bad poker player."

I stared in fascination at the gun pointed steadily at me. "Is that real?" I asked conversationally. Talking was better than getting shot. "I don't think of you as the gun type. Too messy, I suppose. You've always been so fastidious."

"Occupational hazard. It wouldn't do to have a bank manager who couldn't keep accounts neat and tidy, would it?"

"Right. He might misplace your money." I was just chattering, stalling for time, but the look on his face changed so abruptly at my words that I kept talking as though I knew something. "So Gil discovered that you'd been fudging the books at the bank. That answers one question. But why Vanessa?"

He gestured toward the back door. "Shall we continue this discussion in the car? It's out back."

I didn't really want to do that, so I just stood there, waiting for inspiration to strike. Nothing came to me, but I could hardly tell him to go ahead by himself. I kept talking.

The yearbook on the counter was still open to the prom page. Now that it was too late, everything was clicking into place. I looked at the picture again and made a guess. "You didn't go to the prom, did you? And Kurt wasn't the one that Vanessa kept on a string. It was you."

The slight smile he attempted didn't quite work. "Don't be ridiculous."

"After all these years—"

"Let's go!" he ordered. He didn't like this subject.

"I'm not going anywhere." I raised my chin and tried to look resolute. "You'll have to shoot me right here." That always sounded good in the movies, but I was really hoping he wouldn't take me up on the offer.

"Oh, Jane, I'm not going to shoot you," he said. His voice suddenly dropped back to its usual agreeable tone and he smiled broadly. What a chameleon. "I merely need to keep you briefly out of circulation, just long enough for me to leave town."

I nodded, hoping he'd think I was stupid enough to believe that. I wouldn't have thought twice about getting into a car with him last week, but that was before he started littering the county with the bodies of his friends.

The telephone beside me began to ring.

"Don't answer that!" His command voice was back.

"I have to. Laurence knows I'm here."

"He'll think you've stepped outside."

"No, he won't. I told him I'd wait for his call." After four rings, the answering machine took over, but no one left a message. A minute later the ringing started again. "He'll know something's wrong if I don't answer soon."

"Do not pick up that phone unless you want something bad to happen to this dog."

Good threat. I didn't answer the phone.

The ringing stopped and Harley smiled. "There. That's better."

"He'll just call back."

"Then he'll be disappointed again."

"Will you at least tell me what this is all about?" I didn't think he'd go for this stall, but it was worth a try.

"No. Get moving."

Maintaining eye contact with him as though considering his order, I thought about the box of tacks spilled on the floor between us. They ought to slow him down, but they wouldn't be of any use against a gun. Besides, what was I going to do about Wendell? I couldn't leave him with Harley.

I pictured the contents of the shelf next to me under the counter. Pens, Scotch tape, rubber bands...none of them very useful in a fight. Cleaning cloth, telephone book, stapler. Could I throw the stapler at him? It might be heavy enough to do some damage. I slid my hand along the shelf and encountered the smooth plastic side of the Windex bottle. A dose of Windex in the eye ought to sting plenty, possibly giving me enough time to run if I could squirt it before Harley could pull the trigger. He wouldn't risk the sound of a shot if he could avoid it. I gripped the handle of the Windex bottle, still trying to figure out what to do about Wendell.

As if on cue, the ringing of the telephone pierced the air once more. Harley glanced at it just long enough for me to bring up the spray bottle and blast him full in the face. From the depths of my subconscious, inspiration surfaced at last.

"Wendell, dinnertime!" I shouted. Wendell leaped to his feet and raced out the front door of the store, just as he had after book club. Harley was between me and the door, so I dashed the other way, toward the back of the store. Though I didn't wait around to check the results, Harley's roar of pain gave me a pretty good idea that the Windex was doing its job.

It would take too long to get the bolt unlocked and the security bar off the outside back door, so I sprinted up the back stairs three at a time instead. Just around the corner at the top, I whirled and crouched out of sight. Now what? Though I didn't have any idea what I was going to do next, I did know that getting into a car with Harley would have been a spectacularly bad idea.

TWENTY-NINE

"JANE? COME ON NOW." Harley's disembodied voice floated eerily up the back stairwell. "You're over-reacting." He sounded genuinely regretful, the kindly banker disappointed that his client had failed to take his investment advice. Funny how having that gun pointed at me had made me wary of his suggestions.

"You might as well come down. You can't stay up there forever." That last part was true enough, but any delay that I could promote sounded good to me and would improve my chances of escape. He knew that, too, so I didn't expect that he'd stick with his falsely reasonable persona for long. This situation was too much like a chess game for my taste, move and counter-move. Unfortunately, chess was a game at which Harley excelled, whereas I was never able to map out more than one move ahead when Tony used to challenge me to a game. My mind always skittered off to wondering whether the laundry needed to come out of the dryer, or whether we had enough milk for dinner.

"You're afraid I'm going to hurt you," Harley said gently. "Is that it?"

The urge to answer was almost unbearable, but I didn't want to give away my position. The threadbare hallway runner for once did some good instead of just soaking up dust. It deadened my steps as I edged toward the front staircase. His voice had sounded as though it still came from the bottom of the back staircase, but I couldn't be sure.

"I give you my word that nothing will happen to you. All

I want is to get away from Juniper. You can understand that. The sooner I leave here, the sooner Bianca will be set free, so you and I really should be able to work together on this. Imagine how terrified she must be by now. A young girl like that…this must be an awful experience for her!"

And whose fault is that? I thought. His indignant tone merely reinforced my belief that he was truly a chameleon. He must consider me an idiot if he expected me to surrender to him.

"I know you want her released as soon as possible, Jane, but I simply can't allow you to talk to Arnie yet. I have to lock you up for just a short while. I'll tell you what. Come down now and I'll tell you everything that happened. Will that make you happy? Once you're free, you can contact Arnie and clear Bianca. We can have a win/win situation here, Jane."

I tiptoed to the door of the original master bedroom of this house, the room that now housed our history and current events volumes. Besides its one dirty window, it also had an outside door. Now I looked at that door longingly, well aware that its decaying outside staircase had been dismantled when Laurence first bought the place. Even if I could get the old door lock to turn—and that was a big "if"—I'd exit into thin air and a straight drop from the second story. Peter Pan might be able to fly to the branches of the never pruned apple tree which flourished a short distance from the side of the building, but I was no Peter Pan. If I could get that door open, maybe I could tie something together and shinny down the outside wall though.

Meanwhile, I turned my cautious steps toward the front staircase. Running down the staircase leading to the front door of Thornton's seemed more my style than a daredevil circus descent from twenty feet in the air. Just as I edged one foot onto the top step, still undecided, Harley spoke from nearly beneath me.

"I'm very disappointed in you, Jane. You're no more reasonable than your daughter." He was starting to sound aggrieved. Waiting for me to come out and play must be getting on his nerves. "Opposing me is not going to do you any more good than it did Gil and Vanessa. They thought they could outsmart me, and look what happened to them. You're smarter than they are. I knew you didn't want to go out with me, but that's fine. Really. I've never been one to hold a grudge. I like you, Jane, and I don't want to hurt you, but you're smart enough to see that you're going to force me into it if you don't cooperate. It's sad but true. I can't wait here all night for you to make up your mind. This place could go up in flames very fast, you know."

I considered and dismissed his threat to set fire to the building. Harley had no intention of attracting outside attention. Too great a chance that I'd be found alive. I remained silent.

"How come you tried so hard to accommodate your daughter and you won't cooperate with me at all? You listened to her, even when she made no sense. I'm presenting you with a very clear and sensible set of options."

His voice was rising to a pitch I'd never heard before, almost a singsong. "I'm getting really tired of this. Why are people never reasonable? Take Vanessa. She badly misjudged things. I gave her every opportunity to come to me. You have to believe that. Every opportunity. Even when I carefully explained how much more I had to offer her than Gil, she didn't get it. Sometimes I thought she was starting to understand. She'd come to me after they'd had a fight or something, and I'd take her back, but it never lasted. Even after she agreed to go to the senior prom with me, she backed out when Gil finally got around to asking her. That wasn't right, but she couldn't see it. She always thought she could play me for a fool, but I got the last laugh on both of them."

Harley's rambling commentary was punctuated by the sounds of things hitting the floor. "I'm making it look like burglars vandalized the place," he explained, now returning to a conversational tone, "but you can explain the truth later. Maybe Kurt or his stupid son will get blamed for this, too, but you can clear them. Take care of things however you want. Just not for a few hours. Okay?" He paused and then announced the time, as though it had any relevance to this bizarre situation. "It's almost nine o'clock now. We'll go soon, unless you want me to start a fire down here instead."

He didn't really want to march me out of here until it got darker, so I had a few more minutes before he'd get serious about flushing me out. I planned to spend whatever time I had left making a rope ladder and getting that locked door open.

Suddenly a tremendous crash sounded from downstairs, in the front. Silence, followed by a low moaning that set my hair on end. Had Harley fallen? I raced silently down the dim hallway toward the back stairs. Maybe I could be down them and out the door before he recovered. I paused at the top, clutching the sturdy banister and listening. Nothing.

I descended one step, and then another. Was this a trick? If Harley caught me part-way down the stairs, he might get close enough to grab me. Also, if he were willing to risk a shot, I'd be a sitting duck, but I didn't think he wanted the noise. The grounds surrounding the refurbished old house were large, but not that large. Every instinct I possessed was telling me not to go down those stairs. Harley urged rational thinking, so that was a good enough reason in itself for me to stick with instinct. I whirled and retreated upstairs again.

"Changed your mind, eh?" Harley's voice came from under the back staircase, where he'd been hiding. Score one for instinct. "We are going to walk out of this place together, either now or later, so you might as well accept the situation and save us some time. Jane, are you listening?"

Oh, I was listening all right, but only to determine his location. The icy reasoning that had led Harley to kill his two childhood friends as easily as he might knock pieces off a chess board was still controlling his behavior. His place in the world was built around this town, and I knew he had no intention of leaving alive someone who would make it necessary for him to flee. Given his recent treatment of Vanessa and Gil, his assertion that he wasn't one to hold a grudge didn't ring quite true.

If he could get rid of me, he'd be safe. He wouldn't be able to blame my disappearance on Bianca for a change, since she was still in jail, but I had faith in his powers of invention. Maybe he'd make my death look like a suicide, or else he would concoct some yarn that would implicate Kurt or Jenna, and enjoy the challenge in doing so. He seemed to have been three moves ahead of everyone so far, but I wasn't ready to concede the game.

Now that he was in the back part of the store, I would break for the front door. I ran to the top of the front stairs, but skidded to a halt before I could start down them. Across the bottom lay a barricade of books and splintered wood, the remains of the massive bookshelf in the office which had contained all the books we were holding for specific customers. That must have been the crash I'd heard. Harley was making sure that I couldn't easily get down those stairs, and he had added the moaning to trick me. Good moves. He really was thinking ahead, so I needed to match his concentration. Unfortunately, I couldn't seem to get my mind off the thought that someone was going to have quite a time straightening out the mess below. I sincerely hoped I would be around to help with the project.

From the back of the store came the thunder of another shelf toppling and I realized the bookcase that displayed newly released hardback selections had now become another barricade. The immediate question was whether Harley was now above it on the back stairs or below, biding his time. Straining to hear footsteps, I held myself ready to run in the opposite direction from whichever way Harley might come. I even held my breath in an attempt to gain just a little bit more stillness. Was he coming or not? Sweat sprung out all over my body as I braced for a rush. No sound. No movement.

It was getting harder to see now. Was that an advantage to him or me? Maybe someone would notice the lights shining at night in the supposedly empty store. As though Harley had read my thoughts, all the lights suddenly went out. The good news was that the light switches were downstairs, on the other side of his barricades, so I was safe for the moment. He had decided to wait for full darkness. Once my heartbeat slowed again, I was encouraged to realize that maybe I was matching him move for move. Now all I had to do was get one move ahead. He was sure he had me trapped up here, so, obviously, I had to leave.

My search for suitable ladder material turned up nothing but a frayed extension cord and half a ball of twine left over from an uncompleted effort to box up unsold Christmas books. Another project I'd avoided before, but one which I'd be only too happy to tackle in the future, if I could stay alive long enough to do it. I went back to work on my ladder.

It was hard to check each room for useful supplies while simultaneously keeping an ear cocked for the sound of Harley's approach on the stairs. Since each room was stuffed with books and bookcases, it was even harder to maneuver with any speed. We really needed to get serious about weeding the stock, not just the Christmas books, but every other category, too. Slipping out of my sandals so as to move more quietly, I realized that before tonight I hadn't given nearly enough consideration to the need for a floor plan that facilitated escape from a killer. The two staircases were a nice start, but they weren't quite enough.

How much weight would the twine hold? I had no idea. I should have paid more attention to physics and less to Elizabethan dramatists, though Shakespeare provided me with an appropriate line that ran endlessly through my head as I laid out the extension cord along the hall floor and added multiple lengths of the twine for reinforcement. Shakespeare's words provided as good a mantra as any: "For courage mounteth with occasion." If ever there existed an occasion that called for courage, this was it.

The flimsy ladder wouldn't get me clear to the ground, but if I put the part reinforced with the extension cord at the top, it might break my fall for a good part of the distance. With any luck at all, I'd merely break an arm and still be able to run for help before Harley figured out what I'd done. Even if I broke a leg, I vowed to out-hobble him. He was not going to beat me, no matter how smart he was. I wasn't skilled at chess, but so what? This wasn't a game.

I carried my makeshift ladder through the room piled high with books on history and military campaigns, the twine snake following me in a not very impressive manner. Surely, no military operation had ever rested on such a ridiculous plan. I gloomily surveyed my two possible escape routes—the door and the window—in the dim light still making its way through the grimy window. After trying without success to raise the window sash, I conceded that it had been painted closed too many times and was not going to budge. I could break the glass, of course, but that would bring Harley up the stairs in a flash. Next, I turned my attention to the heavy wooden door that opened to the outside. It was secured with an old-fashioned bolt.

"Aren't you ready yet?" Harley called from below. He

sounded like an irritable husband waiting for his wife to put on her lipstick before a Sunday drive. "It's time."

I took a deep breath and pushed against the bolt with all my strength. It didn't move. It needed grease, but where would I find some up here? The front drawer of a desk in one corner provided an eraser and a sheaf of yellowed paper for a typewriter no longer in the room, two pennies, a skeleton key, some paper clips, and a half-eaten roll of Lifesavers. My mouth was dry enough that even the desiccated candies tempted me, but I might not live long enough to swallow one of them if I didn't get that door open soon. What else? On the desk top lay a roll of masking tape and some unshelved books.

Could I trick Harley into thinking I'd gone out the window and throw books at him from behind the door? Not likely. Besides, unless I beaned him with a really heavy encyclopedia, I'd be in worse shape than ever once he turned around and found me.

I felt in the pockets of my shorts, but found only a wadded-up Kleenex and some cherry-flavored lip balm that tasted good, but wouldn't even protect me from the harmful rays of the sun, let alone a bullet from Harley's gun. Tears pricked my eyes. I had no good options.

Listlessly, I picked up the two heaviest books and went to my hiding place behind the door. Shakespeare still droned in my head, but what good was courage without WD-40?

At this point I almost wanted Harley to get up here soon so we could get this thing over with, no matter how it ended. I was hot and tired and I had done everything I could think of. When he came at me, I'd yell and scream, but that was about all I had left.

Licking my dry lips, I considered again the lowly lip balm in my pocket. Might as well put some on while I waited. I had nothing else to do. I put down the books and took out the tube, smoothing the creamy substance over my lips. Maybe

I'd even splurge and go get one of the candies in the drawer. It would ease my parched throat so I'd be able to scream all the louder when I needed to. I hoped there was a cherry Lifesaver left. That had always been my favorite flavor.

There were two Lifesavers left in the crumpled package, lime and...cherry. Ah, yes. Appreciative of small victories, I popped it into my mouth, savoring the sweetness before putting the remaining candy into my pocket. I resumed my post behind the door. Things were looking up. I soon reached for the remaining Lifesaver, but found the lip balm first. My heart started to thud as I considered. Could the lip balm possibly be greasy enough to unstick that lock? Probably not, but even as I denied the possibility, I was racing across the room to the door in the outside wall.

Smearing the red stuff all over the bolt action of the lock, I felt like a vandal. It was now dark enough that at least I didn't have to look at my graffiti, but old habits die hard and it bothered me to deface the lock. The girls and I would have a good laugh about this later...I hoped.

Even if all my efforts failed and Harley caught me, I was stubborn enough to hope I had created enough of a mess that he wouldn't be able to get away. Harley would be caught though only if I could force him to kill me on my terms, not his. I swallowed hard at the thought, but it had to be faced. I was determined to make things as difficult for him as possible. If I could make him shoot me somewhere publicly, rather than giving him the chance to choose a private setting where I might never be found, even Arnie would get the picture that something was fishy. He might even get smart enough to take a closer look at the murders of Vanessa and Gil, particularly with the hounding he'd be getting from my tenacious friends in the Murder of the Month Book Club and Nick, who had wisely disliked Harley on sight.

I pushed against the lock until my hands were sore, but the

lock didn't budge. Then I picked up a book and used it as a hammer, hoping the sounds would be too muffled for Harley to hear. I struck once, twice, and the bolt started to move. I struck it harder, and it moved more until, finally, it cleared the hasp altogether. I dropped the book and wrenched at the knob. Locked, of course. I ran back to the desk and pulled out the skeleton key I had seen earlier, thankful for once that we never discarded anything in this chaotic store. After two tries, I steadied my hand enough to fit the key into the keyhole, and turned it.

The door swung open without a sound, leaving me bathed in the softness of the summer night air. The breeze cooled my superheated cheeks as I reached for the ladder so I could tie it to the doorknob.

"That won't be necessary, Jane." In the gloom I could hardly make out the figure standing in the doorway behind me, but that didn't matter. I knew who it was.

THIRTY

"READY?" HARLEY'S CASUAL tone made it sound as though we were about to set off for the class reunion we had planned to attend together. My flesh crawled at the very idea. And to think that I had agreed to go because I felt sorry for poor Harley, carrying on so valiantly after the death of his close friend Vanessa.

"Actually, I'm not. Why don't you just leave me here?" My voice sounded so normal that I was tempted to add, "Have a nice trip."

"Oh, I'm afraid that won't work at all. Shall we go?"

"That is the question, isn't it?" I agreed. And it was. The choice I made in the next minute would determine whether I was going to live or die. It was just that simple, and never in my whole life had I been so aware that I wanted to live. In the first days and months following Tony's death, I'd been too anguished to think about choices. As a responsible parent, I just kept plodding ahead because that's what a parent does. I had often felt like a sleepwalker, but I took care of my family. When any of the girls needed me—when Susannah couldn't get Kevin to sleep through the night, or Emily wanted me to critique the essay that would get her onto the archeological dig, or, yes, even when Bianca accused the Russell County District Attorney of murder—I tried to help. However, now that I was faced with death, I did a quick mental check and concluded that my kids would be okay no matter what happened to me now. They had healed after their father's death, probably better than I had. For a long time my job had been to care for them, but I had already completed that task. They could care for themselves, and they knew that I loved them.

Now I had the luxury of making choices for myself, and I could feel the cocoon of grief that had imprisoned me for so long breaking apart. In one glorious burst of energy, I knew that I wanted to live and I would fight for my life, which was expanding in ways I couldn't even have imagined a year ago. I wasn't going to be cheated out of experiencing it.

Harley and his gun stood between me and my future. I stood between Harley and his future, too, but I was armed only with determination. It would have to do. He was not going to get away with three murders and then live happily ever after as one of Juniper's leading citizens.

A slight shuffling of his feet alerted me to the likelihood that he was about to rush me. He still wanted to get me out of here without firing the gun or making unnecessary noise.

"Wait," I said, putting as much fear and resignation in my voice as I could. "Just a minute, please." The fear wasn't hard to convey, but I was far from resigned. "I'll go, but first, tell me what happened. You said you would." I waited, hoping that he would relax as he registered the defeat in my voice.

"What do you want to know?" he asked eventually. He'd concluded that he didn't have anything to lose by talking now. That, in itself, was tacit confirmation that he wasn't going to let me go.

"Why did you kill Gil? He was your friend. He practically grew up with you…in your house—"

"Yes, he did. He certainly did grow up in my house. In fact, my dear departed parents thought he could walk on water. It was 'Gil this' and 'Gil that' and 'Why can't you be more like Gil?' More like him? I was better than he was! I was the Valedictorian, not Gil. I was the chess champion, not Gil, but that wasn't enough. My parents even displayed a bigger picture of Gil on our mantel than of me! I could out-think him any day of the week, but Gil could throw a football, and Gil was charming, and everybody thought Gil was just great. How do you think he got through chemistry? I swiped the tests, coached him so he'd look good...and oh, how good he looked. People fell all over him, even people who should have known better—"

"Like Vanessa?"

"Especially Vanessa. I kept trying to explain it to her, but she knew he'd always be the one with his picture on the mantel. She always went back to Gil. And when Gil found out that I was borrowing money from the bank, Vanessa joined right in with him in holding it over me. For years!" He was shouting now, almost forgetting my presence. "It was 'Harley, can you get us into Edgecliffe?' and 'Golf lessons would be a great Christmas present for Vanessa' and 'How about throwing a fundraiser for me, old buddy?' I did everything they asked, and still, they treated me like an errand boy. Well, they found out. They both did. The look on Vanessa's face as she went over the cliff—"

"So you did kill Vanessa! How did you do that?"

"I told her about Gil and Jenna. She was furious, of course. She begged me to help her catch them on tape. Vanessa wasn't as smart as she thought she was, but she could see the writing on the wall. She wasn't going to leave her meal ticket though. No, sir. She just needed a little private insurance so that Gil wouldn't be able to dump her. She wanted to be Oregon's First Lady someday."

"How did you know that Gil and Jenna would be in the gorge?"

"I sent them each a secret note, supposedly from each other, saying it was vitally important for them to meet. When Vanessa came crashing down beside them, Gil didn't have any idea what was going on, but his political instincts kicked right in. He grabbed the videotape and ran. He didn't care what happened to Vanessa as long as it didn't cause a scandal. One less problem, as long as Jenna backed his alibi."

"Which she did."

"Everything was fine until your daughter started meddling."

"But Bianca didn't know anything—"

"Gil wasn't sure of that. When she sent him that note saying she knew what he had done, he thought maybe she had seen him there with Jenna, or maybe she had seen him leaving before Vanessa died, and he couldn't let either of those things come out. Vanessa's death had to be ruled a simple accident. Anything else, he couldn't risk politically."

"So Kurt had nothing to do with it."

"Kurt was just being stupid, same as always. All bluster."

"Gil's house. I still don't know what happened at Gil's house," I put in quickly. Harley seemed to be enjoying the chance to brag about his cleverness, and I was more than willing to take the time to listen.

Harley laughed. "That was the best part. Gil didn't know how to get Bianca to leave him alone. He kept crying to me about it." He imitated Gil's voice, "'Do something, Harley.' Just like always, I was supposed to fix things. Then she showed up at his house."

"She hid in the trunk of his car."

"Is that how she got there? I wondered about that. Gutsy. Anyway, Gil spotted her scarf on the windowsill and figured out that she must be in the closet. He called me and asked what to do, same as always. That was easy. I told him to sit tight. Said I'd send Arnie out so that Gil would get his chance to show what a nut case she was, get her out of his hair once and for all. I never called Arnie, of course. What made it perfect was the look on his face when he saw what I was going to do. I'd waited my whole life for that look. I just wish Vanessa could have seen it."

"So you called from your cell—"

"That's right," he answered. "Okay, that's enough, Jane. We're going now. I've been fair with you, so please don't try to back out of our deal. We can make this easy or hard, but, it's going to end the same way, no matter what."

"I don't think so," I said slowly. "I really don't. There's a line from *The Tempest,* 'On the bat's back do I fly...'" I was coiling up my makeshift ladder as I spoke, using the words to distract him. Drawing a deep breath, I wondered whether it would be one of the last breaths I'd ever take.

"You misunderstood my promise. I said I'd go, and I will... but not with you!" On the last word, I threw the puny extension cord-twine tangle at his face, hoping to disorient him in the darkness just long enough for me to turn and get a running start toward the doorway to the outside behind me.

Even though I couldn't see much, I knew that the closest branches of the apple tree stood a good ten feet from the side of the bookstore. But at this point, I was out of sensible options. I raced for the opening and jumped.

THIRTY-ONE

"HELP! HELP!" AS I SAILED through the air, I shouted as loud as I could. No need for silence now. Time slowed to a crawl and I spewed more words than I'd have thought possible before whacking the first branches of the tree with my outstretched arms. Clawing at the leafy wall which suddenly became porous and insubstantial, I broke off leaves and twigs as my forward momentum stopped and I began to fall. Heedless of the damage to my bare skin, I grabbed at anything within reach, skinning branches and detaching bunches of leaves as they slipped through my hands. The fresh smell of newly exposed bark reminded me of climbing trees as a kid, only I didn't remember the experience as being so painful.

The side of my leg glanced off a particularly solid branch beneath me and peeled a strip of flesh from ankle to thigh as I slid by. Though the pain caused sparks of light to flash behind my closed eyelids, I grabbed blindly, desperately, at the branch. My arms briefly encircled it, just long enough to give me an instant of hope before I lost my grip. The brief stop slowed my descent only marginally before I completed my fall, landing flat on my back beneath the tree.

I lay stunned for an instant, drawing breath back into my lungs and absorbing the fact that I had survived the jump from a second-story window. The scent of recently mown grass was so normal and welcoming that I wanted to lie there forever, but I had to escape before Harley could get down the stairs. He hadn't fired the gun, even when I shouted, so he was still hoping for silence. If I yelled again, it would merely tell him exactly where I was. I couldn't take the chance that he'd find me before someone else responded to my cries.

I heard Harley on the front staircase. There was no time to waste, so I rolled to my knees awkwardly, favoring the injured leg which had smacked the branch as I fell. Before trying to stand up, I looked at the shadowy bulk of darkened stores too far away across the lawn. For the first time ever, I was sorry that the mansion which had become Thornton's Books sat regally on half an acre of grounds. I'd always loved the graceful setting, but now the open expanse was nothing but a hazard. If I could outrun Harley and reach those buildings, maybe I could lose myself long enough to summon help, but I had a long way to go and he still had the gun. Still, what was my choice?

I took exactly one step before crumpling to the ground with a muffled cry. The injury was worse than I thought. My right ankle was either sprained or broken and wouldn't hold my weight. So much for running. As I crawled into the shadows beside the front door, my hand encountered something smooth and cold. I pulled back, expecting a telltale rattle. This was no place to be crawling around in the dark. Rattlesnakes were attracted at night to the warmth retained by stone foundations after a hot day.

All I heard was a gentle gurgling, which caused me to relax a fraction. Not a snake then, just a hose with water trickling through it. Oh, yes, the hose that Tyler hadn't gotten around to moving. My earlier worries about someone tripping over it were replaced by a vague notion that maybe the hose could be useful.

I pulled tentatively. The hose was caught fast on something on the other side of the front door. I pulled harder, but it didn't budge. So far, so good. Harley's muttered curses were interspersed with the slamming around of books and shelves. He'd been delayed by his own barricade at the bottom of the stairs, but it wouldn't be long before he came storming out the door.

I propped myself against the side of the building and yanked the hose up to what I judged to be about knee level. It remained taut. Temporarily, I laid it back down and pulled on the free end of the hose until at last the metal nozzle leaked a cool stream of water against my leg. It felt good on my lacerated skin.

Could I turn the nozzle and spray him? I tried it on my hand. Not enough water pressure. I'd have to trip him and then use the nozzle as a club. All things being equal, I liked his chances with the gun better than mine with the garden hose…but all things weren't equal. Once again I pulled the hose taut across the doorway and braced myself. Just in time.

Harley's running footsteps came straight toward the door and he rushed out. Assuming that he had his gun ready for action, I gripped that clumsy trip wire as I'd never hung onto anything before. Harley smashed into it and sprawled head-first onto the sidewalk. His breath whooshed out, but he still had the gun, and a lot of pent-up anger. Scrambling to his knees faster than I expected, he turned in my direction.

The white blur of his face in the starlight provided a perfect target. I swung the hose like a lariat, once, twice, and whacked him square on the nose with the nozzle. He let out a shout, but I didn't stay to watch what happened next. I scuttled away around the side of the store and toward the back door.

How long would it take him to recover and realize that I hadn't had time to run away? It hardly mattered, as I couldn't get too far anyway. I decided my best chance was to edge around to the back of the building. Maybe I could break a window and crawl inside to the telephone. That would make unwelcome noise, but if I just stayed put, sooner or later he'd find me.

No sound but the chirping of crickets. Apparently, those

insects weren't worried about all the crashing and falling and yelling that had been going on around them. It would be nice to be a cricket on a balmy summer night, surrounded by fragrant grass. Shouldn't this be the ultimate peaceful experience?

Unfortunately, I wasn't a cricket, and the night wasn't the least bit peaceful. The minute Harley came close, I'd scream bloody murder. I hardly recognized myself tonight. I'd always been the mediator, the voice of reason for my family and friends, but this situation had brought out a side to me that I'd never suspected. After jumping out of that second story room, everything else seemed easy. Up against a murderer, I was determined to do battle…and to win. If I lived through the night, I might take up sky-diving.

I scooted noiselessly along the building, touching the uneven stone of the old foundation at intervals, as much for reassurance as for location. Spider webs coated my hands as I crawled. Now, in addition to rattlesnakes, I was worrying about the poisonous brown recluse spider, also known to favor the stone foundations of buildings in Central Oregon. Which would be the most lethal: a rattlesnake, a poisonous spider, or Harley with a gun? Nice choice. I reached the corner and listened again for sounds of pursuit.

Did I hear breathing? I paused in an agony of indecision, angry at myself for losing track of Harley's location, yet impatient to get inside to that telephone before he could find me. I remained motionless for what seemed like a long time. A car slowed on nearby Easton Street before speeding away.

Okay, I reasoned. It's a fifty-fifty chance that he came around the building the other way and is waiting for me around the corner. Either he's there or he isn't. I figured that if I saw him, the adrenaline would kick in so fast that I'd run whether my ankle worked or not. I poked my head around the corner.

Immediately, a hand clamped itself over my mouth and I was dragged, kicking and twisting, into the deep shadows. I tried, but couldn't bite the hand restraining me, so I grabbed at it with both hands in an attempt to claw my way free. My fingernails were too short to do much damage, but I dug them into the flesh as best I could.

I smelled cinnamon. What on earth? A burst of hissing sounds issued from the person holding me, sort of like the sounds a defective snake might make. I immediately stopped struggling and nodded to indicate my understanding. I didn't know why she was there, but I knew I was being held in Minnie's firm grasp. Once I stopped thrashing around, the hissing stopped and she let me go. I turned to look at her in the darkness, but could make out only her shadowy bulk, flanked by two other familiar and very welcome shadows. Behind them stood a smaller shadow with a wagging tail. The Murder of the Month Book Club—complete with mascot—had arrived.

"Harley," I whispered urgently. "The killer is Harley. He's coming. We have to—"

"Harley, eh?" Alix said. "Well, that's a surprise. I didn't think he had it in him. Still waters and all that."

"You don't understand," I continued. "He's got a gun and—"

"So does the sheriff," Tyler said, the excitement of the chase evident in his voice. "Deputies, too."

"Shh," Minnie said. Her usual fondness for talk seemed to have deserted her tonight.

"But he doesn't know about Harley," I insisted.

"Well, he knows someone was holding you hostage, and he'll figure it out soon enough," Alix whispered. "Minnie ordered Brady to tell Arnie to come over here and arrest anyone who wasn't one of us."

"Well, I *was* his Sunday school teacher," Minnie reminded me.

"Brady was too confused to argue," Alix agreed. "Probably thought she was crazy when she just kept repeating that Wendell had shown up without Jane and he wouldn't eat a thing at the potluck. Of course, we knew that meant you had to be in trouble."

"The police will be here any minute," Minnie said. "Brady promised."

"We got here first because Alix was driving." Tyler's admiration was clear. "She should give the cops lessons!"

Within seconds police cars converged from four different directions, sirens wailing. Apparently Brady had convinced the Russell County sheriff that if a dog wouldn't eat at a potluck, that must signify a crisis, especially if his old Sunday school teacher said so. An amazing number of uniformed officers from both the Russell County Sheriff's Department and the City of Juniper jumped out and began to set up portable lights around the perimeter of the bookstore property. In minutes the entire area was as bright as a carnival midway.

We hugged the back wall of the bookstore and shielded our eyes from the glare. I kept a tight hold on Wendell's collar.

A bullhorn cracked the silence as soon as the last of the sirens died away. "This is Sheriff Arnold Kraft of the Russell County Sheriff's Department. I am speaking to everyone on the premises of Thornton's Books. Put up your hands and do not move after that."

Obediently, we raised our hands and stayed where we were.

"Don't shoot, Arnie," Minnie called out.

"We see you, Minnie," Arnie answered. "And everyone with you, including the dog. Please, for once, just stay put." Arnie's command sounded more like a plea.

"It's Harley Cunningham you want," I shouted. "He tried to kill me."

"Harley?" Arnie was skeptical. "You can't be serious."

"Be careful! He has a gun and he's out front somewhere." I wasn't about to look around the side of the building myself.

"Harley, if you're there," Arnie still sounded only half convinced, "throw down your weapon and come out with your hands up so we can straighten out this whole—"

"Arnie, look!" Brady interrupted, his voice carrying to us through the bullhorn Arnie held. Arnie didn't think to click it off, so we also heard Brady's next question, "What's that on the sidewalk?"

A short pause ensued. At length we heard Arnie's incredulous voice, "Well, I'll be damned. It is Harley, and he's out cold."

THIRTY-TWO

THE NEXT MORNING LAURENCE'S hospital room was filled with the entire membership of the Murder of the Month Book Club. We all interrupted each other, vying to give Laurence our own versions of what had happened the previous night. At length he put his hands over his ears and said, with a broad smile, "Just tell me straight out. Is my bookstore still standing? I left Thornton's in your charge for only a few days, Jane, and—"

"You ungrateful wretch!" I waved one crutch at him from my chair, which had been located so that my leg in its elegant purple cast could be propped on the frame of his bed. "Not only is your bookstore still standing, but the publicity from our…heroics, as I prefer to call them…will probably double or triple your business." I paused to bow at the applause of my friends ringing the room.

"But what about the damage? Bookcases knocked over… in both the front and back, you say?"

"We should leave it the way it is and advertise it as sort of a theme house," Tyler said.

"Good idea," Alix said. "Come and see the room where it all started, with Wendell and his frosted bran bars. For only one extra dollar you can step over and around the hundreds of books Harley tried to use to trap the fearless Jane. You could sell the books as collectors' items. Some of them look as though they've been there long enough to qualify. And the ones Jane had picked out to throw at Harley ought to be worth a lot more."

"I could make cookies to sell," Minnie volunteered. "Let's see. What kind?"

Bianca was right in tune with this insane chorus. "You could make them in the shape of little handcuffs."

Minnie looked thoughtful, and then clapped her hands. "I've got it! Instead of cookies, I'll make funnel cakes. They're like little doughnuts."

"Great," Bianca said. "Maybe some non-fat ones, too, so we could appeal to a wider clientele."

"How do you make non-fat doughnuts?" Alix asked.

"I don't know, but if anybody can do it, it's Minnie," said Bianca. "Anyway, the handcuffs would really tie together the whole mystery theme. They'd advertise the fact that Mom caught Harley and at the same time they'd advertise our book club."

"Oh, no," I said. "Never again with the book club. That's how we got into this mess."

"But we never got to discuss *Prove It, Puppy!*"

"We were sort of busy," Tyler said indignantly, "looking for you, mostly."

"If you'd looked a little faster, you could have saved me a lot of trouble," Bianca teased.

"I wasn't even supposed to be in that garage," he protested. "You're lucky I popped the trunk of Gil's car at all."

"We all are, Tyler," I said. "I never thought I'd say it, but let's hear it for insubordination."

"Wait a minute. I have to live with this kid," Laurence said. From the smile on his face, it was clear that he didn't mind the prospect at all.

"Hello," said Nick from the doorway. "This is the most popular room in the hospital today." He looked around until he found where I was sitting. My heart raced just the tiniest bit. "Nice cast, Jane."

"You might as well come in," Laurence said, "whoever you are."

"I'm a customer at your store, as well as Jane and Bianca's attorney."

"Better stick around," Laurence suggested. "They may need you again if they persist in removing evidence from crime scenes."

"Oh, I intend to stick around all right," Nick responded, smiling and handing me a newspaper. "I thought you'd be interested in this morning's *Juniper Journal.* Great headline: 'The Murder of the Month Book Club Closes Chapter on Local Murders.'"

I groaned. "Why'd they have to mention the book club?"

"You're famous," Nick said, "and it's great publicity for the bookstore. The whole town will be clamoring to join your club. You'd better schedule a meeting quick."

"We will!" Bianca turned to me and added, "At least I hope we will."

"Well, we did promise to discuss your book," Minnie said.

"We can show people the cool fake pictures we took," added Tyler.

Alix joined the chorus. "Oh, hell, Jane. Why not?"

Everyone was looking at me expectantly, and Bianca most of all. I thought of the various rules Raymond Morris had laid out in *Making Peace With Your Adult Child.* I'd have to write and suggest a few things he probably hadn't considered. I smiled at Bianca.

"Wouldn't miss it for the world."

* * * * *